Jack fished the keys out of his pocket and dropped them into Charlie's palm. The heat radiating from the metal nearly caused her to dump them on the pavement. Charlie tried to avoid thinking about where the keys had picked up their warmth, but it was hard not to picture gray flannel stretched over a muscular thigh. She took a deep breath and lifted her flushed face to the cold drizzle.

"That's a nice pose but I'm getting wet." Jack's voice had lost all its southern charm.

"Sorry," she muttered, unlocking the car and sliding behind the wheel.

She focused on starting the car rather than the man whose shoulder was only a foot away from hers. "Since I'm going to be in the city tomorrow, I could stop by and do the interview with you then, if it's convenient."

"I'll check my calendar," he said with a sardonic edge to his voice.

"Fine. No problem. Whatever time you're available, I'll be there."

The trip back to Jack's apartment was accomplished mostly in silence. As Charlie stopped the car in front of Jack's door, he suddenly said, "Oh, hell, I might as well get it over with. Tomorrow at ten o'clock."

Charlie repressed a whoop of triumph. "Ten's good."

He got out of the car, then turned to lean back in through the door. "On one condition."

"What's that?"

He smiled. "No bun. No braid. Wear your hair down."

He closed the door.

Praise for

A Bridge to Love

"A heart-warming story . . . Step into Kate Chilton's life and fall in love . . . with not one but three heroes!"

—Karen Kendall,
author of *I've Got You Babe*

"*A Bridge to Love* is Nancy Herkness's debut, and it is evident that the romance world has a wonderful new voice."

—Sandra Brill,
Romance Reviews Today

"Written for today's smart woman, [Nancy Herkness] offers educated characters with family concerns and adult decisions. [*A Bridge to Love*] is fast-paced and well written, a turbulent roller coaster ride of emotions . . . This is an impressive debut."

—Alan Caruba,
Bookviews.com

"Entertaining plot . . . thrilling climax . . . sharp dialogue and a heroine worth rooting for."

—Donna Carter,
Romantic Times Bookclub Magazine

"Every once in awhile, a debut author comes along who makes you sit back and say 'wow.' Nancy Herkness is that author for me. Even with the paper cuts I got on my fingers from turning the pages so fast . . . I would definitely recommend *A Bridge to Love* to all true romantics."

—Jennifer Wardrip,
RomanceJunkies.com

Shower of Stars

NANCY HERKNESS

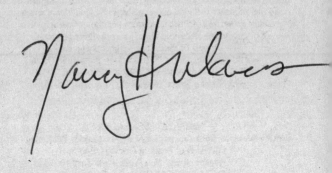

B

BERKLEY SENSATION, NEW YORK

This is a work of fiction. Names, characters, places, and incidents either are the product of the author's imagination or are used fictitiously, and any resemblance to actual persons, living or dead, business establishments, events, or locales is entirely coincidental.

SHOWER OF STARS

A Berkley Sensation Book / published by arrangement with the author

PRINTING HISTORY
Berkley Sensation edition / July 2004

Copyright © 2004 by Nancy Herkness.
Cover photograph of a comet shooting through sky at night by Joseph de Sciose/Nonstock.
Cover image of woman by és/Nonstock.
Interior text design by Kristin del Rosario.

For information address: The Berkley Publishing Group, a division of Penguin Group (USA) Inc., 375 Hudson Street, New York, New York 10014.

ISBN: 0-425-19711-5

BERKLEY SENSATION™
Berkley Sensation Books are published by The Berkley Publishing Group, a division of Penguin Group (USA) Inc., 375 Hudson Street, New York, New York 10014. BERKLEY SENSATION and the "B" design are trademarks belonging to Penguin Group (USA) Inc.

PRINTED IN THE UNITED STATES OF AMERICA

10 9 8 7 6 5 4 3 2 1

To Rebecca and Loukas,
who have shown me that love is truly infinite

ACKNOWLEDGMENTS

Friends are a treasure in all aspects of one's life. However, for a novelist, friends become an invaluable resource in one's work. My hearty thanks go to:

John Lacey, Esq., for his assistance with the legal aspects of my story. I will never forget his expression when I sat down beside him at a child's baseball game, and said without any preamble, "John, how hard is it to get a divorce in New Jersey?"

Elena Brunet, translator extraordinaire, for making Miguel linguistically correct, right down to his *fondillos*.

James Sturm, professor of electrical engineering at Princeton University, for his help with the Princeton commencement ceremony, and recommending just the right restaurant for the graduation celebration.

Kathleen Brower, EMT, for her information on how an ambulance squad would check for concussion. From her description of the symptoms, I think I may have one.

Lynn Freeman Scott, for donating her professional proofreading skills and for never doubting that I would be published someday.

Robert Jenkens (who also happens to be a relative) and John Fahey, for giving me the most wonderful food and shelter so I could spend my days at the Smithsonian Institute reading every single label in the meteorite exhibit.

All errors and/or omissions are entirely my own.

CHAPTER 1

A DOG THE size of a pony streaked across the New York City street.

Charlie Berglund slammed on her brakes, sending her Volvo station wagon into a skid on the drizzle-dampened pavement. The taxi driver in the next lane wasn't as alert, and she gasped in horror as the dog bounced off the cab's bumper and crumpled in a heap.

"Heartless creep!" she yelled, putting her car in park and leaping out.

The car behind her honked angrily, and she made a rude gesture at the driver as she ran to the dog. He looked like a mountain of matted gray fur piled up on the pavement. Crooning softly, Charlie knelt down to see if he was alive. "Poor fellow. That rotten cab driver didn't even stop. How can people be so hardhearted?" She found a steady heartbeat but the creature's eyes were closed, and he didn't stir when touched. She checked for blood and conspicuously broken bones but found none. She stroked the unconscious dog's head. "Now how am I going to move you? I have a blanket in the car, but you must weigh about a hundred pounds . . ."

She checked her wristwatch, swiping her sleeve across the crystal to clear off the rain droplets. *Three o'clock,* exactly time for her interview with Jack Lanett, the newly famous meteorite hunter. *I'm going to be late. And wet.* Looking down at her silk blouse, now clinging transparently to her skin, she muttered, "Damn, damn, damn!"

She had wangled an interview with the man who had found the most valuable space rock in the world: Sahara-Mars, a meteorite that almost certainly held proof of life on the red planet. Not only that, he was a man who *never* gave interviews. Was she really going to blow this chance at a killer article for the *Times*? The dog whimpered under her hand, and Charlie instantly made her decision.

"Your need is greater than mine," she said, giving his unkempt fur one last pat.

She stood up and scanned the street for a likely assistant. All she could see were two elderly ladies shuffling along under umbrellas, and a young woman briskly pushing a plastic-covered baby carriage. The rain had sent everyone else indoors. . . . Well, Jack Lanett lived one block up, and he was expecting her. Charlie left her battered Volvo where it was, protecting the dog from oncoming traffic, and sprinted up the street to Lanett's building.

Nice entrance, she thought as she pushed the highly polished brass bell labeled J. LANETT. "But no doorman. Tsk, tsk."

"Yes?" a male voice with a trace of the deep South came through the loudspeaker.

"Mr. Lanett, I'm Charlie Berglund from the *Times*. I have a favor to ask you. A very large dog was just hit by a taxi, and I need some help getting him into my car. Would you mind giving me a hand? You might want to put on a raincoat."

For a moment, there was silence. Then the voice came through the speaker again, this time with a pronounced drawl. "You want me to come out in the rain and carry a dead dog to your car?"

"He's not dead." *Yet.*

Charlie heard a muttered string of what she assumed were curses before he said, "I'm on my way."

I hope you walk faster than you talk, she said to herself as she took a quick look out the entrance door. Her car was still standing sentinel over the motionless heap of gray. She hoped the poor thing wasn't bleeding internally. Catching sight of her reflection in the brass plate around the doorbells, she quickly tucked stray pieces of blond hair back into her bun. She pulled her damp blouse away from her skin, flapping it wildly in an attempt to dry it enough so her lace bra wasn't outlined in quite such vivid detail. She should have followed her own advice and worn the raincoat slung over the passenger seat in her car.

The elevator dinged. Charlie let go of her blouse and peered through the glass of the vestibule door. The man striding impatiently across the marble floor looked nothing like the one grainy photograph she had been able to track down of the reclusive Jack Lanett. In the photo, jet-black hair had reached his shoulders. Now, its color ranged from dark iron to steely silver, and it waved neatly back away from his face to just touch the top of his collar. Of course, there was no raincoat over the sky-blue polo shirt tucked into gray flannel slacks. *Typical macho man!* She just had time to observe that he moved like someone who gets where he's going efficiently when he opened the door and stopped.

"You're a woman!"

Charlie sighed. With her nickname and her gravelly voice, people who spoke with her by telephone often assumed she was a man. "I'm afraid so."

A look of purely male appreciation softened Jack Lanett's scowl for a moment. Charlie was used to that too; she was very blond and tall enough to have long legs men noticed even when she was wearing slacks.

She looked back appraisingly; the polo shirt outlined a broad set of shoulders. He was tall too, at least six inches above her own impressive five nine. He should be more than equal to the task of lifting a large limp animal.

"Let's get the damned dog," Jack growled as he pushed open the entrance door.

"Don't you like dogs?" Charlie asked as she led the way to the car.

"Only if I'm very hungry."

"I know this is an inconvenience, but you don't have to be snide."

"*Snide?* Lady, when you're stranded and starving in some godforsaken country most people can't find on a map, you'll eat anything."

The reporter in Charlie filed away that piece of information for future use, but her attention was focused on the poor creature lying in the rain. His eyes were open now, so she approached him slowly and spoke calmly, "There's a good dog. Poor hurt puppy. I'm here to help you." She'd been bitten a few times in her animal rescues and always took basic precautions. This dog, however, tried to lick her hand when she knelt down to stroke his head. "What a sweet boy," she said, probing his filthy fur with her fingers. "I don't see any blood but I'm afraid he may have internal injuries. There's a blanket in the back of the car. Would you get it so we can slide it under him?"

After a moment, Jack appeared beside her, shaking

open the old plaid wool picnic blanket Charlie kept for such emergencies.

"What are you, the Florence Nightingale of the animal world? There's enough dog and cat food in your car to feed an army."

"I was a Girl Scout so I'm always prepared." Charlie took an end of the blanket and laid it beside the dog's back. "Could you help me shift him back onto this?"

Jack had already slid his hands under the animal's rump and was gently lifting and easing him onto the wool. "He smells worse than a wet camel," he complained, but he continued to help Charlie carefully slide the dog farther onto the faded plaid fabric.

"If you were homeless, you'd stink too. He doesn't have a collar but he's not hostile toward people so he must have been treated well for part of his life." Charlie was working the wool under the big creature's legs. Except for an occasional whimper, the dog offered no resistance.

"You're a good boy," Charlie assured him, stroking his head whenever she was about to move him. "Okay, he's centered. Now we have to get him into the back of the wagon."

Charlie glanced up to see the meteorite hunter frowning down at the dog.

"I don't want to risk hurting him by picking him up alone," he said. "I think that if you take the blanket corners by his tail and I take the ones by his head, we can keep him relatively flat and still. He's heavy. Do you think you can hold him?"

"I'm an alumna of the Navy SEAL Training Academy. I can manage," Charlie said as she walked around to the other side of the dog.

Jack's gaze focused on her for a long moment, and Charlie discovered he had the iciest blue eyes she'd ever seen. The rain hitting her neck and shoulders suddenly seemed frigid against her skin, and a violent shiver shook her body so hard that her teeth clicked together.

"Let's get him in the car before you catch pneumonia," Jack said as he knelt by the dog's head.

Charlie rubbed her hands up and down her arms in an attempt to erase the goose bumps. Then she knelt opposite Jack and took a firm grip on the corners of the makeshift stretcher.

"Now," he commanded, holding the fabric taut and braced against Charlie's counterpull.

She saw the muscles in his arms flex as they both slowly rose in such perfect synchronicity that the dog seemed to float upward between them. Glancing up, she once again met those cold eyes, the blue so pale that the black of his pupils seemed bottomless. But now she felt heat rather than cold radiating over her skin.

"You'd think we did this every day." Charlie spoke to dispel the disquieting sense of connection.

"I get the feeling that you *do*," Jack said as he backed slowly and smoothly toward the rear of the wagon. Charlie followed him at an equally deliberate pace.

"You know, for someone who considers dogs starvation rations, you're doing a great job of handling this one gently."

"I've learned to go along with other people's obsessions," he said as they slid the blanket and their burden into the station wagon's capacious storage area.

"It's not an obsession; it's my small attempt to help a fellow being," Charlie said.

Jack stretched forward to shift the dog farther into the car, and their shoulders brushed. She expected to see steam rise from the point of contact between his warmth and her chill.

"He's in." Jack lowered the door and then closed it firmly.

Charlie resisted the urge to ask him to wrap his arms around her for just a minute to share his body heat. Instead she held out her hand. "Thank you so much for your help. I know you weren't expecting this when you agreed to an interview, but you've been terrific. I apologize for the inconvenience. I'll call you to make another appointment." She wasn't nearly as confident as she sounded about setting up another meeting; he would probably tell her to go to hell after this.

He reached out to take her hand, and the warmth of his skin was delicious against her palm.

"As much as I hate to say this, I'm coming with you. Wherever you're driving this monster, you'll need help getting him out of the car."

Charlie couldn't stop the grateful smile that tugged at her lips, but she shook her head. "You've already done more than enough. I can get help at the animal hospital."

Using the hand he still held to turn her around, her self-appointed assistant placed his left palm in the small of her back and propelled her toward the passenger door. Swinging it open, he said, "I'll drive while you make the arrangements. I assume you have a cell phone."

Stunned to silence, Charlie nodded as she slid into the seat. In the seconds it took him to walk around to the driver's seat, she found her tongue. "You're bossy, aren't you? Where exactly do you think you're going?"

Jack had turned the key and put the car in gear. "Out of the middle of the street before we get hit," he said, tucking the Volvo neatly in beside a fire hydrant.

"Oh." She covered her discomfiture by grabbing the cell phone out of its hands-free cradle and scrolling down to the number for the animal shelter in her hometown of Bellefont, New Jersey.

"Hey, Allan, it's Charlie. I'm on the Upper West Side in New York City, and I need some help." She explained her problem and got directions to the nearest emergency veterinarian.

"That's in the Bronx," Jack said scowling.

"People who help animals for a living can't afford Park Avenue," Charlie said.

As her unexpected chauffeur took the car out into the flow of traffic, Charlie looked up the vet's office on one of the maps she kept handy in the car. She also called the office to warn them of the emergency coming in. Allan Schumann, the director of the Ocean County Animal Shelter, had already been in touch and smoothed her path. Pushing the disconnect button, she dropped the phone in her lap. "Everything's set for Major's arrival."

"You've named him already?" Jack's voice held a hint of amusement, and Charlie glanced sideways. For the first time since she'd met him, the man was smiling—only slightly—but the corners of his mouth were definitely turning up. Instead of straight angry slashes, his eyebrows had relaxed into a slightly ironic arch. And Grumpy had a dimple! She bet he hated that.

"I've been reading up on the stars—for obvious reasons—and an appropriate name just popped into my head."

"Stars, eh? Let me guess. Major?" he said, frowning in concentration. "*Canis Major*. The Big Dog."

"Exactly!" Charlie said, pleased he got the joke. "One of Orion's hunting dogs in the sky."

"Congratulations on doing your homework, *Ms.* Berglund. By the way, why did you fool me into thinking you were a man? Did someone tell you I don't talk to female reporters?"

About to protest that she hadn't tried to fool him, Charlie found she was more interested in his second question. "Is that true? I thought you just didn't talk to reporters, period."

He made no response.

She sighed. "I wasn't trying to fool you. I have a raspy voice and a man's nickname. You're not the first person to get the wrong idea."

"You have a voice like the air inside an Irish pub: pipe smoke and whiskey. It doesn't match the Norse ice princess look."

Should I be flattered or insulted? It wasn't her fault she had blond hair, greenish gray eyes, fair skin and a husky, contralto voice. "Sorry my mixed-up genes don't meet with your approval."

Suddenly the dimple and the drawl were very much in evidence. "Your genes have my *full* approval, sugar."

"Thanks *so* much," Charlie said, as she tried to counteract the delicious but distinctly undermining effect of being called "sugar" by a tall, good-looking male.

"However," Jack continued, "I distinctly remember your editor telling me that you were the best *man* for the job."

"That's his little joke. He probably assumed you knew who I was since I've been writing *The Average Adventurer* articles for five or six years now."

"I assume these articles are well-known?"

"In certain circles."

"No need for false modesty, Ms. Berglund. I'm out of the country more than in it, so don't take it personally that your fame hasn't reached me."

She knew he said it to irritate her, but Charlie loved the

way he drawled slowly through the "Ms." every time. It reeked of grits and Spanish moss. Unlike hers, his voice was as smooth and golden as honey, pouring easily over and around his words.

"What's an *Average Adventurer*?" he asked.

"A regular feature in *American Traveler* magazine. Instead of some highly trained athletic type going helicopter skiing or enduring the SEAL training academy or whatever the latest 'in' trip is, I go and report back truthfully on how difficult it is for a normal human being."

"I'd hardly call you normal." The corner of his mouth twitched again. "You go around rescuing woolly mammoths like the one in back. You seem to be something of an Amazon."

Another backhanded compliment. However, being an Amazon was definitely a good thing. She pretended to peer out the side window in case her pleasure showed on her face. "Turn right here. The hospital should be on the next block."

Jack double-parked the car in front of the hospital. Reversing the earlier loading process, they carried Major into the waiting room. When the receptionist saw the size of their burden, she summoned help, and soon the dog was on a metal examination table being checked over by a veterinarian.

Once she had answered the vet's questions, Charlie glanced around to see Jack lounging against the wall with his hands in his pockets. Raindrops still clung to his hair. The knees of his formerly immaculate gray flannels were dark with wet and smeared with grime from the street. His shirt was also patched with drizzle and dirt. She felt a pang of guilt for ruining his clothes. It occurred to her that she probably didn't look much better, and she had worn her best pants suit and blouse for the interview.

"We're going to take him in for X rays. You can wait in the reception area," the young doctor said.

Jack held the door for Charlie as they walked back into the corridor. The hospital was immaculately clean, smelling of disinfectant and bleach, but the linoleum floor was peeling away around the edges and paint was flaking off water stains on the ceiling. They settled in across from each other on two of the mismatched chairs crammed around three walls of the small waiting room. When Jack stretched out his legs and crossed them at the ankles, his tasseled loafers practically touched the leg of the chair next to her.

Charlie carefully tucked her feet under her own chair. Her companion had folded his arms across his chest and seemed to be fascinated by a photograph of a basket of puppies that hung on the wall behind the reception desk. She took advantage of his distraction to study him more closely.

His skin was deeply tanned, not surprising in a man whose job was tracking down rocks that fell out of the sky all over the world. In a way, he seemed like a meteorite himself: every line of his face was clean and hard-edged as though any soft substances had been burned away. What she could see of the rest of him looked the same: nothing but necessary and useful muscle filled out those broad shoulders and long legs. She had the unwelcome thought that he'd look terrific in a bathing suit.

"Would you like to call a taxi?" she asked, holding out her cell phone and attempting to channel her thoughts into a more professional direction.

The ice-blue gaze focused on her. "A gentleman would never abandon a lady in the Bronx."

"Think of me as a journalist and you might have less of a problem with it."

An arch of his eyebrow was the only response.

She gave him a dazzling smile and switched gears again. "What made you become a meteorite hunter? It's a rather unusual occupation."

"Is this the interview?" The dimple was nowhere in sight.

"No, it's a conversation."

"With journalists, it's hard to tell the difference."

Charlie shifted forward in her seat and gave him her most open and honest look. "Did someone write something bad about you? I couldn't find a single article that did anything more than mention your name in passing. And one photograph from ten years ago."

He uncrossed his ankles and crossed them the opposite way. "Journalists focus on the wrong things. You should ask questions about the meteorites, not about why I hunt them."

"It's called the human interest angle. People relate better to other people than to rocks. Or maybe they can relate better to the rocks *through* the people who find them." Charlie was rather pleased with that twist. She didn't add that a certain segment of the female population would find Jack Lanett interesting no matter what he did for a living.

"The meteorites speak for themselves." He leaned forward so his face was only inches from hers. "When you hold a carbonaceous chondrite in your hand and know that it was traveling through space before life was even a tiny spark on this planet—in fact, before this planet was even a planet—no interpretation should be necessary."

He had cupped his hand as though holding the meteorite, and Charlie couldn't help but notice how long his fingers were. She forced her gaze upward and encountered a blaze of passion in the usually icy eyes. *So he gets ex-*

cited about his space rocks. What else might fan those flames?

She shook her head sharply to banish such thoughts, and her bun came loose. It sagged lopsidedly down her neck, and she automatically reached up to take out the last few hairpins. Sitting back and tilting her head sideways, she combed her fingers through the tangled strands until they uncoiled enough to braid.

"What are you doing?" Jack's mellifluous voice sounded slightly strangled.

Charlie glanced up to find his eyes riveted on her flying fingers. "Braiding my hair. To get it out of the way." She always twisted her waist-length hair into a bun or braid first thing in the morning, and paid no attention to it after that. She slowed her usually swift plaiting to a crawl. Maybe he had a hair fetish, and she could use it to persuade him to reschedule their interview? Peeking through the strands, she saw Jack swallow and shift in his seat.

"You have extraordinary hair," he said.

"Thanks." *I've got him!* Her lips curved in satisfaction. "Would you be free . . . ?"

She finished her braid hastily as the door swung open, and the veterinarian walked over to lean against the reception desk. "Your hit-and-run victim has a mild concussion and a couple of cracked ribs, but otherwise he's in good shape. I want to keep him overnight to make sure his head injury isn't worse than I think. You can pick him up tomorrow morning."

Charlie stood up. "That's wonderful news. I appreciate your seeing him on such short notice."

"That's what emergency vets are for," the doctor said with a smiling shrug. "By the way, I think you've got yourself a purebred Kuvasz. Under all that dirt, his fur is white. I'd say he's about two years old."

"A Kuvasz?" Charlie didn't see many pedigreed animals; most strays were mutts.

"They were popular with Hungarian royalty in the Middle Ages," Jack's voice drawled from behind her.

The vet nodded. "The kings bred them for guard dogs and hunting. They're still used today but to guard sheep and cattle."

"He must belong to someone." Charlie frowned.

"He hasn't for awhile," the vet said. "Under all that fur, he's pretty undernourished."

"You mean he's usually bigger?!" she exclaimed.

The vet laughed.

"I assume he'll walk out under his own power tomorrow," Jack said from his lounging position.

"Don't worry," Charlie said. "I'll handle dog transportation tomorrow."

She thanked the vet and was about to leave when the receptionist spoke.

"I'll need a name and address in the city."

"I live in New Jersey," Charlie said. "I'll give you my cell phone number." She started to take a card out of her pocketbook.

"It has to be in the city," the receptionist said, shaking her head. "We've had too many owners skip town without paying the bill."

Charlie looked at Jack.

"Thirty-five West 68th Street," he said, then gave his home number. He stood up. "I'll take that cell phone number from you."

Charlie handed him her card. Her skin prickled with sympathetic vibrations when his long fingers brushed over the letters of her name as he slid the square of paper into his trouser pocket.

"Just remember I have a recipe for dog meat stew," he warned.

"Major doesn't look very appetizing," she commented, heading for the door.

The Volvo was still double-parked with the flashers on. Charlie started for the driver's side when she remembered that Jack had the keys. "I'll drive," she said, holding out her hand and expecting an argument.

He fished the keys out of his left pocket and dropped them onto her palm. The heat radiating from the metal nearly caused her to dump them on the pavement. Charlie tried to avoid thinking about where the keys had picked up their warmth, but it was hard not to picture gray flannel stretched over a muscular thigh. She took a deep breath and lifted her flushed face to the cold drizzle.

"That's a nice pose but I'm getting wet." Jack's voice had lost all its southern charm.

"Sorry," she muttered, unlocking the car and sliding behind the wheel.

She focused on starting the car rather than on the man whose shoulder was only a foot away from hers. "Since I'm going to be in the city tomorrow to pick up Major, I could stop by and do the interview with you then, if it's convenient," she said as she put the car in drive.

"I'll check my calendar," he said with a sardonic edge to his voice.

"Fine. No problem. Whatever time you're available, I'll be there."

The trip back to Jack's apartment building was accomplished mostly in silence. Charlie ventured a couple of neutral remarks and was met with monosyllabic replies so she gave up and just steered. As she stopped the car in front of his door, he suddenly said, "Oh, hell, I might as well get it over with. Tomorrow at ten o'clock."

Charlie repressed a whoop of triumph. "Ten's good."

He got out of the car, then turned to lean back in through the door. "On one condition."

"What's that?" she said, glancing over to see an odd smile playing around his lips.

"No bun. No braid. Wear your hair down."

He closed the door.

CHAPTER 2

JACK WAS SMILING as he walked into the living room of his rented apartment.

"What are you smirking about?" a voice rumbled from the depths of a black leather sofa.

"Long, blond hair. What are you doing here, Miguel?"

The man on the sofa sat up. Even sitting, he dwarfed the furniture around him. "I came to rescue you from the dreaded journalist. And instead I find you lusting after a woman. What happened to your interview?"

Jack sank into a steel-and-leather chair and propped his feet up on the glass-topped coffee table. "The dreaded journalist has long, blond hair and *long,* long legs. And a low-cut lacy white bra."

"Before you seduced her, I hope you answered enough questions for her to write a glowing article for the *Times.* Or perhaps you were counting on your performance to create the glow?"

"I didn't seduce her," Jack said shortly. Then his smile returned. "Although it certainly wouldn't be a hardship. I keep picturing her wearing that long hair and nothing else."

"On black satin. I like blondes on black satin sheets," Miguel mused. "You know, I admire a woman with long hair as much as most men, but you have an obsession about it. I've always wondered why that is."

"Rapunzel," Jack said.

"Rapunzel?"

"Didn't your mother read you fairy tales? The prince climbs in and out of the prison tower on Rapunzel's long braid."

"Ahh, an escape fantasy," Miguel said.

"I had many of those at a certain age."

"Understandably," Miguel said. "But if you didn't make love to the reporter, how did you become so intimately acquainted with her bra?"

"She was very wet."

Miguel chuckled lasciviously. "I see . . ."

Jack scowled at him. "I got dragged into a rescue mission in the rain."

"What did you rescue her from?"

"Not the reporter, I helped rescue a dog."

Miguel looked at Jack. "You don't like dogs."

"You want coffee?" Jack stood in a fluid motion. "I've got a dealer coming soon so I'd better make a pot."

"You'd better change your clothes first, *mi amigo.*"

Jack glanced down at his ruined gray flannels with a grunt of disgust.

"Who's coming to talk about the rock?" Miguel asked.

"Eileen Kushen."

"She's a nasty piece of work."

"But she represents Curt Vandermade who wants a Mars rock so badly he'll pay almost anything."

"I'll make the coffee." Miguel rubbed his hands to-

gether. "Including a touch of whiskey to lubricate the negotiations."

"I don't have any whiskey," Jack said over his shoulder as he headed for the bedroom.

"But I do," Miguel said, pulling a flask from his coat pocket. "When I'm visiting you, I always bring my own bottle."

CHARLIE FLIPPED THE windshield wipers to high as the rain came down in buckets. She was still sitting in rush hour traffic on the Garden State Parkway, trying not to think about Jack Lanett's last request.

She focused on the skimpy information she'd dug up on him instead.

He was born in Georgia forty-two years ago. His life was a blank until he was twenty-seven, at which age he had found his first major meteorite, a multi-ton "iron" in South America. From then on, the scientific journals carried regular announcements of his finds from all over the world. These culminated in his current spectacular discovery which he was going to auction off at Sotheby's after letting both the scientists and the general public look at it for the next month or so.

Every article she found had discussed the significance of the meteorites without giving any information whatsoever about the meteorite hunter. Charlie's idea for the science editor at the *New York Times* had been a new angle: what made the mysterious Jack Lanett so successful at his rather unique profession?

Of course, her subject had made it clear that he didn't like her angle.

Which brought her right back to his condition for the interview.

"Men don't ask women to let their hair down so they can talk," she pointed out to her reflection in the rearview mirror. *Maybe he'll be so distracted by the sight of my hair he'll answer my questions without thinking.* "And what if he asks *you* an inappropriate question?" she inquired of the mirror, thinking of his long fingers cupped around an imaginary meteorite and the heat radiating from her car keys. She shivered and cranked the car's thermostat up another notch. *Don't make that mistake again. Keep it strictly professional,* she admonished herself as she resolutely fixed her attention on the bumper in front of her.

As she turned into the driveway of her house two hours later, a welcome sense of sanctuary washed over her. She walked out on the back porch to inhale the scent of mingled salt water and fresh rain wafting up from Corbin's Canal, the channel her property bordered. The narrow finger of water ran from the ocean to an inner harbor, and usually hosted a steady parade of fishing boats and pleasure craft.

Just now the gray, foamy waves coursed past uninterrupted by wakes but Charlie didn't care. She loved the water in all its moods. Three deep breaths and she felt ready to face a dozen recalcitrant meteorite hunters.

She *wasn't* ready for the telephone message that awaited her.

"Hello, Ms. Berglund. This is Candy Mills. I have a family emergency and I won't be able to do the home study for your adoption petition. However, I've referred you to my colleague Rhonda Brown who will be contacting you soon. I'm *so* sorry. I was looking forward to seeing your home."

"Damn!" Charlie said, hurling her handbag onto a big wicker chair by the phone. She stilled as the next message began.

"Charlotte Berglund? I'm Rhonda Brown. I'd like to set up an appointment for your home study sometime this week. Candy Mills says that your paperwork is all progressing well so we want to move the process along. Call me at the same number, extension 12."

"Whew!" Charlie flopped into the other wicker chair as relief washed over her. "She doesn't waste any time. That's a good sign." Her current foster cat leaped onto her lap. Rubbing his silver-gray head, Charlie glanced at the grandfather clock by the fireplace. "Seven o'clock. Well, Twinkle, do I call and leave a message now or wait until tomorrow to try to reach her in person?"

She picked up the phone. "I'll call her now. That way she'll know how gung ho I am."

After leaving a message on Rhonda Brown's voice mail, she sat with the cat purring in her lap. She couldn't resist picturing herself in this very chair, stroking the shining dark hair of a baby girl from China instead of Twinkle's soft fur. She closed her eyes and was swamped by her longing to cradle a small, warm child's body, to inhale the sweet scent of innocence only a child possesses. She imagined carrying her little girl onto the back porch to watch the boats go by. Charlie would read the names off the sterns until her daughter could read them for herself. They'd wave to all the captains and hear the friendly honk of maritime horns, from the bass of the commercial fishing boats to the toot of the little runabouts.

Another six months and this dream should come true . . .

Every aspect of Charlie's life had been validated, notarized, and notarized again. She had been fingerprinted and checked for criminal records. All that stood between her and the child she wanted so badly was the home study. She'd been so confident Candy Mills would approve her;

she and the social worker had spent so much time on the phone together they knew each other's birthdays, favorite foods, and pet peeves. Now she had to start all over again with Rhonda Brown, a total stranger . . .

"At least, my daughter will *have* a mother," Charlie said to Twinkle. "She won't be raised by a series of reluctant aunts, uncles and cousins like I was."

The doorbell rang, and Twinkle leaped off her lap to dash under the sage velvet sofa. Charlie sighed. "Trust comes slowly to you, doesn't it? No one's going to hurt you here, kiddo." She opened the door to find Isabelle Starling standing there, wrapped in her usual collection of fringed shawls and ponchos, with a Tupperware container in her hand.

Isabelle, her favorite next-door neighbor, ran both the local organic foods co-op and one of the most powerful environmental advocacy groups in the state of New Jersey. Charlie could never figure out if she was fifty or seventy years old, although given her rich and colorful life history, Charlie guessed closer to seventy. But you'd never know it from looking at her. Eating all those pesticide-free vegetables must work; Isabelle had few wrinkles, no extra flesh, and was bursting with vitality.

"Good evening, Charlie. I made some butternut squash soup and thought you'd like some on this rainy old March night."

"Sounds delicious. Come in and share it with me," Charlie invited.

"With all the traveling you do, I figure you need every bite of healthy home-cooked food you can get." Isabelle walked straight into the kitchen and began laying out soup bowls, spoons and mugs on the trestle table by the bay window. "I brought some herbal tea too," she said, producing teabags from under a shawl.

"Did your hearing in Trenton go well?" Charlie asked as she filled a kettle with water and set it on the stove.

Isabelle tsked. "That Frank Santino doesn't care if it's a green belt or a parking lot as long as it means money for his district."

"I guess green belts don't generate much cash."

"Oh, you'd be surprised. Tax breaks are almost as good as money in the bank. It's amazing what you can finagle if you put your mind to it." Isabelle swooped into the chair opposite Charlie's and ladled soup into their bowls. "How did your interview with the mysterious meteorite hunter go?"

"It didn't." Charlie swallowed a spoonful of warm soup. "I hauled him out in the rain to rescue a dog that got hit by a taxi. By the time we finished, it was too late to interview him. And he wasn't in a very receptive mood anyway."

Isabelle laughed, a sound that always reminded Charlie of a wind chime in a breeze. "You look like a warrior queen, but you have the heart of a marshmallow."

"You should talk, you professional tree-hugger."

"So true." Another silvery laugh rippled through the kitchen. "We're two of a kind, you and I. You were obviously destined to live in the Inner Circle."

The five houses that made up Charlie's neighborhood were on a tiny cul-de-sac officially known as Winter Circle. The street was named in the twenties when these were among the few houses in the beachfront community of Bellefont whose owners stayed through the winter. The current residents called their street the Inner Circle, referring to the tightly knit group of people who lived there.

"I guess I owe Greg a debt of gratitude for that," Charlie said.

"How *is* your ex-husband?"

"I haven't heard from him since I had to get a copy of the divorce papers for the adoption." Charlie shrugged. "He was fine then. His wife's pregnant with their second child."

Isabelle reached across and touched Charlie's hand gently. "Don't let that hurt you still. I know you wish it were you pregnant with Greg's child. Just remember, when a woman conceives, Mother Nature handles all the complicated parts until the delivery. You've been given a special gift: the strength and desire to take over for Mother Nature just when the going gets tough. There's a little girl over in China who is very lucky you aren't able to have your own biological children."

"If you don't stop now, I'll ruin the flavor of your soup by crying in it." Charlie swallowed hard and turned her hand under Isabelle's to give it a gentle squeeze. "But thank you."

AT 9:59 A.M. the next day, Charlie pushed the shiny brass doorbell at 35 West 68th Street and braced herself. When she had called the emergency animal hospital at seven o'clock sharp, the receptionist informed her that Mr. Lanett was already on his way to pick up Major, at their request. The dog was too big to fit in their pens comfortably, and they had too much activity to leave him loose as they had done overnight.

Mr. Lanett was not going to be happy with her.

She used her blazer sleeve to rub off the fingerprint she had left on the bell. Jack's voice made her jump. "Come on up. Fifth floor."

The inner door swung open before she could touch it. "Weird," Charlie muttered as she walked across to the brass elevator doors. They too opened before she could find a button to push.

"Weirder."

She strode into the lavishly paneled car. The doors were the same polished brass as the doorbells, and Charlie could not resist checking her appearance. The camel-colored pants suit and pale blue, man-tailored blouse reeked of professionalism and competence. However, the effect was completely spoiled by the torrent of hair that fell over her shoulders and down her back to her waist. She twisted it up into a bun and then let it fall again. *Blast the veterinarian!* She might have risked a bun if Jack hadn't been inconvenienced a second time.

The elevator doors slid soundlessly apart. Charlie stepped out onto an exquisite Oriental runner and headed for the only door visible in the foyer. "Open, sesame," she said before pushing the intercom buzzer.

The door swung open.

"Did you say something, Ms. Berglund?" Jack Lanett asked, flashing her a quizzical smile. He was dressed in what was evidently his daily uniform: slacks and a polo shirt. Today the pants were a dark heathered blue and the shirt was a cream that made his deep tan especially noticeable.

"Just checking the password." She smiled and moved past him into the most spectacular space she had ever seen in a Manhattan apartment. His living room took up at least half the floor of the building. The woodwork was extensive: shoulder-high wainscoting, deep crown moldings, and a heavily carved mantel above a marble fireplace. In Charlie's eyes, the beauty was ruined by the starkly modern furniture, all chrome angles and square black leather cushions. She made a quick mental note to create an opportunity to examine the contents of the display stands positioned around the room.

Then she gasped.

A man the size of a mountain rose from a chair by the fireplace. He had olive skin, a mustache and a long, dark ponytail.

"Charlie, this is my friend and business associate, Miguel Antonio de Gonzaga y Silva MacPherson. Miguel, my interviewer Charlie Berglund." Jack made the introductions with the fluency of a courtier.

"My pleasure," Miguel said, raising Charlie's hand to within a centimeter of his lips.

"Nice to meet you, Mr. MacPherson," she said. If it hadn't been for the noticeable twinkle in his eye, she would have been very uncomfortable with his absurd gallantry.

He lowered her hand and held it between both of his. "Call me Miguel, please."

"And here's Major," Jack said with a sweep of his hand toward a door which opened off the living room. Charlie heard the click of toenails on the inlaid wood floor. A large fluffy white dog with a bandage around his ribs walked gingerly into the room.

"That's Major?"

"Someone at the vet gave him a bath, probably to preserve their sense of smell," Jack said.

The dog was clearly heading for Charlie but the discomfort of his cracked ribs slowed him down. She met him halfway, kneeling down to ruffle the fur around his ears as he licked her enthusiastically. "What a sweetheart you are! Such a handsome fellow! Yes, it's great to see you too," she laughed as the dog nearly knocked her over with his affection.

"That's what women usually say to *me*." Miguel sighed.

"He obviously knows to whom he owes his life," Jack commented. "I barely get a tail wag."

"That's because he senses you're thinking about ways to roast him," Charlie said. She stood up, picking white dog hairs off her jacket and slacks. When she realized she was dropping the fur on another magnificent Oriental rug, she stopped guiltily.

"Don't worry. I rented the apartment fully furnished, and there's a cleaning service," Jack said, removing a clump of fuzz from her sleeve and letting it fall.

She could feel the brush of his fingers even through two layers of fabric, and quickly moved away from him, almost tripping over Major. "I'm truly sorry you had to pick him up. I wish you had told the vet to call me. Did you pay his medical bill too?"

"You're apologizing to the wrong person. Miguel gets credit for all of the above."

That made Charlie feel slightly better. She turned to the other man with her warmest smile. "Thank you so much! Please tell me what I owe you for the drive and the bill."

"Not a penny," Miguel said with a flourish of his hand. "Unlike my friend here, I am a great admirer of dogs, and this is an especially impressive specimen. *You* saved his life. I did nothing but bring him to you."

"For which I'm very grateful, but I insist on paying the bill."

"I can't remember how much it was, and I've thrown away my copy."

"Miguel has a *very* poor head for numbers," Jack remarked.

Charlie made a silent resolution to call the animal hospital and send Miguel a check for whatever amount he had spent. However, all she said was, "You're very kind."

"Beautiful women have a beneficial effect on my personality. And now I will leave you and my friend to discuss meteorites. I look forward to meeting you again soon," Miguel said, bowing over her hand.

Jack went to the door with him. Miguel said something to him in low, rapid Spanish, and Jack snapped out an answer in the same language. Neither Charlie's hearing nor her Spanish were good enough for her to understand the exchange.

She was petting the dog when Jack walked back over and lifted a handful of her hair. Letting it slide slowly through his fingers, he said, "You kept your side of the bargain. I guess I have to keep mine."

CHAPTER 3

THE SIFTING OF her hair through Jack's fingers sent a tingle across her scalp that vibrated over every inch of her skin. She was sure her face held the same expression of idiotic bliss as Major's had when she'd scratched behind his ears.

Fortunately, the meteorite hunter's eyes were focused on the strands of hair slipping across his hand. "You almost changed your mind."

"Changed my mind?" Charlie asked vaguely.

"You almost put it back up in the elevator," Jack said, as the last piece of hair fell from his fingers.

"How do you know that?" Her pleasant trance evaporated.

"Security cameras," he said, turning toward the kitchen. "Would you like some coffee?"

"Do you always spy on your visitors?"

"Only if they're reporters. To make sure they don't decide to investigate somewhere they're not welcome."

That wasn't very promising. And he'd seen her checking her reflection. Charlie hoped a strong shot of caffeine might overcome her humiliation so she briskly followed him into the kitchen. Fitted out in modern stainless steel, it had all the latest gadgets including an impressive coffee/cappuccino/espresso machine that Jack was flipping various levers on. As he passed her a filled mug, she inhaled appreciatively.

"Straight from Brazil," he said with an understanding nod, and filled a mug for himself. "Miguel supplies me with it."

"Is he a friend or a business partner?"

"Both. He's an expert metalworker and does all the cutting and polishing of the meteorites I sell."

This was an improvement; the man had actually volunteered some information.

"I'd think that cutting the meteorites would lower their value," Charlie observed.

"Depends on the meteorite. Some are valuable because of where they come from—like Mars or the moon—so it doesn't matter what they look like. Some, like a stony-iron with large olivine crystals, are valuable because of their beauty. But you can't see the crystals unless you slice into the meteorite. That's where Miguel comes in. He makes the displays too."

He led her back into the living room. Taking the mug from her hand, he put it down beside his on a low table and steered her over to one of the stands Charlie had noticed earlier. "You've done your homework, I'm sure," he said, giving her one of his there-and-gone smiles, "so you know the three basic classes of meteorites: iron, stone and stony-iron."

Charlie nodded, hoping he'd continue.

"This is a slice of a stony-iron pallasite from the Atacama Desert in Chile."

The meteorite seemed to float above the square, white, waist-high base, balanced on delicate curves of black wire rising from a slender stem of the same dark metal. It was a thin, roughly rectangular slab about a foot long and six inches high. The highly polished silvery stone was pierced by irregularly shaped, pale, brownish-golden crystals. Two of the edges were perfectly straight lines, courtesy of Miguel, she supposed. The third edge was outlined by a line of charcoal black. The top edge exhibited a weird terrain of bumps and gaps.

Jack pushed a button with the toe of his shoe. Charlie gasped as a brilliant beam of light poured through the crystal "windows," bathing the meteorite in an exquisite glow.

"It certainly *looks* as though it's from another world," she said. She glanced up to see the light shimmering across her companion's face, as he gazed at the rock. Almost as if hypnotized, he reached out and ran his fingers over the black encrusted edge.

"This is the fusion crust. It formed when the meteor burned its way through our atmosphere after Earth's gravity ended its journey from some distant corner of the galaxy."

Charlie started to reach out herself, then hesitated. "May I touch it?"

Dropping his own hand, he nodded.

She carefully traced the strangely gnarled top edge. It was smoother to the touch than she expected.

"It must have broken off from a larger piece there," he explained. "Miguel polished it but left the edge in its natural shape. You can see the holes where crystals once were embedded."

Her fingers slid down to the sliced surface, skimming over the cold gleaming metal and making shadows on the luminous olivine.

"So you don't know what corner of the galaxy it came from?" Charlie asked, shifting her gaze from the alien stone to Jack.

He shook his head. "We can speculate, but scientists don't have enough data about the various heavenly bodies yet to say definitively. However, they *theorize* that the pallasites form at the point where the parent body's core and mantle come together. The iron-nickel alloy—the silvery part—is from the core, and the crystals are from the bottom of the mantle. It would have to be from a fairly large body to have both a core and a mantle."

"It's absolutely beautiful. Is it valuable?"

"Not particularly. A few thousand dollars." He toed the button again to turn off the light. "The ones in this room are just for display. I keep the really unique specimens in special cases under lock and key. Then there's my *private* collection," he added with an infinitely slow smile this time, and a drawl so thick you could have cut it with a knife.

"I'll bet you keep it right alongside your etchings," Charlie said tartly, as she braced herself against the impact of those blue eyes warmed by an interest in something other than meteorites.

He laughed. "The only etchings I collect are the Widmannstatten structures on my iron meteorites." He held her gaze as he stepped close to her side, causing her to involuntarily tilt her head back. Weaving his fingers into her cascading hair, he slowly slid his hand around her waist to rest lightly on the small of her back.

Charlie stifled a gasp as heat rippled upward and downward from his touch.

A low, threatening rumble made them both look down. Major's upper lip was curled away from his teeth, and his head was lowered in a hostile stance. His dark eyes were fixed on Jack.

Charlie began to laugh. She had acquired a guardian Kuvasz.

"It's okay, Major," she assured him, ruffling his ears.

Jack dropped his hand, and Major stopped snarling.

"Your dog doesn't understand the difference between a gentleman and a mugger."

"Oh, doesn't he?"

"No."

"Maybe he sees you as a rival," she said, stroking the dog's head and taking slow deep breaths.

Incredibly, she heard him chuckle, a rich sound from deep in his chest. "I'm flattered." He took the dog's muzzle in his hand and gently tilted Major's head. "Just remember I can close the bedroom door, and you can't open it."

"But I can," Charlie pointed out.

"Not if I tie you to the bed." He let go of the dog and straightened with a wicked gleam in his eye.

Charlie backed up four paces. She *really* needed to get this interview back to business. "Sahara-Mars is at the Museum of Natural History, isn't it?"

Jack took one step in her direction, then stopped and huffed out a sigh of exasperation. However, he answered her question. "That's right. I'm giving the scientists time to study it before the auction."

"Can they study it without causing any damage?"

"They'd better be able to," he said, with a menacing smile. He strolled over to a couch and sat down.

Charlie chose a chair across from him, reclaiming her coffee as she began to formulate another question.

He spoke without prompting, his voice back in what she thought of as "business mode": just a touch of southern molasses and no hint of personal interest. "Right now, that rock is worth a couple of million dollars because the experts have confirmed it's a very old—about four *billion* years—achondrite from Mars. That's the same kind of meteorite as ALH 84001, the one some scientists think shows there was life on the Red Planet. Mine was found in the desert, and it's a very recent fall so there's little biological contamination."

Charlie knew all this. She also knew that if some trace of life could be found in the interplanetary stone, it would become virtually priceless. She hoped the thought of all that money would mellow Jack enough to tell her a few things she *didn't* know.

"How did you find the meteorite?"

"Now, sugar, I can't give away trade secrets, can I?" he said, crossing his arms over his chest.

Damn. She tilted her head so that her hair swung away from her shoulder. "Isn't it named for the Sahara Desert?"

He looked at her a long moment before he raised an eyebrow in acknowledgment of her tactical move and said, "It was found by nomads in the Western Sahara. People know I buy strange black rocks from the desert—and pay them fairly in whatever currency they most want—so they found someone who could get in touch with me."

Her hair was driving her crazy, but Charlie left it streaming over her right shoulder and puddling in her lap. She tucked a strand behind her ear and waited.

"I was in Africa at the time and went to collect it myself. The tribesman who found it wanted to negotiate with me in person. When he pulled the rock out of his camel bag and put it in my hands, I knew it was something rare."

This was good. The man's eyes seemed to be focused on the scene. Charlie longed for her tape recorder but didn't dare interrupt the flow. *If he would just keep talking . . .*

He did, leaning forward suddenly and cupping his hands as he had at the vet. His blue eyes were burning with their own inner flame. "Sometimes a meteorite just *feels* different; something radiates through that black crust. There's no sense to it. This one had a beautiful shape with deep flow structures on the surface, showing how it was pointed when it plunged through the atmosphere. And the fusion crust was perfect: no breaks, no chips. The meteorite was intact. That nomad was a smart fellow. He could read me like he could read a sand dune." He laughed, startling Charlie. "I gave him more for that rock than I've ever given anyone before, and I hadn't even analyzed it."

Suddenly he was on his feet and then beside her chair, holding out a hand to her. "Come here."

She put her hand in his without thinking. The warmth and strength of his grip were shocking but she had no time to react as he pulled her up and toward another display stand. Taking a small black stone from its metal cradle, he turned her hand upward and placed the meteorite in it.

"Feel how heavy it is, heavier than an Earth rock of the same size would be. See the conical shape and the lines radiating out from the tip; that makes it oriented. It didn't tumble during its flight through our atmosphere and the friction shaped that blunt tip and liquefied the surface of the rock so it flowed backward in rivulets. This is what the Mars rock felt like." He closed her fingers around the small stone by wrapping his hand around hers. "Except it radiated something else too. It was extraordinary to hold."

This was what she wanted to write about, a man who could feel the difference in a meteorite just by touching it.

"Is this one from Mars?" she asked.

"No, it's probably from an asteroid." He released her hand.

She opened her fingers. The meteorite's surface gleamed darkly against her skin. She traced a flow structure from the tip to the base with her index finger. "I can't believe I'm holding a piece of an asteroid in my hand." She glanced up to find his gaze locked on her. The blue flames still blazed but their focus had altered. She was glad to feel Major push between them.

Jack frowned at the dog but stepped back.

"How do you feel the differences in meteorites?" Charlie asked.

"I can't really." He shrugged. "I have to have them analyzed by the experts." There was a slightly ironic emphasis on his last word.

"Have you had trouble with the experts?"

"Some. The scientists don't like it when I sell my finds to private collectors."

"Isn't the bio-astronomer Peter Burke especially vocal in his opposition to your business?"

"Dr. Burke doesn't understand that it *is* a business," Jack said.

"I read that you always donate a piece of any rare meteorite you find to research," Charlie said to soften his mood.

"Whenever possible. Some meteorites would lose their value if I cut them. Like the one you're holding. The beautiful fusion crust is what makes it worth something." He smiled unpleasantly. "I give them their pound of flesh but they want blood." The opening bars of Beethoven's *Fifth Symphony* suddenly emanated from Jack's trouser pocket.

"Excuse me," he said, walking toward the hallway as he pulled out the cell phone. He disappeared through a doorway.

Charlie stood absolutely still. Guests didn't eavesdrop, but reporters did. After a few opening pleasantries, she heard a distinctly steely tone enter her interviewee's voice.

"I'll make sure that you and your client get an invitation to the preview party." Silence, then an even firmer statement. "Mr. Vandermade can see the meteorite at the same time as the other serious bidders."

Charlie recognized the name Vandermade; he was a billionaire who collected geological rarities rather than Old Masters, spouting something about Mother Nature being a greater artist than man. She thought he was just trying to be different from the rest of his super-wealthy friends. If Curt Vandermade was interested in the meteorite, Jack Lanett was going to make a *lot* of money on this auction.

"The crust is intact. All analyses have been done without invasion of the meteorite. Yes, you can bring your own geologist to confirm that. I'll fax you the verification reports today."

A few more curt formalities, and Jack Lanett emerged back into the living room.

"I'm sorry; business intrudes. That's the private line for folks who are seriously interested in buying Sahara-Mars." He glanced at his watch. "I hate to end this delightful conversation, but I have an appointment at the Museum of Natural History. I hope you have enough for your article."

Not nearly enough, but Charlie smiled sweetly.

"You've started me down some interesting paths. I'd like to find out more about the metal-working aspect of meteorite dealing. Would Mr. MacPherson be willing to talk with me? I'd also like to thank him again for picking up Major."

It was hard to maintain her air of innocence when the man was looking at her as though she were a particularly venomous subspecies of cobra.

"Reporters are all alike," he muttered as he pulled a card out of his wallet and scrawled a telephone number on the back of it. "Call him and see what he says."

"Thank you," she said, tucking the card in her blazer pocket. She gathered up her shoulder bag and headed for the door. "I'll be in touch if I need clarification on anything."

"Don't forget your dog."

"Oh. Of *course!*" Charlie felt heat in her cheeks. She was so frazzled she had completely ignored the dog limping after her.

Major caught up as she stopped.

"There's a leash on the table, courtesy of the vet. Miguel said the young doctor sang your praises. Evidently, you have a reputation as a good foster home for emotionally disturbed strays. You straighten them out, and they get adopted."

"*Animals* trust me," Charlie said pointedly.

He laughed as he sauntered toward her. Giving the dog a hard look, he stepped in close and combed his fingers through her hair from the base of her skull to the base of her spine.

"Don't ever cut your hair." His voice was back in the South.

"No, no, I won't," Charlie stammered, flustered again as she felt the stroke of his fingertips all the way down her back. She grabbed the leash and hooked it on Major's collar. Trying to end the meeting on a professional note, she held out her hand. "I enjoyed the privilege of holding a meteorite. Thank you for your time."

A half-smile played over his lips as he bypassed her hand and brushed a strand of hair back behind her shoulder. "Consider it my contribution to the human interest angle."

CHAPTER 4

CHARLIE WALKED AS fast as the dog could manage down the hallway to the elevator's open doors. After practically vaulting into the paneled cubicle, she pulled a tortoise shell clip out of her shoulder bag and twisted her hair into a torturously tight bun. She spent the rest of the brief ride to the first floor fussing over Major even as she wondered if Jack was watching on the security monitor.

He was and he chuckled when she snapped the clip into her hair. "I guess my little game worked." Unfortunately, it had worked on him too. He knew he would spend the rest of the day trying to banish visions of that glorious hair spread across a black satin pillow . . . and worrying about what she meant by "interesting paths."

He and Miguel had known publicity would be risky, but they both wanted the big payoff it would bring. Being subjected to the glare of the press would be worth it as long as some African country didn't decide to lay claim to the profits—or some reporter didn't unearth a past he had buried as deeply as humanly possible. He dialed Miguel's number.

"Hey, *amigo*. I want to give you the heads-up. The 'beautiful lady with legs and hair that go on forever' is going to call you."

"*¡Que belleza!* I envy you your interview."

Jack snorted. "By the way, how do you know she doesn't speak Spanish?"

"She may, but she could only be flattered by such a description. So, what do you want me to tell her?"

"Whatever you think is appropriate and safe." Jack paused a moment. "Why don't you invite her to our lecture on Wednesday?"

"Because you limited attendance to scientists only."

"How bad can one reporter be? Tell her to sit in back and keep her mouth shut." His drawl thickened. "Use that Spanish *machismo* of yours. Maybe she'll write her article on *you* and then go away."

"Perhaps I'd like her to come closer."

"She's a reporter. Don't mess with her."

"Ahhh." There was a grin in Miguel's voice. "Perhaps *you'd* like her to come closer."

"Her dog might have something to say about that," Jack muttered.

"Your favorite bio-astronomer was on the *Today Show* this morning." Miguel smoothly changed the subject.

"Was Peter doing his usual rant?"

"Of course. Why don't you explain to him what his entire career is based on?"

"I don't think he'd be grateful," Jack said. "Why don't they get bored with him saying the same thing all the time? *I'm* certainly tired of hearing that meteorites are the rightful property of scientists, etc., etc., etc."

Miguel sighed heavily. "He looks good on television, and he's got that irresistible southern charm. Reminds me strongly of someone else I know. You should suggest a face-to-face debate."

"Too risky."

"If you included me, no one would be looking at you and Peter."

Jack snorted again. "I'm leaving for the museum now, Miguel."

JACK UNDERESTIMATED CHARLIE'S ability to focus. After helping Major into the back of her Volvo, she pulled out a pad of paper and furiously scribbled the notes she had filed in her mind during the interview. She finished with a list of follow-up questions, and called Miguel MacPherson to set up a time for them to speak the next day.

He was surprisingly willing to meet with her.

"Lanett must have called him as soon as I walked out the door," she said to the dog as she pulled out of the parking garage. "Otherwise he would have been cagier. He's not going to tell me anything new, I know it." Major whined sympathetically. She eased out into traffic, and used the drive to speculate on the less factual aspects of her interview.

Lanett obviously has a long-hair fetish. . . . Trying to use it to pry more information out of him had backfired, partly because she seemed to be developing a Jack Lanett fetish. *How could I possibly enjoy being called "sugar"!* "It's that damned southern accent, nothing else," she swore out loud, glancing at the dog. He wagged his tail. *Not to mention that those blue eyes were lit with intentions I should have been insulted by.* . . . To her own horrified amazement, when he had mentioned tying her to his bed, she had been far more tantalized than outraged. "What am I thinking?" she said. "I don't even like the man, and he certainly doesn't like me!"

But even as she said it she knew one of those statements wasn't entirely true.

MAJOR PRECEDED HER into her house. Twinkle took one look at the monster and streaked off down the hall to Charlie's bedroom.

"Oh—now that's not a good start," Charlie said, dropping her keys on the hall table. "I'm going to have to introduce you two more formally." Major was sniffing the chair where the cat had been sitting. Suddenly, he put his head down on the cushion and gave a soft yelp. "What's the matter, boy? Do you like cats? Or hate them? There's no time like the present to find out."

They walked slowly to Charlie's bedroom, where the cat was cowering under the antique four-poster bed. Charlie pushed aside the crocheted dust ruffle and slid under the mattress on her stomach to try to coax him out. Twinkle backed up hissing and spitting, and Charlie realized Major had wedged his head and shoulders under the bed beside her. "I don't think Twinkle wants you here just yet," she said, starting to push the dog backward as gently as possible.

Major dropped his chin to the floor and gave a low whine.

Twinkle stopped hissing. Major inched a little farther forward and whined again. The cat's ruffled fur smoothed out. Another whine and Twinkle stretched forward to delicately sniff the big dog's nose. Charlie held her breath. Twinkle rubbed her head along the dog's snout and strolled out from under the bed. Charlie and Major had to wriggle backward to make their undignified exit.

"What *are* you? Some kind of cat whisperer?" Charlie asked, smoothing loose strands of hair away from her face with one hand as she scratched the dog's ears with the other. Twinkle was sitting on the rug, calmly bathing herself not two feet away from the enormous Kuvasz. The dog lay with his head on his paws and watched. *Animals never cease to amaze me.* "I'll leave you two to establish whatever relationship this is blossoming into while I play my phone messages."

The first recording was the editor at the *New York Times* checking on the status of her article on Jack Lanett. Charlie groaned. The second was Allan Schumann from the animal shelter asking about Major's health and inviting her out to dinner. Charlie sighed. The third was Rhonda Brown scheduling a home study for Friday at ten o'clock. Charlie grabbed her calendar from her shoulder bag and scrawled "HOME STUDY!!!" over the two appointments she had already written down for Friday.

The cat and the dog emerged from the bedroom side-by-side to see their human spinning and leaping around her living room.

As CHARLIE DROVE to the Rose Center for Earth and Space the next evening, she reflected that the interview with Miguel MacPherson had gone surprisingly well. He described Jack Lanett as a new breed of meteorite hunter, one who developed a network of contacts all over the world to notify him of falls and finds. She learned that Jack spoke seven languages and even more dialects, all self-taught. Miguel told her several entertaining if unrevealing anecdotes about meteorite hunting with his partner, and described his own role in the business. He even flirted with her in a very mild way, but she found, to her relief, she had no interest in being tied to *his* bed.

By far his most valuable contribution was an invitation to the scientists-only lecture where she was now headed.

Before the interview, she had pulled every string she could find to get in, but no one could get past the dragon lady who controlled the guest list.

She wondered if Jack knew about his partner's breach of his defenses.

She already had a pretty good first draft of her *Times* article; this exclusive would put it over the top. She'd add her take on the lecture, give her prose a final polish, and send it off with the beautiful photo of Sahara-Mars Miguel had presented to her. The science editor was going to swoon with delight.

Parking took longer than she expected, and Charlie strode into the lecture hall with only minutes to spare. She found an empty seat in the back row and sat down. Flipping open her leather portfolio to a yellow pad of paper, she glanced around the room. Almost all of the fifty or so seats were occupied. The spectators were mostly male, but a few women were sprinkled in the mix. Charlie noticed her ensemble of navy blue blazer and slacks and blue-and-white striped shirt was among the more formal outfits there. The auditorium was endowed with a raked floor so all the seats had a clear view of the empty podium and table standing on the raised platform at the front of the hall. Two men stood by the lower entrance, checking their watches every few seconds. When they relaxed and smiled, Charlie sat up straighter and waited for Jack Lanett to appear.

He walked in with his hand outstretched. As he shook hands with his hosts, Charlie could just catch the rich tones of his voice but not his words. He was dressed in a silver gray suit that clearly had been tailored for him. His shirt was light blue and his tie swirled with blue and gray. He looked more like a corporate vice president than a renegade meteorite hunter. Then Miguel MacPherson walked through the door, carrying a large, shiny, dark cube that he placed on the empty table. Miguel had on jeans, a black T-shirt, and a black leather jacket. Charlie chuckled at the obvious statement he was making. She stopped laughing when his jacket gapped open to reveal a gun holstered underneath.

Jack stepped up to the podium, and tapped the microphone. "I'm Jack Lanett. This is my colleague Miguel MacPherson. And this," he gestured toward the cube, "is Sahara-Mars."

Miguel touched a switch and the cube lit up.

A collective gasp arose from the audience.

The glittering black rock still seemed to be blazing through the Earth's atmosphere. The meteorite was large enough that even from where she sat, Charlie could see the cone shape and flow structures. Miguel had suspended it pointing diagonally downward, creating the illusion of flight. The display case's lighting shifted subtly every few seconds, making the fusion crust sparkle.

Barnum and Bailey couldn't have done it any better, Charlie thought.

Jack let everyone in the auditorium stare for several moments, and then introduced a Dr. Wayne Fletcher who would summarize the results of the analyses conducted on the Mars rock. Dr. Fletcher quickly plunged into incomprehensible scientific jargon, and Charlie put down her pen. She watched Jack and Miguel instead.

Miguel stood behind the meteorite looking large and menacing. She could see him scanning the room and concluded that he had neglected to mention security was another of his responsibilities in the firm of Jack Lanett Meteorites. Jack, on the other hand, had taken a seat behind the speaker and appeared totally absorbed in the description of thermographic scans, chemical comparisons and new developments in X rays. He nodded occasionally, and once jotted down a note on a small pad he pulled from his breast pocket.

Dr. Fletcher registered the complaint that his team had not been permitted to probe inside the meteorite, and so his conclusions were incomplete. Jack frowned. But the doctor stated his conviction that this stone was an achondrite from Mars, similar in age and composition to the famous ALH 84001.

Jack returned to the podium. "Thank you for that fascinating report, Dr. Fletcher. I appreciate the thoroughness of your examination, given the constraints placed upon you by the exigencies of economics." He looked out over the crowd. "You were threatened with a lecture," he continued, eliciting a few cautious chuckles from the audience as he picked up the microphone and walked out to the front of the platform. "But you already know what you want to know, so I'm going to open up the floor to questions instead."

After a moment, an astronomer stood and identified himself. Charlie couldn't quite follow his question, which dealt with comparing Sahara-Mars to another meteorite, but she did catch the condescending tone in which it was asked. Jack answered pleasantly and without hesitation. After a follow-up question, the astronomer sat down. There was a brief pause, and then two people stood. Jack knew one of them and, presuming on their acquaintance asked him to yield to the unknown scientist.

The man left standing was an astro-geologist. His question was so technical Charlie couldn't understand it after the third word. When he finished his query, the man sitting in front of her muttered, "Let's see you get past *that* one."

Jack launched into an explanation as jargon-laden as the question had been.

Charlie sensed the atmosphere in the room shifting.

Outright laughter burst out when Jack finished his answer to the third question. *Obviously some inside joke in
the astronomy industry,* Charlie thought. Suddenly questions were coming thick and fast, and the lecture hall's
hostile formality disintegrated into a lively discussion. The
woman beside her leaned over to say, "He's got all these
self-anointed geniuses eating out of his hand."

"It's that southern accent," Charlie whispered back.
"Yankees can't resist it."

She saw Jack stiffen and move back behind the podium.
She craned her neck to see what had caused the change. A
tall good-looking young man with coal-black hair stood at
the back of the room.

"Dr. Burke from Princeton," Jack said before the man
could speak. "An unexpected pleasure."

"I wouldn't have missed this opportunity to see Sahara-
Mars. I apologize for interrupting with my late arrival," Dr.
Burke said. His southern accent was even thicker than Jack's.

"We're honored to have such a notable expert in our
midst."

The woman whispered again. "That's Peter Burke, a
world-class bio astronomer. He's published piles of papers
about the chances of finding sentient life in the universe.
And he hates Jack Lanett for selling a meteorite that could
crown his career."

Charlie knew this, of course. She had seen a tape of Dr.
Burke's interview on the *Today Show*; he had charmed
Katie Couric right out of her designer pumps. Had Charlie
not met Jack, she might have sympathized with the scientist's point of view: it seemed reasonable that a find this
rare should be turned over to research. On the other hand,
Dr. Burke was not bumping over sand dunes on a camel
and risking his own hard-earned cash to acquire the meteorites he wanted to study.

"I wonder if I might pose a question," the scientist said as he sauntered down the center aisle, ostensibly in search of a seat.

"Of course," Jack said, relaxing his posture to lounge casually against the podium.

"By what right do you claim ownership of this meteorite, this gift from space, flung to Earth to help us solve the riddles of the universe?"

The silence was absolute.

"By the right of risk and reward," Jack said easily. "I take the risks and I reap the rewards."

"There would be no reward without years of painstaking research by people like these." He made a sweeping gesture around the room. "Without *science*, your million-dollar stone would be a worthless black ro—"

"Without meteorite *hunters*, scientists would have nothing to study." Jack laughed, but he did not look amused. "Face it, Dr. Burke, we're in this together."

"If you auction this meteorite to the highest bidder, a crucial piece of evidence in the search for life in the universe will be lost to science."

"I would like nothing better than to have the winning bidder be a museum or university. In fact, I have given the scientific community every opportunity to put together a consortium to purchase it. You have been unable to do so for reasons which do not do your profession credit."

Peter Burke stopped partway down the aisle so he was exactly at eye level with Jack. Charlie was struck by how evenly matched the two men were in their thrust-and-parry. They each seemed to sense how the other would respond before they spoke.

"As you know very well, an institution of research cannot hope to compete with the wealth of private collectors such as you cater to," Dr. Burke said.

"Console yourself with the thought that my meteorite may in fact be just another black space rock, and the private collector will have wasted all that wealth. After all, even an expert such as Dr. Fletcher cannot *guarantee* it carries signs of Martian life. Are there any other questions?"

A hiss of whispers flooded the hall. Charlie was astounded that Jack would throw doubt on his own discovery. Dr. Burke appeared to have touched a nerve.

She glanced at Miguel to check his reaction, but his face was impassive.

No one ventured to ask another question publicly, but when Jack formally closed the program, a dozen scientists surged forward to talk with him at the podium. Two dozen made a beeline for the meteorite. Charlie was tempted to join the latter group but she stuck to her promise to stay out of the way of the trained professionals.

She closed her portfolio and watched Jack chatting with the scientists. He was taller than everyone else in the group. She admired his posture: head bent courteously, attention focused on the speaker, yet there was no hint of inferiority or currying favor. He clearly considered himself the equal of any man there, but he paid them the compliment of his respect at the same time. It was a neat trick. Suddenly, he raised his head and looked straight at her.

Charlie felt his blue gaze go through her like an icy wind.

Then he did something that caused her pen to clatter to the floor.

He winked.

CHAPTER 5

FRIDAY MORNING THE house was spotless. Sunlight streamed through the French doors that opened onto the back porch, giving the rose and mossy green hues of the living room a warm, earthy glow. The small spare first floor bedroom sported brand-new curtains, an antique hooked rug with Noah's ark on it, and space just begging for a crib and changing table. An apple-cinnamon cake sat cooling on the kitchen counter, and the smell of fresh coffee issued from the spout of a china pot decorated with cavorting dolphins. Major lay on the braided rug in front of the fireplace with Twinkle curled against him.

"Could you two stay posed like that *after* the doorbell rings? You're better than all the Noah's ark rugs in the world," Charlie said as she paced from the kitchen to the front door and back for the tenth time. She checked her watch, adjusted her hair clip, and straightened a puffy throw pillow.

The doorbell rang.

Major and Twinkle raised their heads as their mistress sprinted for the door.

"Hello, Ms. Berglund. I'm Rhonda Brown."

"Please come in. And please call me Charlie."

Rhonda Brown did not offer the use of her first name as she stepped into the living room and looked around. She was about fifty, with short iron-gray hair and deep brown skin. Tall and imposing, she wore a flowing, calf-length dress in a swirling pattern of earth tones, decorated on the left shoulder with a large silver and garnet pin. She placed her bulging brief case on the floor by the couch.

"Would you like a cup of coffee?" Charlie asked. "And some cake? I just made both."

"Coffee, thank you."

Charlie carried the tray laden with the dolphin pot, cups, spoons, sugar and cream into the living room. She found Rhonda Brown, Major and Twinkle engaged in a silent staring match.

"The dog is Major, the cat is Twinkle. They're just here temporarily. I foster stray animals until they can be adopted."

"Candy noted that in your file." The social worker accepted the cup of coffee and took a sip, closing her eyes appreciatively at the flavor. "Thanks. Caffeine is one of my favorite vices."

Charlie smiled, grateful that her guest had shown a small gleam of humanity.

"I'd be happy to give you a tour of the house, Ms. Brown."

"You may call me Rhonda," she said, inclining her head with all the regality of an empress.

"Thank you."

Charlie led her through the kitchen, dining room, the master and spare bedroom and the bath-and-a-half downstairs. After touring the upstairs, which consisted of another bedroom and bathroom and Charlie's office, Rhonda said, "This house is much larger than it appears from the outside."

"I know. 'Capes' are very deceptive that way."

"I imagine you and your ex-husband bought it expecting to start a family."

"Yes. Yes, actually we did." For some reason, Charlie was startled by her perception.

"And you still want that family."

Charlie nodded.

"Let's go downstairs and talk."

They settled in the living room, and Rhonda accepted a piece of coffee cake. For two hours, she probed Charlie's views on discipline, education, toilet training, medical care, and a myriad of other topics related to nurturing a child.

"Would you like a sandwich?" Charlie asked when the discussion paused for a moment.

"Thank you but no."

Rhonda deliberately collected all the files she had pulled out in the course of their conversation and carefully put them back in her briefcase. "I believe that you will make a very good adoptive parent."

Charlie couldn't stop the grin that spread across her face. "That's great!"

The older woman held up her hand in a warning. "I have a serious reservation though. I've read your financial file, and the numbers demonstrate an ability to support a child. However, I then looked up your articles as the 'Average Adventurer,' your steadiest source of income. Your writing is most enjoyable. Your subject matter concerns me."

"My subject matter?"

"In order to write those articles, you must travel widely and often to remote locations. By definition, the expeditions are somewhat hazardous." Rhonda paused. "You will be a single parent," she continued, leaning forward. "There's no spouse to take your place while you are away, or in the event that you are seriously injured or possibly even killed. You are proposing to adopt a child from halfway around the world. She will have no safety net in this country, no network of relatives such as you had when you were orphaned. Think about that."

She sat back.

Charlie was stunned. Candy Mills had expressed no such concerns, and she knew very well what Charlie did for a living. They had even discussed her plans for childcare when Charlie had to travel. The possibility that she would die on one of her expeditions was remote; she wasn't stupid, she didn't take unnecessary chances. A near-fall on a poorly organized rock-climbing trip flitted across her consciousness, but she dismissed it. She had chosen two guardians from among her cousins, in any case. "My daughter will have the same family I have."

"How satisfactory was *your* upbringing?"

Charlie opened her mouth and then closed it. She had obviously revealed more about her childhood than she had realized.

"Exactly," Rhonda said.

"What do you want me to do?"

"That's up to you. You're an intelligent, principled young woman. Prove to me you can earn a living less hazardously. Or find a guardian whom you would genuinely want to have your child raised by."

Charlie looked away and blinked furiously to fight back tears. The interview had been going so well; she was so sure that Rhonda Brown liked her. And now this.

"What happens if I can't?"

The social worker shrugged. "I'll probably approve you anyway, but I won't revisit your file for six months unless you tell me something has changed."

"Six months," Charlie whispered. A year had already elapsed since she had started the adoption process. Even if Rhonda approved the adoption today, it would be six months before all the paperwork cleared, and Charlie could bring home her new daughter from China. Now the social worker was adding another six months to the process. That meant another *year* before she had her baby. It seemed like an eternity.

"Six additional months isn't long when weighed against a child's lifetime," Rhonda said, standing up. "But frankly, I expect to hear from you before that."

Charlie stood as well, escorting her new nemesis to the front door. "I appreciate your confidence," she said with a distinctly ironic inflection.

"Honey, you've gotten this far." Rhonda reached out and patted her cheek. "You'll be a mother soon enough."

She left Charlie openmouthed.

"WHAT ABOUT A husband?" Mike asked.

"Oh, please," Charlie said, rolling her eyes.

Four of the residents of the Inner Circle were sitting around the polished mahogany table in Mike Phillips and Ernst Haufmann's dining room, sipping brandy over the remains of dinner. The two men had bought their house four years ago when they retired from law and investment banking respectively. Although the newest comers to the neighborhood, they had quickly become the organizers of all Inner Circle gatherings. Now they were applying their formidable minds to the latest roadblock in Charlie's adoption process.

"Allan Schumann would marry you in a New York minute, given the least encouragement," Mike persisted, his green eyes twinkling.

"Allan likes animals much better than he likes people," Isabelle said.

"Have I just been insulted?" Charlie asked.

"He's not the man for you, my dear," Isabelle responded placidly.

"Are the trips you take really dangerous?" Ernst asked, his square face and blue eyes serious.

"I haven't considered them dangerous for a long time. But when I started my 'adventures,' it was right after my divorce and part of my thinking was that I had nothing to lose if something went wrong."

"I see," Ernst said, steepling his fingers. "So we must find you a new job."

Charlie grimaced. "I like being a writer, and editors like hiring me. I don't want to change careers now."

"Who says you have to change careers?" Mike said, passing a beautifully arranged plate of assorted fruit and cheese. "You just need to do a different kind of writing. How about becoming a food critic?" he suggested as he surveyed the table.

"Charlie's perfectly happy eating beef jerky and trail mix," Isabelle snorted.

Charlie laughed.

"I think it's time you wrote a book," Ernst stated. "Enough of these short pieces that require more action than thought. You're too good a writer to waste any more time on fluff."

"You know, if I were a sensitive soul, I'd be in tears by now," Charlie said, choosing a slice of apple and a sliver of organic Gouda. She stacked the two together and took an appreciative bite. "Maybe food critic isn't such a bad idea. What would I write a book about?"

"Global warming," Isabelle suggested promptly.

"Roe versus Wade," Mike said.

"Enron," Ernst said.

Charlie looked skeptical.

"Whales."

"The Supreme Court."

"The SEC."

"How about meteorites?" Charlie asked.

"And the hunter!" Isabelle interjected.

"Who wants to read about rocks?" Mike asked.

"Rocks from space," Charlie pointed out. "Very *valuable* rocks from space."

Now Mike was interested. "How much is that fellow expecting to get for his Mars rock?"

"He won't really say, but his partner anticipates more than two million. Evidently, they've whipped up a rivalry between some private collectors and a couple of public institutions," Charlie said.

Mike's eyes gleamed; he had been a top-notch litigator so he loved a good fight. "Maybe I'll wangle an invitation to that auction. It'd be fun to watch."

"I have no interest in seeing a group of grown men spend absurd amounts of money on a lump of stone," Ernst said.

"No, but you were happy to help grown men *lose* absurd amounts of money on dot-coms," Isabelle said.

"I'll go with you, Mike," Charlie offered. "It would be very useful for my book."

"Are you really going to write a book about meteorites?" Isabelle asked, as she untangled a dangling silver earring from her shawl's fringe.

"The idea has some merit." Charlie shrugged.

Actually, the more she thought about it, the more it appealed to her. "I could expand the human interest angle I used in the *Times* article. Add a scientist to the mix. Talk about the conflict at the intersection of science and business."

"You can talk to that handsome young astronomer I saw on the *Today Show*," Isabelle suggested. "Peter Burke. *He's* not shy about being interviewed."

"You see, you're ready for a subject you can sink your teeth into. I can tell you're longing to get to your computer already." Ernst was smiling. "Go ahead. You don't have to stay to clean up."

Charlie cleared her place and bolted for her house.

SEVERAL LONG DAYS and nights and a few favors later, she faxed off a proposal and three sample chapters to her agent. Within a week, she had her answer. Two editors wanted the book, and they wanted it *fast* while the topic was hot. Her only obstacle was one recalcitrant meteorite hunter. She didn't have time to beat around the bush so she picked up the phone and called him.

"Hello, Jack. This is Charlie Berglund from the *Times*. I'd like to take you out to lunch and discuss a proposition I have for you." She certainly wasn't going back to his apartment.

"Let me think about this," he drawled. "A beautiful lady with long blond hair wants to proposition me over lunch. How can I say no?"

"You can't." She had made a bad choice of words, but gritted her teeth and somehow injected a smile into her voice. "I'll meet you at the Brasserie Américaine at one o'clock tomorrow if that's convenient."

"Make it two o'clock, sugar, and I'm available."

"By the way, I really enjoyed your question-and-answer session at the Rose Center," she said, buttering him up now that she had him hooked. "You did a superb job of handling an unfriendly audience."

He laughed. "So you noticed the atmosphere was somewhat strained?"

"Only for about three questions. After that, even Peter Burke couldn't destroy the general good will."

"Burke usually knows better than to confront me directly. I'm sure you were unable to resist reporting that little contretemps in your article."

"Controversy sells," Charlie said, stung by his unflattering assumption. The fact that she *had* included part of their dramatic confrontation in her article only made his insult worse.

"I can think of something else that sells even better, but we'll talk about that over lunch," he said, his voice slowing and deepening. "See you then."

Charlie slammed the receiver down, making Major jump and Twinkle dash for the bedroom. "Sorry, guys. But that man is infuriating. And I have to be nice to him."

"I CAN'T DO this," Charlie said, staring at the mirror. "I look like a hooker."

She was wearing the white silk blouse the dry cleaner had salvaged after Major's rescue and a straight blue skirt that stopped a modest couple of inches above her knees. The problem was her hair.

If she left it down, it looked like an invitation.

If she put it up, she lost the softening effect it might have on Jack's attitude.

She rooted around in her dresser drawer and found a

tortoise shell barrette. Scooping up the front part of her tresses, she draped them in loose curves over her ears and clipped them at the base of her neck.

"Half up, half down. Let's see what you make of *that*, Jack Lanett."

As soon as he saw her at the restaurant, his lips curved into a sardonic smile. Although his gaze slid down her legs appreciatively, all he said was, "Hello, Ms. Berglund."

He must buy his polo shirts in bulk. Today he was wearing a navy blue one under a tan suede jacket with an expensively soft drape. She was tempted to reach out and stroke the jacket sleeve, but he shrugged out of the coat and dropped it over the back of his chair before sitting down.

The waiter took their orders and Charlie plunged right in. "I have a proposal for you I think could benefit both of us."

"Ah, now it's a *proposal*," he said as he buttered a slice of French bread. "I'm not interested."

She disregarded his interjection. "I've got two editors at competing publishing houses bidding to publish a book about Sahara-Mars and how you found it. Think of what the publicity could do for your business."

"I assume that you would be writing this book."

"Yes. So you would have a sympathetic author . . ."

Jack raised an eyebrow at that, but Charlie ignored him. "And I'd include a chapter on the buyer of the achondrite," she threw in his meteorite's classification to impress him, "as well as discussions of its significance by scientific authorities. I think it could hit the *Times* bestseller list. You'll be the best-known meteorite hunter in the world."

"Has it occurred to you that I might not *want* to be the best-known meteorite hunter in the world?" he said.

"Why not?"

"I value my privacy."

"This book is about your *business*, not you." Charlie nonchalantly shifted so her hair streamed down over the front of her shoulder. "As a businessman, you can't afford to pass up such a great opportunity—"

He leaned across the table and twisted her hair into a makeshift rope, using it to gently but inexorably pull her face close to his. "As a *business*man, I prefer to conduct my transactions with a certain amount of discretion. A single article in the *New York Times* is one thing; an entire volume on the subject is another. I'm not interested in your *proposal*," he said decisively, then softened his tone as he tugged her just a little closer. "How about trying a proposition?"

She couldn't help herself; she looked at his lips.

"That's more like it, sugar," he said, flicking his eyes downward too.

For an insane moment, Charlie was tempted to close the distance between his mouth and hers, just to see if his kiss was as deep and rich as his voice. As she shifted infinitesimally, the tines of a salad fork jabbed her forearm, blessedly bringing her to her senses. "Please let go of my hair."

He did so instantly, and she nearly fell back onto the banquette. While her hair uncoiled and she collected her scattered wits, her companion sipped his water, watching her over the rim of the glass.

"I would rather have your cooperation," she said with a resolve she was far from feeling. "But I can write this book without it."

"I wouldn't try that if I were you." He put his glass down with such force that several drops of water splashed onto the tablecloth. "I would make it very difficult for you to talk with my clients and associates."

"What are you afraid I'll find?" Charlie asked, genuinely puzzled by his attitude.

"Nothing at all. I'm just protecting my clients' anonymity and my ability to travel freely." He picked up the butter knife again, absently twirling it between thumb and forefinger. "You strike me as an intelligent and fairly decent human being." Then he added, "For a journalist. I'm surprised you would pursue a subject who is clearly unwilling."

"We all have our obsessions. One of mine is rescuing stray animals. Another is pestering antisocial meteorite hunters."

"Well, I won't be a meteorite hunter much longer. After the auction, I'm retiring so your book will be out-of-date."

"Not at all. What better time to reflect on the highlights of an illustrious career?" Charlie pointed out.

"There won't be time for basking in past glories; I plan to return to school."

"To *school*?"

"I never finished college. Hell, I never even started college."

The waiter interrupted the conversation by delivering lunch. Charlie jabbed a shrimp with her fork and jumped back in. "You seem to know just as much as the scientists who authenticate your rocks."

"It doesn't matter. You need those initials after your name." He was neatly cutting his steak when he asked, "So what drives you?"

"Me? The usual: money, fame, immortality." Charlie wasn't interested in a change of focus.

"Tit for tat, Ms. Berglund. Give me a real answer."

He put down his flatware and waited.

Charlie found another shrimp that needed spearing while she considered her answer. "I'm tired of writing short pieces that disappear into the recycling bin within a month. I want to write something with some depth, to make a more lasting contribution." *That sounded pretty darn good.*

"Cut the b.s. and try again, sugar."

She almost choked on her shrimp.

"Fine," she said after a hasty gulp of water and a brief inner debate. "You really want to know? I'm trying to adopt a baby from China as a single parent. I've been in the process for over a year, and my new social worker is worried about my occupation. I need to prove I can earn a living without going on potentially risky expeditions. How's *that* for a reason?"

"It has the merit of being truthful," he said, as he picked up his fork again. "However, I'm having a hard time picturing you with a dirty diaper in one hand and a baby bottle in the other. You seem better suited for climbing Mt. Everest or flying fighter jets."

Suddenly, she was back in the hospital bed after her third miscarriage with her ex-husband Greg's voice searing through her brain. *"Face it, Charlie, you just weren't meant to be a mother."* Lowering her gaze to the remains of the salad on her plate, she felt the pain of her loss all over again. *But she was meant to be a mother!* She could change diapers and boil bottles as well as anyone. She just couldn't give birth herself.

She raised her eyes to challenge Jack straight on.

"I'm not willing to wait any longer for this. I want that baby, and I'll do whatever is necessary to get her. You can either help or hinder me, but I'm going to write the book."

I BELIEVE HER, Jack thought as he walked back to his apartment.

He even admired her refusal to be turned aside from her goal.

But adoptive maternity struck him as a strange goal for a woman who had once been the cover girl for *Xtreme Adventure* magazine. She could just as easily be the cover girl for *Maxim* and fulfill a lot of male fantasies, he thought with a wolfish smile. Yet she had looked downright stricken when he had paid her what he considered a compliment. *What the hell was that about?*

He shrugged away his own question; it didn't matter.

He didn't trust her to be content with just the information he fed her, and he couldn't afford to have a determined journalist poking around in his personal history. No matter how confidential records were, a really good reporter—and after some research, he had concluded she was good—could get into them. So he needed to come up with an alternative solution for her problem, something that would eliminate all thought of the book from her mind. He shoved his keys back in the pocket of his jacket and bypassed the entrance to his building, heading instead for a long, contemplative walk in Central Park.

"You DIDN'T REALLY expect him to cooperate, did you?" Isabelle asked as she ladled carrot-ginger soup into two china bowls in Charlie's kitchen.

"I suppose not," Charlie sighed. "But I didn't expect him to threaten me with stonewalling my other sources either. You know, all my instincts are telling me he's afraid I'll find out something he doesn't want the world to know."

"Like shady business dealings?"

"I'm not sure, but I couldn't find even a hint of that in my research. I think it's something more personal."

"Did you use your hair?" Isabelle asked pointedly.

"Not enough, obviously," Charlie said with a grim laugh. "I can't tell if he has real intentions along *those* lines, or if he's just trying to distract me."

"Call his bluff."

"What? You mean jump into bed with him? I'm not *that* desperate for the book." The telephone rang. "I'd better get that in case it's my agent," Charlie said, pushing back her chair.

"May I please speak with Charlotte Berglund?" Jack's voice seemed to slide through the phone like melted butter.

"Hello, Jack. Have you changed your mind about the book?" Charlie's brisk tone counterattacked his seductive drawl.

"Maybe. I have to do a little more thinking first. Will you be free to talk tomorrow at about four o'clock?"

"Four o'clock? Sure, call me here," she said, quickly flipping her calendar open to double-check. Fortunately, nothing had to be canceled.

"I'll talk with you then, sugar." He hung up.

"Right." She walked slowly back to the kitchen trying to absorb the sudden about-face. And trying to ignore the little frisson of pleasure she felt every time he called her "sugar."

"He's phoning tomorrow at four to talk about the book," she told Isabelle.

"The hair worked!"

CHAPTER 6

WHEN CHARLIE DROVE into Winter Circle the next afternoon, she noticed a big, boxy green Land Rover with Wyoming license plates parked halfway around the cul-de-sac. As she carried her purchases into her house, she wondered who had visitors from so far away. Major was lying in the swath of sun by the back French doors and stood up to greet her. Twinkle watched from atop the refrigerator.

"Have you guys given up on the fireplace rug?" she asked, giving the dog a pat. Inspired by the glorious spring day, she had bought a pink geranium in a plastic pot for the back porch and walked out to put it on the tile-topped table.

"Nice view you have here."

She yelped and dropped the pot, making Major jump out of the way.

"My apologies," Jack said, rising from the rocking chair he had been sitting in. He bent down to scoop up the pot and hand it back to her with a slight bow. "We did have an appointment."

"You're early, and I thought you were going to *call* me." Charlie hugged the pot to her chest in an attempt to subdue her racing heartbeat.

His smile didn't help her. The dimple was out in full force, and he was wearing a polo shirt faded to the exact shade of his eyes. Even his short sleeves bothered her because they drew attention to the play of muscle in his forearms.

"Oh no, sugar. A *proposal* needs to be presented in person."

"What kind of *proposal* is that?" she asked as she pretended to inspect the geranium for damage.

"The usual sort: a proposal of marriage."

"Right," she snorted, centering the pot on the table with great precision.

As she turned, he reached out and took both of her hands in his. "Ms. Berglund, will you do me the honor of becoming my wife?"

She stared at him for a moment. "Has radiation from your space rocks scrambled your brain waves?"

"I see gallantry is wasted on you." He released her hands.

"It was a pretty bad Rhett Butler impersonation." She crossed her arms and tucked her hands safely out of his reach. "What did you *really* come to talk about?"

"Marriage."

"Right. And then you'll tell me you were abducted by aliens who experimented on your mind—"

"Charlie, I need and intend to keep your pretty nose out of my private affairs. I figure the best way to do that is to provide you with a reliable income to show your caseworker. The *easiest* way to do *that* is to marry you."

"You have a very odd view of marriage if you think a wife keeps her nose out of her husband's affairs," she replied lightly, although she was beginning to think he wasn't joking.

"This is merely a convenience for both of us; a mutually beneficial business partnership, if you will," he said.

"All right," she agreed, to humor him as she narrowed her eyes to give him her most astute businesswoman look. "How reliable is the income of someone who makes his living selling rocks that fall out of the sky?"

"I've made some investments in things other than rocks," he said with an edge in his voice. "I don't live entirely on my income from meteorite hunting anymore."

A returning fishing boat honked, and Charlie absently raised her hand to wave a greeting.

"In fact, my investments are good enough that I would want you to sign an agreement waiving any claim to my property in the event of a divorce. Which, by the way, we can get in about eighteen months without any difficulty." He sat down and stretched his legs out, tilting the rocking chair back with the ease of a man who has solved all his problems.

Charlie overcame the urge to stomp on one of the rockers to knock him off balance. "You've thought this through, I see."

"Planning is one of my strengths." He smiled.

"Have you planned on hanging your clothes in my closet and showing up when the social worker comes for the home study?"

"Is that necessary?"

"Do you think I can just announce I've acquired a husband without producing one? And you'd have to go to China with me to pick up the child."

He stood up and came close enough to her that Major rumbled a soft growl.

"I'm not going to strangle her, dog, despite the temptation," he muttered. "You can put some of my clothes in the closet, and I'll meet the social worker. I have contacts in China so the trip won't be wasted."

"I thought you were retiring."

"I might freelance for Miguel."

"You're actually *serious* about this?"

"Deadly serious." Then the molasses was back in his voice. "You know, I'm not such a bad bargain as a husband."

"You have your good points," she said, stepping backward to slowly scan him from head to toe.

"And you don't even know me yet," he murmured, moving close again.

Major wedged his body between them, and another fishing boat tooted.

"Are you on speaking terms with every goddamned sea captain on the East Coast?" Jack asked, as Charlie turned away to wave even more enthusiastically than usual.

"I'm sort of the unofficial welcome home for the fishermen. They like having someone notice their return."

"They like having a tall blonde notice their return."

Charlie decided to get the discussion back to business. She took two long steps away from him before she turned. "Let me get this straight. You're offering me a . . . a marriage of convenience in exchange for what exactly?"

"For dropping the book idea permanently, and telling the editors to drop it too."

"I can't guarantee they'll do that."

"I've seen your powers of persuasion in action. You can convince them I'm an unsuitable subject for a book."

"I'll do my best." Charlie shook her head and leaned back against a wooden column. "This is the strangest offer I've ever had."

"It's better than the chief's sister-in-law, two camels and a tent."

He was smiling again, and Charlie felt the corners of her mouth turning upward in response. "That's not a bad deal," she said. "I've always wanted to ride a camel and a tent would come in handy."

"But the sister-in-law only had three teeth and made the camels look good."

He sauntered toward her, eyeing her in a way that made her wish her shorts weren't so short and her blouse weren't so thin. Bracing a hand on the column above her head, he treated her to the unfamiliar experience of having a man tower over her.

It wasn't unpleasant.

A whiff of ocean-scented breeze prickled over her skin, raising goose bumps on her arms. A strand of hair blew loose from its braid and caught in her eyelashes. If she lifted her hand, it would be hard to avoid touching him. As she debated the wisdom of that, he crooked a finger around the errant hair and pulled it away from her eyes. Then he tucked it behind her ear, brushing the sensitive skin between her hairline and her earlobe with his fingertips. The goose bumps disappeared under a wave of rippling warmth that made her gasp.

"I think this marriage could be convenient in *many* ways," her prospective husband murmured in her ear.

He had shifted almost imperceptibly but now Charlie could feel the slide of his khaki slacks against her thighs and the friction of cotton against her blouse. She closed her eyes and took a deep breath, inhaling the intertwined scents of salt water and warm, clean male.

Then she ducked neatly under his arm, nearly colliding with Major who had been keeping them under close surveillance.

"Sorry, Major," she said, dropping a hand on his head. "Not to be coy, but may I have some time to think about your very flattering offer?" She considered batting her eyelashes but decided against it.

"You have until Monday morning at 9 A.M.," her suitor snapped.

" 'Marry in haste, repent at leisure,' " Charlie quoted.

"Oh, I'm already having second thoughts," he said. He touched his fingertips to his lips in a mockery of blowing her a kiss before he strode off the porch and disappeared around the corner of the house.

Charlie sank into a rocking chair and listened to Jack leave Winter Circle with a bad-tempered squeal of the Land Rover's tires.

Major trotted over to lay his head in her lap, and she scratched him behind his ears. Setting aside the shock of the bizarre proposal, she considered its pros and cons . . .

Despite her brave words, she really didn't want to write a book about a man who didn't want to be written about. Some of her colleagues would call her a wimp, but she didn't enjoy confrontational interviews or unauthorized investigations . . . and, as Mike had pointed out, having a husband would certainly solve her problems in the short term. A two-parent family was more acceptable to an adoption agency than a single parent. Of course, hunting meteorites was not exactly a low-risk profession; he undoubtedly traveled more extensively and more hazardously than she did. *But he's retiring, so that won't be a concern.* His investment income would give her the paperwork cushion she needed to find a good, home-based job. *Not that I'd touch a penny of his money,* she thought, remembering his requirement for a pre-nuptial agreement with indignation.

She had her own savings.

But his would look good on the financial statement.

However, all of that was just the paperwork. Going beyond that, things got more complicated. They would have to pretend to be a loving couple in order to hoodwink the social worker, and Rhonda Brown didn't strike her as an easy person to hoodwink. She would also have to make up a really creative story as to why she was getting married so suddenly. As a writer, that was not beyond her capabilities. It was when she considered the flesh-and-blood reality of Jack Lanett as her husband that Charlie swallowed hard. He had made his interest in physical contact quite clear. *And that wink at the lecture hall . . . that was so unexpected.* She swallowed again.

Would she have the good sense to say no?

Was it good sense to say no?

"Of course, it is," she told Major firmly. "I don't jump into bed with men I don't care about."

Except for Nick. She winced. Less than a year after her divorce, she was assigned a story on an ecology-minded resort hotel in the middle of Egypt's Western Desert. Nick Rogers got sent along to do the photography. Adrère Amellal was one of the most exotic places Charlie had ever been. Since there was no electricity, the hotel was lit by candles at night. The swimming pool was fed by a spring and surrounded by date palms and oleanders. She had thought achingly what a perfect place it would be for a honeymoon.

On their second afternoon there, Nick suggested a swim. They lolled about in the deliciously cool water, talking about other assignments they'd each been on. Then Nick stroked purposefully over to her, and skimmed his hands up her thighs, over her hips, and along the sides of her breasts. Charlie was swamped by a wave of longing so intense she literally couldn't breathe. She answered the question in Nick's eyes by twisting in the water so his hands were cupping her breasts. Without a word, they climbed out of the pool, grabbed their towels and went straight to Nick's room.

Charlie and Nick spent the rest of their five days inventing ways to touch each other without anyone noticing. The moment they landed in New York, though, Nick made it clear that the trip was great fun, but he didn't wish to extend their acquaintance.

Charlie was devastated.

When she had failed to carry a child and her husband discarded her as a result, she had lost belief in herself as a woman; with Nick, she had begun to recover it. She had started to feel that she was capable of touching another person's mind, body and heart but Nick had proved she was wrong—*again*.

"Enough wallowing in self-pity," she said, gently pushing Major's head off her lap and standing. "I need company and a wiser head than mine."

With the dog at her side, she jogged across her yard to Isabelle's back porch and banged on the screen door. No one answered so she pushed it open and walked in.

"Isabelle?"

"I'm out front. Come on through."

Charlie found her neighbor kneeling by a flowerbed, surrounded by flats of pink impatiens and purple begonias, as she sprinkled organic fertilizer on a newly turned bed. "Would it be crazy to get married just to push the adoption through faster?" she asked, picking up a trowel and gouging out an impatiens-sized hole.

"Has Allan, our smitten veterinarian, finally proposed?" Isabelle asked, sitting back on her heels in surprise.

"No, the meteorite hunter has."

"The good-looking fellow who burned out of here in that gas-guzzling Land Rover?"

"Yup."

"Good heavens, your hair had a more powerful effect on him than you thought!"

Charlie explained Jack's proposal, and Isabelle braced her gloved hands on her knees. "If it's *really* just a convenient business arrangement, I think it has some possibilities . . . but a man who will go to that length to protect his privacy has something in his life he doesn't want exposed. For all you know, he's murdered three wives already."

"I checked his background when I got the interview. He has no criminal record."

"So he murdered them and got away with it."

Charlie chuckled. "He's never been married—in this country anyway."

"Aha, he has a harem in the Far East." She looked closely at Charlie. "Seriously, my dear, you need to be careful. This man is a total stranger. A most attractive stranger but a stranger nonetheless." Something in Charlie's face made her say, "Ah, you think he's attractive too."

Charlie flushed.

"That's very dangerous for you," Isabelle said, shaking her head. "Perhaps you should find another topic for a book."

"I can keep it strictly business," Charlie insisted. Then she sighed. "You know how much I want a child. I was so close, and I just can't bear to wait another year. But it's such a bizarre idea."

Isabelle considered for a moment before she shrugged and said, "Marriages have been made for stranger reasons."

*   *   *

By Sunday evening, Charlie had picked up and put down the telephone so many times she had lost count. Finally, she sat down on the sofa, took a gulp of white wine, patted Major and Twinkle, and dialed Jack's cell phone number.

"Jack Lanett."

"I know," Charlie said. "It's Charlie Berglund."

She heard a grinding noise in the background.

"Just a minute. I'll move to a quieter place."

The noise receded, and Charlie took a deep breath. "Jack, I've thought a great deal about your *proposal*. And although I think it's a rather unusual way to handle our, um, situation, I'm going to say yes."

"Fine. I'll have my lawyer contact you on Monday."

"You mean I haven't just made you the happiest man on earth?"

"This is a business arrangement, pure and simple," he said more emphatically than she thought necessary.

"That was a *joke*." Charlie gave up trying to keep it light. "Fine, strictly business. I've checked it out, and we can get married on Friday if we do it here. You'll need to get a blood test and sign some papers. I can fax you the necessary information."

He gave her his fax number.

"We also have to coordinate our story for the social worker and present a convincing picture of a married couple."

"We can discuss that at our wedding." His tone when he reached the word *wedding* became distinctly ironic. "Or are you inviting the social worker?"

"I might," Charlie said just to annoy him.

"Fax me the information, and we'll talk again. And I appreciate the honor you do me by accepting my proposal."

"Better late than never," Charlie said, chuckling. "Good-bye, Jack."

"Until Friday, Ms. Berglund."

Jack hit the "end" button and slipped the phone back into his pocket. He was amazed to discover that he was smiling. He walked back into the sculptor's studio Miguel had rented to work on meteorites while they were in New York. Miguel was cutting an especially fine stony-iron, slicing it into pieces which would highlight the large greenish-brown olivine crystals embedded in the metal. Jack flipped down his safety glasses and walked over to pick up a cut slab. He started toward a grinding machine when Miguel stopped his saw.

"Hey, *amigo,* what are you doing with that?"

"I'm going to finish it for you. You know, I actually did my own prep before you joined the firm."

"Yeah, but I'm better at it," Miguel said, pushing up his welding mask and wiping a sleeve across his forehead. "Leave that piece to the expert. You can work on this one." He picked up a small chunk of an iron and tossed it to his friend.

Jack caught it and turned it over in his hands for a moment. "I can't do much damage to this."

"You have other things on your mind. The pallasite requires concentration."

Jack dropped the iron on the work table. "Will you be my best man?"

"Sure, when the day comes."

"It's coming Friday."

"In which decade?"

"I'm getting married this Friday."

"Tell me you're joking." Miguel sat down hard on his stool.

"No joke. I'm marrying the nosy reporter." Jack filled him in on the details.

"You've done some crazy things in your life, *amigo,* but this one is the craziest," Miguel said, shaking his head.

"What's so crazy about it? It solves both our problems, and then it's over."

"That's what you think *now.* But remember Rapunzel: long blond hair can turn into a very strong rope."

"Have I ever come *close* to getting tied down?"

"This one's different. She's got noble intentions. And we all know what a sucker you are for a good cause."

Jack picked up the small meteorite and studied it a moment. "You know, it's been a long time since I made an iron ring."

"ISABELLE, WILL YOU be my maid of honor?" Charlie asked as she hefted a box of organic mangos onto her neighbor's porch Monday morning.

"So you accepted the hunter?" Isabelle ripped open a box of pesticide-free carrots and began sorting them into clients' baskets.

"The wedding is Friday."

"Friday!" Isabelle's carrots landed on the floor in a heap. "We have to get organized. I know just the place to buy the dress. Mike and Ernst can have the reception on their patio—"

"This is *not* a real wedding. I don't need any of that."

"Nonsense. If nothing else, you need pictures to show your social worker. Authenticity is important in deception. And you *will* be legally married, won't you?"

"Yes. But—"

"Then we plan a wedding."

CHAPTER 7

IN THE END, Isabelle had her way, and the wedding planning was fast and furious. Mike vetted the prenuptial agreement, and insisted on adding several clauses to protect Charlie's assets. He also found a justice of the peace to perform the ceremony. Ernst organized *hors d'oeuvres* and a small wedding cake for the patio reception. He ordered flowers, including a bouquet for the bride and a boutonnière for the groom. Charlie faxed forms back and forth to New York, went to the doctor for a blood test, made two trips to the county courthouse, and cleaned out space in her closet for Jack's clothes. She also endured an exasperated diatribe from her agent when she killed the book idea. Isabelle dragged her to a vintage clothing store and persuaded her to buy an ivory silk crêpe de Chine dress with a square neck, elbow length sleeves and bias-cut skirt.

The morning of the wedding Isabelle helped the bride smooth her hair back into an elegant figure-eight chignon. Charlie had decided *not* to invite Rhonda Brown. A romantic, spur-of-the-moment decision seemed to fit the story she had concocted for the social worker better. So the only people present—besides the bride and groom—were Isabelle and Miguel, the justice of the peace, Mike, Ernst and a photographer Isabelle brought along.

Having not had the nerve to ask Jack what he would wear, Charlie was relieved when he appeared at the courthouse in the same silver gray suit he had worn to the lecture. This time, though, he was wearing a yellow tie that coincidentally matched the spray of yellow alstroemeria Charlie pinned on his lapel.

"How very wifely," Jack commented as she carefully wove the anchoring pin through the fine fabric of his suit.

She made the mistake of looking up.

He was so close she could see the fine lines around his eyes and a few glints of silver in his dark eyebrows. His smile held a disarming hint of teasing. Without thinking, Charlie laid her palms against his chest. It felt like sun-warmed brick: utterly solid and inviting to lean against. She sighed and said, "Not wifely, professional. I have to make my business partner look good."

"I'm going to have a hard time looking as good as *my* business partner," he said, taking one of her hands and raising it to his lips.

"Charlie! Jack! The justice of the peace is ready for us!" Isabelle's voice yanked Charlie out of her bemused trance.

The ceremony at town hall and the reception by the channel passed in a blur.

Isabelle's scruffy-looking young photographer was from one of her environmental groups. She assured Charlie young Warren Bixby was very skilled and would produce portrait quality prints of the festivities within a week. So Charlie and Jack posed and blinked in the glare of the camera's flash.

Jack sailed through the afternoon with almost eerie

poise and good humor. As she stood on Mike and Ernst's lawn, absently twisting the newly acquired ring on her fourth finger—a complete surprise, the one detail she had overlooked—Charlie watched him charming her three friends with a certain amount of irritation. Even the photographer had taken a shine to him. Unfortunately, she was just as susceptible to him as everyone else.

Miguel must have noticed because he stopped by her side and said, "It's an occupational hazard."

"What is?"

"Instant intimacy with total strangers."

"He's good at it," she said, "except I wouldn't call it 'intimacy.' He doesn't reveal much of himself in the process."

"That's an occupational hazard too," Miguel said, chuckling. "*Your* occupation."

"What's he afraid I'll find out?"

Miguel shrugged. "He's a private man, and he likes to be in control."

Just then, Isabelle announced it was time to cut the cake. Charlie marched to the buffet table. "Isabelle, this is ridiculous! We don't need a cake cutting ceremony," she hissed as Jack strolled over looking amused.

"It's just for the photographer," Isabelle said, offering her a silver cake knife.

"Try to be gracious, sugar," Jack said, taking the knife and wrapping her fingers around it by the simple expedient of cupping her hand in his. "Smile for the man, and then we're done with it."

Charlie gave a canned grin, all the while intensely aware of her new husband's body pressed against the length of her back as they leaned over to cut the cake. The thin silk of her dress seemed to evaporate anywhere that he touched her. When he completed the embrace by reaching around to pick up a plate with his left hand, she could feel the buttons on his jacket, the buckle on his belt, and a great deal of muscle beneath his suit.

"Now I know why grooms always seem to enjoy this part of the reception," he murmured in her ear, his breath feathering deliciously over her skin.

She shifted her elbow so it met his ribs, and was rewarded with a grunt of discomfort. But he didn't give an inch.

By the time the photographer released them, Charlie had no doubt her new husband was feeling the effect of their proximity as much as she was.

It served him right.

JACK LOOKED UP from the suitcase he was unloading into an empty dresser drawer. "Do you really think your Ms. Brown will check the drawers?"

Charlie had grabbed a few suit hangers for Jack's clothes from her coat closet, and was returning to her bedroom, followed by Major. "No, but if you're staying here when she comes for the home study, you have to put your clothes somewhere," she said.

She stopped, watching him. The last man who had folded his clothes into that dresser drawer was her ex-husband Greg. To have Jack Lanett looking so utterly at ease in her bedroom was unsettling. Charlie snatched a pair of slacks out of his suitcase and slid them onto a hanger.

"You're taking your quest for authenticity to great lengths." He shook his head. "Although I enjoyed the cake cutting ceremony very much."

Charlie shot him a glare. "Isabelle got a little carried away bringing a photographer, but she wants to make sure Rhonda believes in the marriage. She even gave me a silver frame as a wedding gift."

Jack laughed, a surprisingly pleasant sound.

"I didn't know you were such a clothes horse," Charlie said, using another hanger.

"I'm just making it look like the real thing."

He seemed to be in an extraordinarily mellow mood for a man who had recently endured a wedding, and a fairly fraudulent one at that. Jack in a mellow mood was dangerous to her equilibrium. They still needed to discuss their strategy for hoodwinking Rhonda Brown. She felt slightly guilty about fooling the caseworker, but Rhonda had admitted she'd make a good mother . . . and she had already waited seven years for a baby. She needed to be rational and businesslike to develop a strategy so Charlie decided to hand the hangers to him and get out of the bedroom.

She almost tripped over the dog in her haste to exit.

Charlie went to the refrigerator for a bottle of white wine; a little alcohol might make the upcoming discussion less awkward. She had two glasses poured and a tray of cheese and fruit laid out when Jack came into the kitchen. He had changed into jeans and a long-sleeved black shirt. "That looks mighty tempting, but I have to go."

"*Go?* We have to talk about the adoption!"

"I'm sorry, sugar, but I have an appointment tonight. I'll stop by on Sunday."

"I thought you'd at least spend the night, get familiar with the house, start filling out the adoption forms." Charlie realized tears were about to spill down her cheeks and she turned her back.

"Damnation," he muttered, having noticed the telltale glitter in her eyes. "Fine, come with me. We can talk while we're driving."

"To New York?" Charlie surreptitiously wiped her tears and grabbed a glass of wine.

"I'm not going to New York. I'm going to the Poconos."

"You have an appointment in the *Poconos?*"

"I'll explain on the way. Just pack warm pajamas and hiking clothes." He checked his watch. "We need to get going in a half an hour."

Charlie took a sip of the wine, and debated for a second. They needed to spend enough time together to pretend to be a couple, and here was a good chance. "I have to see if Isabelle can take care of the animals."

"I'll wait in the living room." He picked up the tray of food, and carried it with him.

When Charlie peeked in after her phone call, he was sitting on the couch with Twinkle draped across his lap. Major sat watching intently as Jack cut a piece of cheese and tossed it to him. She smiled. He already looked at home. She raced back to her bedroom and stripped out of her wedding attire. As she was pulling on a pair of jeans, her wedding ring caught the light, and she paused a moment to examine it closely under the lamp. It had seemed to be a simple, wide band of highly polished silver when Jack had slipped it on her finger. Now she moved her hand and a web of tiny, straight lines crisscrossed over the surface.

"Widmannstatten structures," she gasped.

She knew from her research that only iron meteorites formed in the core of a large asteroid or planet exhibited the distinctive geometric pattern she saw on the ring. It was created when the nickel-iron alloy at the center of the parent body cooled very slowly, and the atoms of the two metals separated.

The man had given her a ring made from a meteorite!

She slipped a soft, cream-colored turtleneck over her head and walked out to face Jack in the living room.

"Ready?" he asked, carefully moving the cat off his lap.

"Not quite." She held up her left hand. "I can't believe you gave me a ring made from a meteorite."

"Glad you like it."

"It's . . ." Charlie searched for the right word, "extraordinary. I'll return it to you when the divorce goes through, of course, but in the meantime, I'm honored to be entrusted with it."

"It's nothing special; just a bit of an iron with nothing to recommend it but the Widmannstatten pattern. You can keep it even after the divorce. Something to remember me by."

"No, no, I can't. It wouldn't be right," but she turned her left hand to admire the pattern again. It was too ridiculous to say what she really felt: she was touched to be given something that was unique and important to him.

"Did Miguel make it?" she asked.

"Everyone seems to think I'm incapable of working my own damned meteorites," he said. "No, *I* made it."

"I'd better pack," Charlie mumbled and returned to the bedroom.

She hurled clothes into a duffle bag, stopping every few seconds to look at the ring her new husband had made for her with his own hands. Soon her duffle was stowed in the Land Rover, and they were on their way. Charlie directed him through a few back roads to the highway.

"Okay, why are we going to the Poconos?" she asked. Suddenly, the aptness of their destination hit her. "Does the hotel have a heart-shaped bed? Or a bathtub like a giant champagne glass?"

"What are you talking about?"

"A mirror on the ceiling?" Charlie was grinning widely. "A white fur bedspread?"

"We're going to a very simple cabin which has nothing

but a couple of regular mattresses and box springs and a pull-out sofabed." He was starting to sound annoyed.

"Don't you get it? People go to the Poconos for their *honeymoons*."

His chuckle from the darkness sounded like Twinkle's purr, smooth and deep and relaxed. "Oh yeah. 'Heir-conditioned.' I've seen the billboards. Well, we're not going anywhere near those places. There's too much light."

"So where *are* we going?"

"To Miguel's cabin out in the middle of nowhere."

"And what appointment do you have there?"

"It's not exactly an appointment. It's more in the nature of a pilgrimage."

Charlie waited.

"I hate reporters," he muttered but he continued. "We're going to watch the Lyrid meteor shower. It reaches its peak tonight and tomorrow night."

" 'Lyrid'. That means it looks like it's coming from the constellation Lyra?" More useful facts from her research.

"Actually on the border of Lyra and Hercules, and it's produced by Comet Thatcher. The Lyrids are one of the oldest meteor showers on record. Chinese astronomers mentioned them in 687 B.C."

"What's the ZHR?" Charlie was having fun showing off her newly acquired knowledge. ZHR stood for "zenithal hourly rate" which basically meant how many meteors you could expect to see in an hour.

He raised an eyebrow. "The norm is twenty but it can get up to over a hundred. And sometimes you get fire-balls."

"I'd love to see a fireball. Why is this a pilgrimage?"

He gave a long-suffering sigh. "A long, long time ago—"

"In a galaxy far, far away . . ." she interjected.

"When I was a kid, about fourteen," he went on as if she hadn't spoken, "I couldn't sleep one night. So I lay just staring out the window, and suddenly the sky exploded. Stars were shooting everywhere."

He stopped.

"And?" she prodded.

"I thought the world was coming to an end, and I dove under the bed. But nothing happened. There was no noise, no explosion, no earthquake. So I crawled out from under the bed and lay down again and watched. I was going through a rough patch just then, and somehow this silent fireworks display put on by Mother Nature seemed to be a sign. Of what, I had no idea. I went to the library the next day and looked up everything I could find about space. That library wasn't exactly up-to-date so I didn't find much. But I was hooked. And I've been hooked ever since," he finished.

"So every year, you go somewhere to watch the Lyrids?" Charlie prompted.

He shrugged. "I do my best. It's my offering to the gods of outer space."

She let him lapse into the silence he obviously preferred. It was soothing to sit next to him in the soft glow of the dashboard instruments. He drove the way he did everything else: with effortless competence. She tilted her seat back slightly as she watched his long fingers flex and relax on the steering wheel. Her eyelids drifted closed as she thought what a marvelous opening his story would make for the book she wouldn't get to write.

JACK GLANCED OVER at the woman beside him. Her breathing was deep and even, her legs sprawled in the relaxation of sleep. Wearing worn jeans and a simple turtleneck she still managed to look like an advertisement for Ralph Lauren. He contemplated brushing his fingers up the inside of one of those deliciously long thighs. . . . It was a funny thing about lust. You had no control over it. One minute the woman was a major thorn in his side. Then a gust of sea wind blew off the channel, pressing the thin silk of her wedding dress tightly against her breasts, hips and legs, and he wanted nothing more than to be between those thighs.

The cake cutting ceremony had been a particular pleasure. Standing with his arms around her waist and his hands holding hers on the knife handle, he'd been able to pull her against him from shoulder to ankle. He tightened his grasp on the steering wheel to counteract the stirring in his crotch. Why shouldn't he take his hand off the wheel and see what happened, he thought irritably. There was no real reason *not* to . . .

Except his gut was sending danger signals to his brain.

He started to reach across the space between them. Then he remembered her friends. At the phony reception, every one of them had cornered him and sung Charlie's praises while probing *his* character and background. He had circumvented their questions without a twinge of conscience. All three of them had ended with a warning—some more direct than others—not to hurt her.

He frowned.

Why were they so damned protective?

He looked over at his new wife. Even asleep, she radiated strength and independence. She obviously could take care of herself. He shook his head again.

Maybe her friends sensed something in *him* that worried them.

* * *

CHARLIE'S HEAD BANGED against the car window.

"Ouch!" she said groggily, as she straightened up and rubbed the sore spot.

"Sorry. Miguel discourages visitors by leaving the road unpaved," Jack said, shifting into a lower gear.

"You mean I slept the whole way?" she asked in dismay.

"I understand wedding days are exhausting for the bride."

"And wedding nights are exhausting for the groom," Charlie quipped without thinking. She regretted it when he took his eyes off the road and gave her a look that—even in the dim glow of the dashboard lights—seared deep into the inner space low in her belly. "Oof!" she grunted as the big Land Rover bounced over a frost heave.

She used the rough road as an excuse to turn and grab a handhold on the door.

The skittering headlights suddenly flashed on the windows of a building. Jack pulled up beside it, and Charlie slid out of the car and stretched as she examined Miguel's country home. It was a handsome wooden cabin. A long porch well-stocked with rocking chairs stretched across the front. The windows were tall and multi-paned. The porch itself was built of stone, as were the chimneys at each end of the house. Charlie walked back around the Land Rover to help Jack unload. He had pulled a set of keys out of his jacket pocket and stood weighing them in his hand.

"You know, sugar," he said with a deep drawl, "talk about mirrors on the ceiling and white fur bedspreads can put ideas into a man's head. Ideas which have nothing to do with a business partnership."

Charlie discovered she had to clear her constricted throat. Before she could get a word out, Jack continued.

"So let's get back on the proper footing." The drawl had all but disappeared. "You need me to adopt a baby. I need you to stay out of my private affairs. That's why we're here."

"My footing is perfectly stable," Charlie said. "I'm here to make up some stories to tell Rhonda Brown, and to watch rocks fall out of the sky."

He handed her the keys; this time she was prepared for the heat they emitted.

"Good. Then we're straight. The big silver key opens the front door. I'll bring in the gear," he said, hefting two duffle bags out of the car.

"I can help carry," she said.

He laughed. "You could probably carry the whole load, but I'll handle it."

Charlie led the way up the steps and onto the porch. The key turned easily in the lock. She heard the click of switches behind her as she walked inside and blinked in the flood of light.

She stood in a large room that was open all the way up to the rafters. To her right, stairs led up to a sort of gallery offering access to several doors. To her left, she looked over a high eating bar into the kitchen. In front of her was a male fantasy of a hunting lodge. Big overstuffed chairs and sofas in subdued plaids crouched around the two fireplaces and an enormous television set. A locked gun rack stood against one wall. The chandelier was made of antlers.

"This is real guy territory," Charlie chuckled.

"Paradise," Jack agreed, dropping the duffles by a table made of tree branches with the bark still on them. He checked his watch and headed for the kitchen. "Ten o'clock. We have time. Let's see what supplies the caretaker laid in for us."

Charlie volunteered to make sandwiches while Jack
went in search of the equipment they would need for a
night of meteor-watching. As she slathered Dijon mustard
on whole wheat bread, she contemplated Jack's statement
about being on the "proper footing." *He started this little
flirtation, and now he claims he wants to end it.* The more
she considered it, the more she thought he found her a bit
harder to handle than he expected. A smug smile curved
her lips; there was something very satisfying about rattling
a man like Jack Lanett.

Appearing totally unruffled at the moment, he walked
into the kitchen with two loaded backpacks and an insulated bag for the food. He was also wearing a shoulder har-
ness with a pistol in it. Charlie felt a twinge of unease as
Isabelle's speculation about Jack's secret flitted across her
mind.

"Is it *that* dangerous up here?"

He shrugged. "Just an occasional garbage-raiding
bear."

"I don't see any bearskin rugs scattered around."

"The only animals I've ever actually *aimed* at were two
drunken hunters who wouldn't get off the front porch."

"Did you shoot them?" she asked hopefully.

"Bloodthirsty, aren't you? No, but I was tempted." He
made a long slow survey of her from head to toe but this
time his gaze was flatly analytical. "The sneakers and
jeans are good. Do you have a warm jacket, gloves and a
hat?"

"The jacket, yes. Gloves and hat, no."

A trip to the coat closet unearthed a plaid hunting cap
and a pair of too-large ski mittens that engulfed Charlie's
hands.

"You won't need your hands except to eat so they'll
do," Jack assured her.

He, of course, looked every inch the fashionable explorer with a black leather jacket and gloves, and a gray fedora.

She caught the grin he couldn't quite repress when she fitted the ridiculous hat on over her elegant chignon. "Don't say a word," she warned.

He appeared to debate a moment before saying, "Let's go."

"Wise man."

He helped her on with her backpack and handed her a flashlight. Turning off all the cabin's lights and locking the door, they set off into the woods on a path that Jack followed with the silent surefootedness of a deer. About fifteen minutes later, they emerged from the trees. Charlie swept the area with her flashlight, discovering a large field where flat expanses of stone alternated with dried brown meadow grass. Her companion headed for the center of the open space and swung his backpack onto the ground. Charlie helped him unroll thick egg-crate foam pads over the grass and cover them with insulated blankets and sleeping bags; then he raided her backpack for pillows and binoculars, and positioned a thermos of coffee within easy reach.

"No counters and no logbook," he said almost to himself.

Charlie assumed he was referring to the usual practice of counting the rate of meteors observed and recording them for scientific purposes. "This is a sacred, not a scientific vigil?" she asked.

"You got it." He flipped a corner of a sleeping bag back. "Your observation lounge awaits you."

Charlie smiled and slid into the makeshift bed. Jack switched off his flashlight so Charlie heard rather than saw him settle into his cocoon. She lay back on her pillow, and all thought of the man lying so close beside her flew out of her head. With no artificial lights and no moon to overpower them, the stars powdered the sky like sparkling grains of sand. *Actually,* she thought, *it was more as though a safe filled with the most brilliant diamonds of all sizes had spilled its contents across incomprehensible miles of deep blue velvet.*

"Wow!" she breathed.

Jack's chuckle was pure satisfaction. He began pointing out constellations, and for the first time, Charlie could really trace the outlines of the mythical creatures they were named for.

"Almost straight up is the Great Bear, Ursa Major, which is most famous for the seven stars that form the Big Dipper."

"I see the Big Dipper."

"All right. Follow the line of the two stars which make the end of the dipper and you'll see the North Star which is part of Ursa Minor."

"I just hope all those bears stay up there."

"Once the ancient gods put them in the sky, they aren't inclined to come back to earth," her companion said with surprising whimsy. "Curling around the Little Bear is Draco, the dragon guarding the North Star. One of its stars was actually the North Star about 5,000 years ago. See that bright star near the Dragon's head? That's Vega, the alpha star of Lyra, our meteor shower's radiant constellation. Vega is one of three bright stars that make up the Summer Triangle. The other two are still too low to see but they're Deneb in Cygnus and Altair in Aquila."

"The swan and the eagle. Birds of a feather. How did a lyre get mixed in?"

"Pure magnitude. Vega's the fifth brightest star in the

sky, partly because it's only about 27 light-years away and partly because its fifty times as bright as our sun."

"It's sort of bluish though."

"You have good eyes."

"Not good enough to find Orion," she said, tilting her head to search the sky. "He's the only constellation I can usually recognize."

"Orion set about an hour ago."

"He should be your patron saint."

Jack was silent.

"He's a hunter, just like you," Charlie persisted.

"His methods were more violent than mine. And I try not to anger the gods."

"That's right, they sent a scorpion to kill him, didn't they?"

"And there he crouches on the horizon, waiting to strike."

Her eyes were accustomed to the dark so Charlie turned her head to follow the dim line of Jack's arm toward the constellation Scorpius. "Yeow!" she yelped. The hairpins in her wedding day hairdo had shifted and were jabbing into her scalp. She sat up and took off the hunting cap, fumbling around to find the small implements of torture.

"Let me do that," Jack offered, although he sounded as if he were doing it against his better judgment.

This is a dumb idea, Charlie agreed mentally, but she swiveled to present her back to him. She felt his fingers in her hair, then heard a rustle of blankets and a soft grunt. Suddenly, his hiking boots were planted on either side of her thighs while his knees almost brushed her shoulders. This is a *really* dumb idea, she thought again. But her eyes drifted closed as pins were pulled adroitly from her hair. Her chignon loosened under Jack's onslaught. She shook her head to release the last of the pressure, and then barely stifled a moan as he raked his fingers through her hair, spreading it over her back and shoulders. The exquisite tingling of her scalp radiated downward and across every inch of her skin. She luxuriated in it until the sensation focused between her thighs. When she began to picture his hands skimming around her ribs to cup her breasts, Charlie gave herself a hard mental shake and reached back to braid her hair.

He brushed her hands aside. "I'll braid it."

"Did you learn by making camel bridles?" Charlie was trying to distract herself from the new ripple of pleasure his division of her hair into three strands was creating.

"No. I learned from making lariats out West."

He was taking his time.

"Do you find a lot of meteorites there?"

"Some. I have a cabin out in Wyoming. Sort of like Miguel's here. Do you have something to tie this with?"

Charlie fished in her pocket for an elastic band. His fingers brushed hers as he took it, and she almost winced at the shock the contact gave her.

"All neatly tamed and tied up." He flipped the braid over her shoulder and shifted back onto his own side. "Just the way you like it."

Charlie was annoyed by the mockery in his voice. "You seem to take an inordinate amount of interest in my hairstyle."

"*You* seem to consider it more a nuisance than an adornment."

"I consider it unprofessional to leave it loose," she said. But she didn't consider it a nuisance ever. She clung to it as the last vestige of her femininity. When she felt overwhelmed by a sense of her failure as a woman, she found reassurance in the extravagant sheet of gold flowing over her shoulders and down to her waist.

"And we're being strictly professional now, aren't we?" Jack said.

"Strictly," she agreed.

Charlie lay back down, edging as far away from his disturbing presence as she could get without falling off the padding. She was trying very hard to keep this on a strictly professional basis, but he wasn't exactly doing his bit to help. At this moment, she wanted to hurl herself on top of the very male person lying next to her, and feel his hands running down her back, over her backside, between her thighs and . . .

"Oh!" she gasped.

A meteor streaked through Draco, leaving a trail of light glowing in the sky.

"A falling star!"

CHAPTER 8

"THAT WAS THE first falling star I've ever seen," Charlie said after a brief silence.

"You don't spend much time looking at the sky."

"No, I guess I don't." She was always too busy dealing with matters on Earth.

Jack checked his watch. "It's almost midnight. The show should get better soon."

"That's because before midnight the material from the comet was chasing us. Now the earth has rotated so our side is running into the space debris, right?"

"That's right."

Another meteor drew a glowing line across the sky. The silence of the display was eerie. "I can see why you thought it was a sign of some sort. It seems supernatural."

Her companion made no comment.

Charlie lay quietly, letting her gaze drift across the sky, waiting for movement to catch her eye. But all the stars stood still for the moment, although the woods around them were alive with sound. An owl hooted and was answered from farther away. A night breeze whispered through pine needles and early leaves. Rustling in the undergrowth marked the passage of some larger animal. Charlie glanced at Jack to see if he looked concerned, but his gaze was firmly skyward.

She looked back up. There was another meteor! And another! A third zipped past Cygnus' beak.

"Wow!" Charlie breathed. "It's an entire *shower* of stars!"

"Mmm-hmmm."

Charlie decided to refrain from further comment. Maybe he took this pilgrimage even more seriously than she thought, and he really *was* praying to the space gods.

They lay side-by-side while the sky hurled glowing rocks at the Earth. As fascinating as the sight was, Charlie could feel her eyelids drifting closed.

"Why are you so set on adopting a baby from China?"

Her eyelids snapped open. She had no idea if she had been asleep a minute or an hour. "What?" she stalled.

"Why do you want to adopt a child so badly?"

"Those are two different questions."

"And you're an expert on asking questions," he noted. "Answer the second one then."

"I suppose you're entitled to an explanation," she conceded, "but it's not simple."

"I have all night."

She was relieved to hear a hint of humor in his voice. She took a breath and released it. "I was orphaned when I was four. My parents were killed in a car accident. After that, I lived with a series of relatives, some of whom wanted me more than others. I had one good run with an aunt and uncle who really cared about me. But then Uncle Alfred got transferred to a town where the school system was terrible. So, for my own good, I was sent to an educationally superior location."

"But an emotionally inferior situation?"

"Yes." Charlie sighed. "No one ever abused me or anything like that. I just sensed I was considered a burden." She was silent for a moment, remembering. "So I want to adopt a child who was such a burden to someone they gave her up, and show her what a joy she is to me."

"That's very noble. But why not have a child of your own? It seems easier than adopting." His last statement was heavily laced with cynicism.

"Isn't that incredible?" Charlie agreed indignantly. "No qualifications are required to get pregnant, but it takes years and an entire forest of paperwork to adopt a child no one wants."

"A pretty lady like you should have no problem finding a willing sperm donor."

"Are you volunteering?" she said, then wished she'd bitten her tongue.

"Trust me, sugar, you can do a lot better than me for a biological father."

She had expected a reminder of their deal or an emphatic refusal, not this wry declaration of unworthiness. It made her stop evading his question.

"I can't have children of my own."

"I'm sorry."

"I was married for five years," she found herself continuing. "I had three miscarriages and two ectopic pregnancies. The last one almost killed me, and the doctors decided it was better if I not try again. I had surgery to prevent any further conception."

"And your marriage didn't survive the ordeal."

"Greg wanted his own children. And now he has them."

"He remarried?"

"Within a year of our divorce."

"So I'm your second husband. And I won't be your last, I'm sure."

This was the first time he had referred to himself as her husband. It gave her an odd little thrill so she ignored his last comment.

"Why a baby from China?" he asked.

"Now who's asking a lot of personal questions?" Charlie hesitated as two meteors chased each other through Aquila before she answered him. "Several reasons. Most of the babies in orphanages there are girls because they're considered useless to their families."

"Women don't do housework in China?"

"Very funny. They do housework, farm work and every other kind of work, but they do it for their *husband's* family."

"I like that system."

Charlie elbowed him—gently—in the ribs.

"Watch it. I can hog-tie you in under thirty seconds."

She almost challenged him to try it, but was afraid they would both enjoy it way too much. "Because China has the one child per family policy, parents are almost forced to give away their daughters. It must be a terrible decision to make," Charlie mused sadly. "Anyway, as a single mother, I can provide a role model for a girl, but I can't do that for a boy. I also don't like the idea of girls growing up feeling they're inferior just because they're female."

She waited for another crack but none came so she went on with her list.

"There are generally fewer health issues with Chinese babies than with, say, Russian or Eastern European children. I ruled out adopting within the United States because the legal issues are far more complex here, especially if a biological parent has a change of heart."

"I'd hate to try and take a child away from you once you got hold of it."

"It would break my heart to give up a child I'd considered my own. I thought about adopting an older child to avoid that problem but I've always wanted a baby. They smell so sweet and innocent," she finished awkwardly, afraid to expose any more of her longing.

"What makes you think you'll be a good parent?" he queried after a pause.

"Now that's asking me to sing my own praises," she said with a laugh.

"You don't have to enumerate all your sterling qualities. Your friends have already explained to me what a lucky man I am."

"Sorry about that," Charlie said, glad the darkness covered her flush of embarrassment. "They got a little carried away by the wedding thing. Sometimes I think they forgot it was an unusual solution to our problems."

"So Miguel didn't mention what a great catch I am?"

"Afraid not. He just warned me about your occupational hazards."

He raised his hand. "Don't repeat them, please. Back to the adoption: how can you be so sure you'll be a good mother?"

"I can't," she said with a shrug he probably couldn't see. "But I'm sure I'll do my best. And I'm sure I'm responsible, loving and committed to putting a child's needs at the top of my priorities. What else can a parent—or anyone—guarantee?"

"Sometimes that's not enough."

"Really?" Her reporter's instincts were telling her Jack's statement came from somewhere profound. She tried to see his face, but the starlight only glinted off his eyes, leaving the rest of his features indistinct.

"Let's break out the sandwiches," he said, levering himself up on an elbow to reach for the bag of food.

Charlie knew he wasn't going to elaborate, no matter what she asked, so she gave in with good grace. They devoured the roast beef, gouda and mustard sandwiches and washed them down with still-steaming coffee, always keeping an eye on the sky. The silence was companionable and broken only by an observation on the location of a streaking space rock or a question about a noise in the woods. Fortunately, the bears were all staying in the sky, and once again Charlie's eyes closed in exhaustion.

A CRESCENDO OF birdsong wakened her, and she opened her eyes to a sky washed in the pink and gray of dawn. She could smell the dew on her blankets and the grass around her, damp, fresh, and tangy. A quiet snuffle from beside her made her turn her head in some alarm.

It was Jack. He lay asleep on his back, the arm beside her bent up and around his head, the other thrown out into the grass palm-up. Charlie propped herself up on her elbow so she could get a good long look at him. *Wasn't sleep supposed to make one look younger and more innocent?* The planes of Jack's face seemed starker without the blue of his eyes or the deep music of his accent to provide a distraction. His nose was like a knife blade, narrow and straight. The arch of his eyebrows cast a hint of mockery over his expression. His steely hair had gotten longer since she first saw him, now curling well down his collar. He must be too busy to see a barber. Up close, his hair showed an unusual mix of colors: deep black, pale silver, and every shade of gray in between.

He was a striking man.

Not precisely handsome but eye-catching.

Charlie looked at his mouth. Without the dimple show-ing, his lips looked as chiseled as a statue's.

"What's on your mind, sugar?"

Her gaze flew up to find the pale blue eyes open and looking right into her thoughts.

"You were snoring."

He laughed and threw off the covers. "Let's get back to the cabin, and get some real sleep." When he stood up and stretched, Charlie got busy folding blankets to keep herself from salivating over long, jeans-clad legs and broad leather-covered shoulders . . . and everything in between.

She yawned through the hike back to the cabin.

Jack escorted her up to the second floor where she stripped off her clothes and collapsed onto the comfortable bed without even asking where he was going to sleep. Six hours later her sleep ended abruptly as the scent of coffee, bacon and pancakes swirled past her quivering nostrils. She splashed cold water on her face, threw on some clean clothes and practically fell down the stairs in her haste to get to the source of the delicious smells.

Jack looked up from the griddle. "Sleep well?"

"Like a log." Charlie grabbed a mug from the row hang-ing under the cabinet and poured herself a steaming serv-ing of coffee. The first sip made her close her eyes in ecstasy. "Nectar of the gods."

"My caffeine craving woke me up," he agreed, neatly flipping the browning pancakes. "Can you find some syrup in the pantry?"

Brunch together was surprisingly relaxed. Jack re-sponded easily to any topic Charlie brought up but he wasn't prone to small talk, and he wasn't uncomfortable with silence. She stopped making polite conversation and let the quiet settle around them. Even with a day-old beard, he looked utterly rested and fit in a green-and-blue plaid flannel shirt and clean blue jeans.

"Would you like to join me for a hike to the beaver dam?" he asked, picking up his empty plate. "If you're up to it, that is," he added. "We'll be out again tonight, so if you're still tired you might want to rest . . ."

"Do you really want company?"

"The company of a beautiful woman is always welcome."

"Laying on the accent is overkill when you're making that kind of statement," Charlie said. "I may be average, but I'm an adventurer. I'd love to see a beaver dam."

They cleaned up the kitchen together, showered separately, and set out with water bottles and binoculars slung over their shoulders. For a while the trail was wide enough to walk side-by-side, and Charlie enjoyed her companion's knowledgeable commentary on the flora and fauna.

When the way narrowed, Jack took the lead and Charlie happily walked behind, enjoying the warmth of the sunlight filtering through the still barely-leafed trees. Spring came later here than on the Jersey shore; it was slightly chilly in the shade, especially since she was wearing shorts. Occasionally, she treated herself to a leisurely look at Jack's denim-clad legs and backside, but that sent her thoughts in *un*businesslike directions, so she mostly scanned the woods around her.

A flash of golden brown caught her eye. A chipmunk sat on top of a boulder beside the path, looking straight at her. Another one bolted off a nearby stump; the patch of woods was thick with the little creatures. A high ledge of rock rose from the forest floor about thirty feet from the path. Chipmunks dashed over its outcroppings and in and out of its holes, chittering at each other constantly.

"I've never seen so many chipmunks in one place," Charlie said.

"That colony has been here ever since Miguel bought the place." Jack came back to stand beside her.

"I love the black racing stripe down their flanks," she said, getting a good look at the brave fellow on the rock.

"See how they stick their tails straight up when they run? I get a kick out of that," her companion said.

"They certainly are lively," Charlie said, following as Jack set off down the path again. "Like Energizer bunnies."

Jack laughed. Charlie went back to her woods-gazing, but her thoughts kept returning to the man in front of her. He was still an enigma but now she had discovered he had had a rough childhood, and that his interest in meteorites had helped him through it. There was a streak of the mystical in him too; witness his annual pilgrimage and his refusal to secularize it with scientific observation.

He was smart, capable, self-sufficient and very, very controlled. He turned his charm and his accent on and off like a faucet. He was one of the most successful meteorite hunters in the world, but he wanted a college degree. He thought he'd be a lousy father, and he liked chipmunk tails.

Charlie shook her head.

He was way too interesting for her peace of mind.

The path had been hugging the steep bank of a stream. Now it twisted up and over a rock outcropping. Jack turned around to give her a hand up. When she felt his long fingers close around hers, the contact flashed across her entire body. She locked her gaze with his, but those blue eyes were as cold as Pluto. The moment she came up beside him, he released her hand and started forward again.

Charlie trudged along behind him, wondering if all the by-play between them was simply part of Jack's talent for manipulating people. *What had Miguel called it? Instant intimacy with total strangers.* Maybe now that she was no longer a threat, he didn't need the seduction act. Maybe he had turned off the physical attraction just like he turned off his accent.

Jack stopped, and she almost ran into him.

"What is it?" she asked, glancing around to see what had halted their progress. All that met her eye was the path winding through a stand of pines. "Is the dam nearby?"

"No," he said.

Her braid had fallen forward over her shoulder, and he picked it up. His gaze was directed somewhere off in the woods as he absently brushed the loose tips of hair over the palm of his hand. Charlie tried to ignore the wavelets of delight coursing over her scalp. After all, Jack had no idea that when anyone handled her hair, she was almost paralyzed with pleasure. Her eyelids had drifted closed when a sharp tug on her hair made her open them. Jack had wound her braid once around his fist, and was watching her intently. Charlie noticed little flames were flickering in his blue eyes.

"I was thinking," he drawled, "that in the interest of authenticity, we should rehearse a couple of things before we meet your social worker."

"What sort of things?" she asked, surprised at the direction of his thoughts.

He looped another length of braid around his hand, forcing her closer to him.

"I think a really convincing kiss needs to be practiced," he drawled.

Charlie tried to shake her head, but he held her hair captive.

"Any amateur should be able to do that," she said.

"But only a professional knows how to improve with each performance."

He twisted her hair once more around his fingers, bringing her to within an inch of his chest. She kept her eyes on the third button of his shirt, wondering if he really considered "practice" part of their business arrangement.

Using his makeshift rope, he slowly drew her head back, first to meet his eyes and then to expose the arch of her throat. She gasped as he skimmed his lips down her neck to the hollow of her collarbone and flicked her skin with his tongue.

"That's not exactly a kiss," she managed to say in a husky whisper.

She actually felt his lips curve into a smile. The vibration of his voice and breath on her skin made her moan as he spoke. "Now you're quibbling about semantics?"

In answer, she gave into her craving and ran her hands around his ribcage and up his back, relishing the feel of soft flannel over hard muscle.

He shuddered and released her braid abruptly. Then he became very, very still. Charlie angled her head to look up at him.

His lips were twisted into a strange, tentative smile very much at odds with the blaze of heat in his eyes and the hard arousal pressing against her thigh.

"Are we going to practice or not?" she challenged. He had started this, and he was darn well going to continue it to whatever the outcome might be.

He choked on a laugh and lowered his mouth almost to hers. "I'm prepared to practice until we get it right. Are you?"

Charlie didn't bother to answer. She simply tilted her chin a degree higher and touched his lips with hers. When he didn't respond, she traced the outline of his mouth with her tongue.

"Say 'yes,' Charlie," he rasped against her lips. "Just say 'yes'."

"That's what I've *been* saying," she said in some exasperation. "Yes, yes, *yes!* Is that good enough?"

He brought his hands up between them and flicked a button on her blouse out of its hole. Her nipples hardened instantly at the thought of his fingers on them. She reached up and yanked loose the top button on his shirt. She wanted to lean into him and kiss the pulse she saw beating on the side of his neck but that might impede his progress with her blouse. She started unbuttoning at the bottom of her shirt and beat him to the middle. Pushing her bra up without bothering to unfasten it, he at last cupped her breasts in his hands.

"Oh God, *yes,* Jack!" she whispered as he pressed his palms against her skin.

Heat blazed like lightning from his hands down to the hollow between her thighs. She tilted her pelvis against him, and felt his body harden even more. Now she frantically undid his shirt and tugged it out of his waistband. His torso was stunning: muscle rippled across his chest and carved lines in his abdomen. Three scars crisscrossed over one shoulder. She traced the three lines with her tongue, following one down to his nipple, which she kissed. He groaned and picked her up by the hips, swinging her around so her back was against a pine tree. He bent his head and closed his mouth over her breast.

"Yes, yes, yes, yes, yes," Charlie moaned as Jack swirled his tongue over and around first one and then the other tight, aching peak.

She wanted him to touch her lower and he obliged, running his tongue down the center of her body until he reached her belt buckle. He straightened to unbuckle it, and Charlie seized the opportunity to unbuckle, unsnap and unzip his fly. He slid her shorts and panties down over her hips and legs in one fluid movement, holding them as she stepped out of them. Then he stood and pulled her left knee high onto his hip. She pushed aside his underwear and guided him into her, then set her hands on his shoulders. As he buried himself inside her, he slid his other hand up her leg and cupped her bottom, lifting her and bracing her against the tree.

"Yes, yes, yes, oh yes," she murmured as he stroked into her.

She could feel the rough tree bark rasp against her lower back and a drift of cool breeze brush her bare skin. But the man inflamed her: his hands wrapped around her thighs like steel bands, the skin of his chest softly scuffing her breasts, and the brush of denim and silk against her most sensitive spot as he slid in and out, in and out . . .

"Ye-e-e-e-s!"

She felt the first ripple of climax and then convulsed so hard she whacked her head against the tree. Another wave hit; she dug her fingers into his shoulders. He withdrew and then buried himself inside her with a shout of release. As she felt him pump deep inside her, she exploded one last time. She collapsed with her head on his shoulder and her arms hanging down his back. He braced his weight against her to hold them both in place while they found their breath again. She made a tiny mew of regret when he slid out of her.

"Did I hurt you?" he asked, as he lowered her to the ground and zipped his jeans.

"No, I'm just sorry it's over," Charlie said, brushing bark off her bare backside.

Much to her embarrassment, he turned her around for inspection.

"You have a couple of scrapes but nothing too deep," he said in a tight voice, as he flicked more bits of bark away from her skin.

He reached down to pick up the heap of her shorts and panties.

Charlie took the proffered clothing and turned her back to pull it on. She wanted to tell him how wonderful she felt, what an incredible experience it had been, but everything had happened so fast she felt absurdly shy. She opened her mouth to say *something* when Jack spoke.

"My apologies. That was unforgivable."

"Unforgivable?" She was taken aback.

"I pushed you up against a tree with no thought for your comfort or pleasure."

She had just had the most powerful orgasm of her life and he was worried about her *comfort?*

"Did you hear me complaining?"

"I didn't give you a chance to."

"Well, I'm not complaining now."

He took three steps down the path and stopped, keeping his back to her.

"The most damnable part about this is I want to do it again."

"I might be talked into that."

He turned to face her and shook his head.

Charlie stood twisting her wedding ring for a few seconds. *What was this man's problem?* "You know, I don't want to contribute to your already-inflated ego, but I *really* enjoyed that. And I'm a little insulted you didn't notice."

He gave her a travesty of a smile. "My only excuse is extreme provocation."

"What am I wearing that's the least bit provocative?"

Charlie asked indignantly as she looked down at her white man-tailored shirt, baggy khaki hiking shorts, sport socks and sneakers.

"Sugar, you'd look provocative in a burlap sack."

"Another backhanded compliment," she muttered.

"Some malicious fate sent you to tempt me," he continued.

"I don't believe in fate," she said sharply. He was dousing her afterglow with ice water.

"Don't you?" he asked. He started down the rocky path. "Let's head back."

They walked in silence. Occasionally, she glanced over at him but his face was set, and he kept his gaze forward. He no longer offered his hand when they hit a steep part of the trail. There was definitely no second time in her future. And she should be glad of that, she scolded herself. Hadn't she learned anything from Nick?

As they walked up the porch steps, Jack said without looking at her, "Maybe we should get back to civilization today."

"No," she said. "I'm not going to drag you away from your vigil. I'll go work in my room while you do whatever it is you usually do up here."

So Charlie spent the rest of the afternoon and evening sitting in front of her laptop, emerging only for a quick visit to the kitchen to fix a sandwich. She could hear Jack hammering something, then roaring off in the Land Rover and returning an hour later, then furiously chopping wood.

As HE HUNG up a shiny new axe right beside the two other axes already on the wall, Jack mentally castigated himself yet again for practically assaulting the woman upstairs.

So much for his carefully cultivated self-control.

Miguel had warned him, her friends had warned him, even Charlie had warned him: this "marriage" was going to go in directions he hadn't foreseen.

Now why wasn't he more perturbed about that?

CHAPTER 9

AT MIDNIGHT, CHARLIE lay looking up at the stars. She had come to the conclusion that in spite of his flirtations with her, Jack considered their making love against a tree a serious blunder on his part. He was a control freak, and he had lost control. She let her lips curve upward, and turned to look at the solid three feet of springy brown grass separating them.

Jack was obviously taking no chances of this afternoon repeating itself.

She looked back at the sky, no longer smiling. She hadn't found any satisfying explanation for her own immediate capitulation. Despite Nick, or maybe because of him, she believed strongly in the importance of emotional as well as physical intimacy. She found Jack intriguing and attractive to look at, but she really barely knew him.

Maybe the wedding had removed some barrier in both their minds?

She shook her head against the pillow. That was absurd. She thought of him as her husband in a very ironic way. In fact, she needed to work on that if she was to convince Rhonda Brown this marriage was real. She had no doubt Jack would charm Rhonda the way he did everyone else, but she wasn't as accomplished an actor as he was.

Three meteorites blasted in different directions and she "ooh"ed in appreciation.

"Looks like we'll get a better display tonight," Jack said.

"Great."

Charlie went back to worrying about the display of this afternoon.

What puzzled her most was the suddenness of their connection. There had been no hesitation, no second thoughts on her part. His desire and hers had fused seamlessly, and built to an explosion that made her quiver when she remembered it. For several glorious minutes, she had felt intensely female: open, receptive, and complete, reveling in her power to give and take pleasure. Wielding that power was very seductive. She needed to remember that it was a double-edged sword.

She glanced at her companion again, this time without moving her head. He was wrapped in an air of detachment so vast the three feet between them might as well have been the distance to the North Star. She went back to watching the debris from space immolating itself in Earth's protective atmosphere. The silent streaks of silver were hypnotic; she let her mind drift aimlessly among the stars. A sudden flash drew her eye back toward Lyra as an odd hissing sound seemed to echo from the trees around their clearing. A brilliant ball of light traced a gleaming line across the sky. It moved more slowly than the falling stars, and its light pulsed with colors: yellow, green, red, blue.

"A fireball!" Jack breathed.

The meteoroid cast dancing shadows on the ground as it blazed across the sky. Suddenly it seemed to throw off sparks.

"It's breaking up," he said.

The light went bright white, then turned reddish, and the glowing ball disappeared. Its thin trail of smoky glow continued to hang in the sky for several more seconds, then faded. A rumble like distant thunder rolled toward them, followed by several loud thumping sounds. Then silence settled over the woods again.

"That was *incredible!* What was that noise?" Charlie could barely contain herself.

"That was the shock wave of the meteoroid traveling through the atmosphere," Jack explained.

"Why didn't we hear it when the meteoroid was over-head?"

"Because light travels faster than sound."

Jack had switched on a flashlight and was taking notes on a small pad of paper he had pulled from his pocket.

She sat up and scooted over to see what he was writing. "Do you think that there might be meteorites on the ground from the fireball?"

"Maybe."

"Are you going to go look for them?" Charlie asked, trying to make sense of the numbers and letters he was scribbling.

"No, but I'm going to make a few phone calls after looking at a map. Someone might have seen the fall." He scanned the horizon and jotted a few more notes.

"That would be unbelievably cool if you found parts of that meteorite! Would I be able to buy one? I'd love to have a space rock that I'd actually *seen* fall to Earth."

"If I find any, I'll give you a family member discount."

He appeared amused by her enthusiasm so she asked

the other questions flying around in her mind. "The light seemed to be different colors. What causes that?"

"Some colors come from the materials of the meteoroid itself. Some come from the gases in the atmosphere around it, sort of like the aurora borealis."

"Why did it last so much longer and burn so much brighter than the other falling stars we've seen?"

"It was probably unrelated to the Lyrids, which are the debris of a comet," he said, tucking the notebook and pen back into his pocket. "The fireball is bigger, usually a chunk of an asteroid, and it travels more slowly because of the atmosphere's braking effect." He looked at her for a moment, then continued, "It looks even bigger than it really is because the atmosphere around it becomes incandescent, sometimes for hundreds of feet. Most of the visual drama in a fireball is glowing hot gases."

"In all my so-called adventures," Charlie said, with awe in her voice, "I've never seen anything even remotely like that."

"That was just an average meteoroid. Some fireballs are so bright they light up the *daytime* sky. And some are so large they knock down entire forests just with their shock wave."

"That was in Siberia, right?"

"Yes, in 1909. No meteorites were ever found where the fall should have been so the current theory is a large meteoroid exploded about five miles above the Earth."

"I guess we're lucky that didn't happen over New York City. Of course, the dinosaurs weren't so lucky, were they?" She was literally vibrating with the thrill of the experience and couldn't stop talking. "I still can't believe I actually saw a fireball. Thank you so much."

"I'd like to take credit for arranging it, but it was pure luck."

"If I hadn't been out here staring at the sky with you, I would never have had the experience."

Charlie suddenly became aware she had pressed herself up against his arm and shoulder while she was trying to read his notes. She pulled back and bent her knee to lever herself to her feet when he said in a voice about an octave lower than the one he had used to explain the fireball, "Don't move. I owe you something."

"What?" she asked, halting in surprise.

He reached around to yank her blankets over beside his.

"I owe you one of these," he said, taking her by the shoulders and brushing his lips slowly over hers. "And this." He shifted to run his tongue around the outside of her ear at an exquisitely leisurely pace. "And a lot more of this." He turned and lowered her onto the blankets, coming down with her so she felt him along the whole length of her body. When his hand swept up her body to rest ever so gently on her breast, she choked on a moan.

"I'm all in favor of honoring your debts," she said, trying desperately to recall her dispassionate analysis of their afternoon encounter. She felt his other hand slide under her waistband seeking bare skin and gasped, "But I don't think you owe me anything."

"Let's just call it a southern gentleman's sense of obligation," he drawled.

As Charlie started to protest, his palm did a slow, exquisite dance over her chest. "I may have to rethink my opinion of *Gone with the Wind*," she managed to say before she threaded her fingers into his hair and pulled his face down to hers.

He checked his descent an inch above her. "Call me Rhett and I'll divorce you tomorrow."

"Jack," she said, and lifted her head to kiss him.

He sank into her kiss, half-covering her body with his

while his hands roamed over interesting places. She could feel him hardening against her hip but he seemed in no hurry to satisfy himself. So she wedged her hands between them and unbuttoned his flannel shirt one button at a time, spreading her palms over the skin she bared, running her fingers along the scars and wondering briefly what accident had put them there. She licked his throat and felt him shudder, but all her encouragement had no effect on his pace.

He shifted and worked her shirt loose from her jeans, pushing it up and unhooking the front catch of her bra. She arched into his mouth when it came down on her breast, and for a moment felt the marvelous scrape of his whiskers before he eased back to just flick her nipple with his tongue.

"Please," she groaned, arching again.

"Yes, ma' am," he said and took her into his mouth, letting her feel just the edge of a bite before he swirled his tongue over and around and then drew away to tug her nipple ever so gently in his teeth.

"Again," she begged, twisting to offer him her other breast.

He obliged, and Charlie pulled him up to thank him with a kiss that had him rock hard against her. She reached down to unbuckle his belt but he was already sliding down her body, using his tongue to trace a line down to the top of her jeans. As he unsnapped and unzipped, she raised her hips to wriggle out of the impeding denim and cotton. She toed off her sneakers, and he pulled her pants down and off her ankles, then crouched over her and ran his lips up the inside of her leg and thigh.

She was so ready to feel his mouth between her legs that she almost wept when he moved to her other thigh and down. Her hands fisted in the blankets and her toes curled into the pad as he moved upward again, the flannel of his open shirt brushing her sensitized skin and adding more delicious torment to his slow journey.

"Oh, Rhett!" she moaned.

He laughed, and the sound and breath of it vibrated against her just before his tongue touched right where she most wanted it. She tilted her hips to give him better access, but he kept right on stroking her toward her climax in his own agonizingly slow, absolutely wonderful rhythm.

As she reached that moment of suspension when all sensation was focused in the pool of heat between her thighs, before the ripple of release began to spread outward, he drew away to unfasten his own jeans. Then as she felt the first clench of orgasm, he slid inside her, instantly triggering another spasm so hard that she dug her fingernails into his shoulders. He moved again, and she locked her legs around his waist to keep him there while she came over and over until her muscles quivered with exhaustion. His own release was a rush of warmth inside her, causing an echoing tremor in her belly.

She let her arms and legs sprawl across the sleeping bag, still enjoying the scrape of denim and flannel against her bare skin and the weight and warmth of him between her thighs and on her breasts.

"I'll overlook you calling me 'Rhett' just this once," Jack said, propping himself up on his elbows to look down at her.

"You know it was your own fault," she said, smiling up at him. "You were deliberately torturing me."

Then she closed her eyes and wriggled slightly under him. "God, I feel good."

"You certainly do," he agreed, cupping her bare breast.

"Do your worst. I can't move," she claimed.

"You're a liar, sweetheart. I felt your hips tilt up just now."

"It was involuntary muscle movement, like when chickens run around with their heads cut off."

That warm, honeyed chuckle poured into the night and Charlie chuckled back. Her laughter turned to an "oh" of deprivation when he pushed away and stood up.

"If you could see yourself . . ." he said, staring down at her for a long moment before raising his face to the sky.

"If I could see myself what?" she wanted to know, enjoying in equal parts the shock of cold air on her heated skin and the knowledge that he still wanted her.

"Don't fish, sugar, and put some clothes on before you catch your death."

He flicked her jeans toward her with the toe of his boot.

The darkness covered any awkwardness she might feel about dressing in front of him, but Jack kept his back politely turned. Dressed, she stood up and wrapped her arms around him from behind, burying her nose in his back and inhaling the scent of man and shirt and outdoors.

"Ummm, you smell good."

He laughed. "In your current mood, everything is good."

"Thanks to *you*," Charlie murmured. She felt a sudden stiffening in his back and shoulders.

"You give me too much credit." He laced his fingers with hers and gently pulled her hands away from his waist. Turning, he kissed first one of her palms and then the other before releasing them. "You provided all the inspiration."

"Still, you can consider your debt paid," she said, stung by his smooth but obvious withdrawal. *He had started this.*

"Glad to hear it." He stood three feet away in the darkness so she couldn't read his expression.

She squinted up at the sky, only to find the heavens as

inscrutable as her companion. "Is the meteorite shower over?" she asked.

"No, it's just passed its peak. From now on, you'll see only occasional activity."

Charlie wondered if his statement applied to more than the sky.

"Why don't we pack up and head back?" he said, bending over and starting to roll up a blanket.

"Avoiding temptation?"

"You got it, sugar. Temptation with a capital 't'."

She noticed that he had given up his attempt at neatness and was simply stuffing the wadded-up blanket into a backpack. She smirked into the darkness as she deftly rolled her own blankets and mat into a tidy bundle. *Inspiration or temptation, either one meant he was more affected than he wanted to admit.*

Jack was thinking exactly the same thing.

THEY SLEPT, THEY loaded the car, they drove halfway back to New Jersey, all as if they had never touched each other. Charlie couldn't stand it any longer.

"You know, I'm all for keeping this 'partnership' businesslike, but I'm not sure I can just forget what happened this weekend."

"Forget it?" He laughed. "I'm not going to forget it for a very long time. I'm just going to put it behind me and get back to the original intent of our arrangement."

She frowned. He seemed much too confident in his ability to do that.

"Face it, Charlie. Put a man and a woman together out in the woods, and they start to feel like they're in the Garden of Eden." He shrugged. "There's nothing surprising about it, and now we've gotten it out of our systems."

Charlie didn't particularly care to be cast as Eve. "You're right," she said. "It was just the excitement of seeing fire blazing across the sky that got me all hot and bothered. Any man who had been there would have gotten the same reaction. Maybe even a woman."

He had been looking like a thundercloud, but her last comment cleared the storm and made him smile. "A dose of my own medicine, eh? Be careful what you suggest."

"I thought we were being strictly business from now on," she pointed out.

"We sure as hell are," he agreed, but he sounded as though he was reminding himself.

"THIS IS WHERE you list your assets and liabilities and your income," Charlie said, passing the forms to Jack. She tried not to touch him as he sat beside her on her couch.

His focus seemed entirely on the paperwork. "I'll fill this out in New York where my records are." He gestured toward a pile of papers on the table. "What are those?"

"Proof of citizenship, INS forms, birth certificate, criminal record, fingerprints, etc. They don't require any thought, just filling out, notarizing and sending in. Those are the easy ones," she laughed.

He didn't smile.

"Is there a problem?" she asked. *Maybe in all his international travels, he had done something to annoy the INS? Or maybe Isabelle was right: he had murdered his first three wives.*

"No, no problem. I had no idea there was so much red tape involved in adopting from China."

"Now you see why I didn't want to wait any longer for my home study approval. It will be another six months after it's done before I can bring home my baby."

"You have a pretty nice life here." He waved a hand around her living room. "Why are you so eager to have a child who will gum up the works?"

"I have a pretty lonely life," Charlie said quietly. "I grew up without a permanent family. I don't want to live that way any longer. And since I can't have a family in the usual way, I'm going to create one."

"You've already done that with your neighbors. They think very highly of you."

"The ties aren't the same. They'll move. Or die."

"We're all going to die, sooner or later."

She made no response so he gathered up all the documents and tapped them into a neat pile. "I'll have these done for you by the end of this week."

"Then I'll call Rhonda Brown and guilt her into an appointment for the following week."

He picked up the garment bag with his wedding suit in it. Charlie went with him to the door. "Call me if you have any questions about any of those forms."

"I will." Taking her chin in his hand, he looked down at her and said, "Watching the Lyrids will never be the same again."

Then he straightened and walked out into the dusk.

CHAPTER 10

"CHARLIE, THIS IS Rhonda Brown. I'm sorry to call so late and on a Sunday, but I have an emergency situation I need help with. Can I come over and talk with you in person?"

"Of course. I'll be here."

What on earth could Rhonda Brown need my help with?

Charlie fixed some coffee and put leftover wedding hors d'oeuvres on a plate before the doorbell rang. Rhonda swept into the room with the same majesty she had displayed on her first visit. Tonight she was dressed in a swirling purple shift that matched the heavy amethyst-and-silver necklace around her neck. When she saw the coffee, she took a mug, and buried her nose in it, saying, "I need this desperately."

"Bad day?" Charlie said, offering her the plate of food.

"I left Brooklyn to get away from this sort of day," her guest said, eating a miniature quiche with a sigh of pleasure. "Thank you."

"You're welcome. Would you like something more substantial, like a sandwich?"

Rhonda sat back on the couch with the coffee mug cradled in her hands. "No, thanks. I don't have much time. I just came from the police station in Atlantic City."

"That doesn't sound good."

"A young woman from Tennessee who came to live here about a year ago was murdered early this morning."

"I'm sorry to hear that."

"She has a nine-year-old daughter. We can't locate a father or any relatives here. And so far we haven't been able to reach anyone in Tennessee either." Now Rhonda sat forward and looked straight at Charlie. "I don't want this little girl to go into the foster care system. I think we can find a family member who will want her, but it may take some time. You know what it's like to be an orphan, and you're prepared to adopt a child. Would you take her in until I can find the right person?"

Charlie put her mug down with a thud. "I-I guess so."

"I could get into a hell of a lot of trouble for not putting her in a certified foster home," Rhonda said, "but I think you could make a difference for this little girl. She's as cute as a button, has a southern twang, and says, 'yes, ma'am' every other sentence. Her mother raised her right."

"Do you know why the mother was murdered?" Charlie asked.

"She was working as a prostitute and a john got violent," Rhonda said, looking grim. "I hate those damned casinos. They don't do anyone any good." She shook her head. "Evidently, she rented an apartment in Bellefont because the schools were good, and she didn't want her daughter anywhere near what she did for a living."

"Of course I'll take the child," Charlie said, with a conviction she was genuinely beginning to feel. "What's her name?"

"Sallyanne McGraw."

"Where is she now?"

"With a neighbor. I'll go pick her up and bring her here."

"Shouldn't I go with you?" Charlie said, rising too.

"No. You get her room ready, and think about what you want to say to her. I'll tell her a little bit about you."

"Any suggestions?"

"I think you'll figure it out." Rhonda had reached the door, and paused as she opened it. "You're a smart lady, and you have good instincts. I'll be back in under an hour."

"Right." Charlie closed the door after her, and turned around to lean against it.

She needed to get the guest room ready. She wanted to bake some chocolate chip cookies. She had to make a nine-year-old girl whose mother had just died a violent death feel welcome in a strange house. *How exactly did one do that?*

Major came over and pushed his nose into her hand. She stroked him a couple of times and said, "You're great with cats. How are you with children?" She pushed off from the door and headed upstairs to make the guest room look inviting.

Flowered sheets and a patchwork comforter brightened the bed. A friend had given her two Beanie Babies as a joke; they went on top of the quilt. She hung yellow-and-white-striped towels in the bathroom and unwrapped a lilac-scented cake of soap someone had given her as a houseguest present. Somewhere in her attic was a set of the *Chronicles of Narnia* but she didn't have time to dig them out.

That would have to wait for tomorrow.

Checking her watch, she dashed downstairs to the kitchen and started whipping up a batch of chocolate chip cookies. They wouldn't be ready to eat but the smell should make a child feel more at home. She had just pulled the first tray out of the oven to cool when the doorbell rang again.

She took a deep breath and opened the door.

Standing beside Rhonda was a small girl with blond pigtails and blue eyes. A pink plastic purse hung from her shoulder, and Rhonda held a small suitcase in her hand. Charlie got down on one knee and offered her hand to the child. "Hi, I'm Charlie. It's nice to meet you, Sallyanne."

"Hello, Miz Charlie," the child said, shaking hands gravely.

Charlie reached up and lightly stroked the little girl's pigtail. "Just 'Charlie' is fine. Come in."

Rhonda stepped forward but Sallyanne stood still. "Charlie is a boy's name."

"My real name is Charlotte, but everyone calls me 'Charlie'. I have some chocolate chip cookies cooling. I baked them especially for you."

"Mama and I bake cookies together," Sallyanne said. "We make the best cookies of anyone."

Charlie could see the exact moment Sallyanne remembered she and her mama wouldn't be baking cookies together anymore. She swept the little girl into her arms and hugged her close. "Well, maybe you can show me how you did it." The little body was stiff in her arms, but Charlie held on until Sallyanne relaxed and put her head on Charlie's shoulder just for a second. It was enough. When she pulled away, Charlie let her go.

They eyed each other, and then Sallyanne stepped past Charlie into the house.

And screamed.

"What is it? What's wrong?" Charlie asked, racing after her.

Sallyanne stood frozen two feet from Major.

"Oh, sweetheart, I'm sorry. That's just my dog Major. He's as gentle as a lamb."

"I'm allergic to dogs," the little girl announced in a trembling voice.

"Oh dear. Well, then Major will have to go live somewhere else for a while. In the meantime, I'll shut him up in my office," Charlie said, grabbing the dog's collar and leading him up the stairs.

"Are you allergic to cats too?" she asked when she returned to the living room. Twinkle had bolted as soon as she heard voices, but Charlie wanted to avert any more drama from Sallyanne's day.

"No, ma'am. They're little and soft, and they don't bite."

"Ah, I see," Charlie said. "Would you like to come with me to the kitchen, and we'll take the cookies off the cookie sheet and put some more in to bake?"

Rhonda nodded her approval and sat down on the couch. "I'll just sit here a little while and read the paper."

"Thanks," Charlie mouthed and took Sallyanne into the kitchen.

Sallyanne wasn't boasting when she said she knew how to bake cookies. Even though the first batch had cooled so much they stuck to the pan, the girl expertly wedged the spatula under a cookie and carefully separated it from the metal.

"Wow, you're really good at that," Charlie said with honest admiration. "I would have broken that into at least three pieces."

Sallyanne smiled a tiny, tentative smile.

"Thank you, ma' am," she said before returning to her task.

When the cookies, all intact, had been arranged on the Noah's Ark plate, Charlie handed Sallyanne the cookie dough and a clean cookie sheet. The young chef carefully spooned the proper-sized mounds of dough onto the pan and handed it back.

"We may have to go into competition with Mrs. Field's," Charlie said as she put the second batch in the oven. "Why don't you invite Rhonda in to eat some?"

They all sat down to milk and cookies at Charlie's kitchen table, the scent of baking enveloping them. And Charlie was happy. She berated herself for the sudden flood of joy that flowed through her because it sprang from a little girl's terrible misfortune. But having a child sitting at her kitchen table felt so good she had to hide a smile behind her milk glass.

In the last few hours, Rhonda had become family too.

She had come to Charlie when she needed someone to take care of a child. She had even broken the rules to do it. Charlie wanted to reach over and take her hand but restrained herself. "Oh my gosh," she exclaimed suddenly. "Rhonda, I completely forgot to tell you. I got married on Friday."

"Wasn't that rather sudden?" Rhonda asked as she arched a skeptical eyebrow. "And where's the lucky man?"

"He had to go to New York on business. He's Jack Lanett, the meteorite hunter who found the Mars rock."

"I've read about him."

"It wasn't really sudden. We've been . . . involved for several years, but we both traveled so much we never made the relationship more formal."

"What changed your minds?"

"He's retiring after he auctions off the Mars rock. And

I'm staying home for . . ." she glanced at Sallyanne, then said vaguely, "reasons you already know. We had always planned to get married when our circumstances were more settled, and we decided to go ahead with the wedding now so we could be together for the Chinese, um, situation."

Rhonda looked dubious.

"We had the most marvelous honeymoon in the Poconos."

"Don't overdo your story. I can't see you in a heart-shaped tub."

"Not *that* sort of place," Charlie said, laughing. "We went to a cabin out in the woods and spent two nights under the stars, watching the Lyrid meteor shower." Turning to Sallyanne, she said, "We even saw a fireball," and explained the phenomenon to her guests. They both had questions, and Charlie spent a half an hour fascinating them by describing the shower of stars she and Jack had witnessed.

Finally, Rhonda glanced at the kitchen clock and stood up. "I have to go. And you, young lady, need to get to bed. Do you want to go to school tomorrow or would you rather stay home for a day?"

"I'd like to go to school, ma'am. My mama says school is very important."

"Your mama is absolutely right, but you can take one day off if you'd like to."

Sallyanne shook her head.

"All right. Do you mind sitting in here while I tell Charlie all she needs to know about your school?"

"No, ma'am."

Rhonda and Charlie went into the living room and held a low-voiced consultation about Sallyanne's life for the next week. When they had worked it out to both their satisfaction, Rhonda said, "That was a good idea, baking the cookies."

"I felt horrible when it reminded her that her mother is dead."

"No, it was a good thing. She needs to grieve, but she can't do that until she accepts her mother is truly gone."

"She doesn't have to do it so soon, does she?"

"Everyone is different," Rhonda shrugged. "Some folks, even children, need to deal with harsh realities immediately. It's healthier than denying them indefinitely."

"I suppose."

"You're doing just fine," Rhonda assured her as she walked to the door. "By the way, best wishes on your marriage. I'll need the adoption paperwork from your husband."

"I know. We're working on it already."

"I don't think you'd be crazy enough to get married just to adopt a baby, or if you were that crazy, that you could find a man who was equally insane. But I want to meet Jack Lanett as soon as possible."

CHARLIE GOT SALLYANNE into her pajamas, supervised tooth-brushing and face-washing, knelt awkwardly beside her when the little girl reminded her about bedtime prayers and swallowed hard when Sallyanne asked God to be nice to her mama in Heaven. The girl's face lit up when Charlie told her the Beanie Babies were hers to keep, and she carefully arranged them so their heads rested on the pillow beside her. Charlie left the closet light on as a nightlight because she remembered waking up in strange houses in the middle of the night and not knowing where she was in the dark. Then she kissed Sallyanne on the forehead and wished her sweet dreams.

She went down the hall to let Major out of her office. He licked cookie crumbs off the floor while Charlie cleaned up the kitchen. "You're going to have to go live with Isabelle until Sallyanne gets over her 'allergy,'" Charlie said, taking Major's muzzle in her hand and looking him in the eye. "If anyone can help someone get over their fear of dogs, it's you. I'm going to bring Sallyanne over to visit as soon as I think she's ready."

Twinkle strolled into the kitchen, having emerged from whatever hiding place she had been sleeping in.

"You!" she said, opening a can of cat food. "What kind of a therapy cat are you? You vanish just when I need someone soft and cuddly the most."

She sat down at the table. The cat jumped in her lap and Major laid his head on her knee. She stroked them both absently as she stared out the window toward the channel. "My new hubby is going to find the works all gummed up, isn't he? This is going to be interesting."

HER ALARM WENT off at 6:30 the next morning. Charlie hit the snooze button, then sat bolt upright as she remembered she had a child to get ready for school. She threw on slacks and a T-shirt, fed Major and Twinkle, shut the dog up in her bedroom and went upstairs to waken Sallyanne.

The child lay on her side facing the Beanie Babies. She looked peaceful, but when Charlie brushed against the pillow it was damp. *The poor little thing.* Charlie's heart ached for the girl. She sat down gently on the side of the bed and touched Sallyanne's shoulder.

"Sweetheart, it's time to wake up."

"Mama?" a sleepy voice whispered.

"No, it's Charlie."

Sallyanne opened her eyes, and the misery in them

made Charlie gather her up onto her lap. The little girl clung to her and sobbed.

"I'm so sorry, sweetheart. I'm here. Go ahead and cry," she whispered as she stroked the girl's sweet-smelling silky hair. "It's fine to cry. I'm here as long as you need me."

"I'm sorry for wetting your shirt," Sallyanne said after the storm passed and she was wiping her eyes and nose with the Kleenex Charlie handed her. "I miss Mama so much."

"Of course you do. I know all about missing mamas."

"What happened to your mama?"

"Both my parents were killed in an accident when I was four years old."

"I'm sorry, ma'am."

"I was too but I'm okay now. I still wish I had them, but I've learned how to be happy even without them. You will too but it takes time—and some crying."

"Yes, ma'am. Should I get ready for school now?"

Charlie reached out to smooth the little girl's hair back from her face. "You don't have to go today if you don't want to. Your teacher will understand. You can stay home with me, and we can watch the boats going by in the channel."

"I'd like to, ma'am, but I'm going to do what Mama wanted."

"Then let's get you to school."

While they were eating pancakes, Rhonda called to say she was setting up a meeting with the school officials and wanted Charlie to come. "I'm introducing you as a friend of the family who is temporarily taking care of Sallyanne until relatives can be found," the social worker said. "You might want to coach her a bit, so she doesn't tell her teacher something else."

"I hate to ask a child to lie," Charlie said in a low voice, glancing at the kitchen.

"It's for her own good, believe me. And I'm doing more lying than anyone here so don't be so queasy."

"I like you, Rhonda," Charlie said, grinning. "You surprise me, but I like you."

"That's a great comfort to me. I'll call you when the meeting's set."

Charlie was still smiling when she walked into the kitchen. But her good humor evaporated as she explained the necessary white lie to Sallyanne, who didn't think it was right because God and her mama objected to lies. Eventually, Charlie got her to promise she simply wouldn't discuss where she was living with anyone at school.

Packing lunch was an adventure. Charlie's pantry wasn't supplied with much in the way of a children's menu. She borrowed all-natural peanut butter from Isabelle and used the least peculiar mixture of organic preserves she possessed. Potato chips were an immediate hit as were the Junior Mints Charlie was addicted to. All in all, she thought she improvised pretty well.

Making sure the little girl was securely buckled in, Charlie drove her to school. She ascertained that Sallyanne's mama did not walk her to "line-up," and much as Charlie wanted to do it, she decided not to change the routine any more than was absolutely necessary. However, she did get out of the car and give Sallyanne a hug and a kiss.

"If you decide you need to leave school any time today, you ask the teacher to call me. I put my cell phone number in your backpack, and I'm going to call the school office and give it to them too. I'll come pick you up right away. Your mama would understand if you got upset or tired today. You're allowed."

"Thank you, ma'am," Sallyanne said dutifully.

Then she turned and marched off toward the big brick school building, joining the stream of children headed for the lines forming on the playground.

Charlie waited and watched, and was relieved when two other little girls ran up to join Sallyanne. Having friends always helped. It had been a rare pleasure in her own childhood since she had been moved so often.

She went to the grocery store on the way home. After unloading the groceries, baking a chocolate cake, arranging for Major to stay with Isabelle afternoons and nights, and unpacking the newly-unearthed *Chronicles of Narnia* into the bookcase in the guest room, Charlie picked up the phone. "Hello, Jack, it's Charlie."

"I think I can recognize my wife's voice."

Hearing him call her his wife brought memories of the weekend's activities back to vivid life. "Yes, well, I suppose so. Listen, I have to be in New York on business tomorrow," she lied. "I wondered if you were free around noon." That gave her time to meet with Rhonda and the school officials first thing in the morning.

"Noon? Sounds good. Come to my apartment and we'll have lunch."

"Hmmm." The last thing Charlie wanted to do was commit to sharing a meal with him after she dropped her bombshell. And she had to be home to pick up Sallyanne at school. "I'll take a rain check on the lunch, thanks. I have a lunch meeting already scheduled."

"Fine. See you then."

She was not looking forward to announcing they had acquired a child slightly ahead of schedule, since it meant he was going to have to play father whether he liked it or not. During the night, it had occurred to her that she could probably have done some negotiating with Rhonda and negated the necessity for a husband. She had disclosed her marriage before she had thought things through. *It can't be helped now.*

She and Jack would just have to make the best of it.

The phone rang. "Hello, Mrs. Lanett. This is Warren Bixby."

She was about to tell him he had the wrong number when he continued, "The photographer at your wedding."

"Of course," she said, shaking her head.

"Your prints are ready. Can I drop them off about five?"

"Sure."

After she hung up, she looked at Major. "Mrs. Lanett." He wagged his tail. She shook her head again.

CHAPTER 11

"COME ON UP, *dear!*" the voice from the intercom said.

"On my way!" Charlie took her finger off the talk button. "Babycakes."

The doors swung open, the elevator beckoned, and soon Charlie was facing Jack in the doorway of his apartment. "You know, all this automation is sort of creepy," she commented. "I'm glad you at least have to open your own door."

"Actually, I don't. I could press a button and it would open itself."

"Weird," she said, walking beside him to the living room.

"Good security. Doormen can be bribed. That's why I rent this place. It used to belong to an art dealer."

"I see." She had safely navigated past the issue of whether to say hello with a kiss and sank onto the couch with a sigh of relief.

"Something to drink?" he asked. Jack was wearing a

black shirt, black trousers and a blazer in a salt-and-pepper fleck. He looked quite devastatingly attractive.

"Some water would be great." She stood back up and followed him into the kitchen. "Did you track down any meteorites from the fireball?"

"Not yet, but I have some leads." He poured a glass of water and handed it to her.

"I know I can't write a book but would you object to an article about meteor-watching with the world's foremost meteorite hunter? It would be such a great story, especially if you actually find some meteorites," she said wistfully.

For a moment she thought he was going to blast her. Then the corners of his mouth quirked up just the slightest bit. "And who would you sell it to? *Hustler*?"

She gaped at him a moment before realizing what he was hinting at, then laughed. "No, I'm going for a G rating, so I'd have to do some editing."

"If I have final approval."

"Deal." She thought of offering a handshake but decided against it on the grounds that touching him was risky.

"I have a wedding gift for you," he said, gesturing her back to the living room. He picked up a large black envelope from an end table and handed it to her.

"I didn't know we were exchanging gifts . . ."

"We're not. Open it."

She lifted the flap and pulled out a large rectangle of black paper. Glittering bits of silver were embedded in the thick handmade stock. In stark silver letters she was invited to a private viewing of the Sahara-Mars meteorite at the Rose Center for Earth and Space in New York City the following Tuesday. She had read about this event in *Page Six*. Only the most serious dealers and collectors would be there. It was an invitation to die for.

"This is a wonderful wedding present! Thank you *so* much." She tilted the invitation back and forth in her hands, creating little flashes of silver, and a thought occurred to her. "Will I be attending as your wife or a journalist?"

"That's a question I debated at length," he said "On the one hand, a wife might distract serious attention from the meteorite. On the other, she would definitely attract more publicity, as a sort of double story."

"And any publicity is good publicity," Charlie interjected.

"Also, it will make for more photographic coverage. A tall blonde is more interesting than a black rock. However, a tall gorgeous blonde standing beside a black rock from space will make the photographers salivate. So I'd like you to come as my wife who's also a prominent journalist."

"Why do I feel I'm being treated as an object? I'll let it go only because you used the word 'gorgeous.' "

"It's black tie. If you need a dress, I can recommend someone."

"I can dress myself, thank you." Although she had no idea how—she couldn't wear a pair of black silk pants and a beaded top, her usual formal attire. Lots of *very* rich people would be at this party and, of course, the photographers. She could feel a small bubble of panic forming in her throat.

"I'll send a limousine for you." As she started to protest, he cut her off. "I'm not having my new bride arrive in a beaten-up Volvo station wagon."

"I understand. You have your image to consider." She took a sip of water. "Jack, there's something else we have to discuss."

He raised an eyebrow.

"I'm fostering a nine-year-old child, temporarily."

"What?"

She quickly told him Sallyanne's story. By the end, she was relieved to see him looking more irritated than furious.

"That's a hell of a way to start out in life," he said with surprising compassion. Then his tone changed. "But if this Rhonda Brown trusts you enough to drop a nine-year-old in your lap without any paperwork whatsoever, why are we married? It seems to me we can file for divorce immediately."

Charlie winced. "Being married for five days wouldn't look good on my record."

"So keep it off your record—"

"I can't. Rhonda already knows."

"Damnation." He sat down, drumming his fingers on one knee.

"I've explained that you're not going to be around much until the auction is over, but I think you're going to have to spend a couple of days playing father and husband." She tried to make a small joke. "Rhonda has an inside source now."

Jack wasn't smiling. He pulled an electronic calendar out of his jacket pocket and punched a few buttons. "I can come down Thursday afternoon and stay through Friday night. I have to be back here on Saturday to meet some dealers."

"Great. That's great!" Charlie said. He was taking the news with remarkable equanimity. She glanced at her watch, and put her glass down on the end table. "I have to get to my lunch appointment."

"An editor? An agent?" He rose fluidly.

"Editor." She couldn't bring herself to embellish her lie anymore than that.

"What project are you discussing?"

"A travel article." She made a beeline for the door.

"An interesting location?"

"Very." She stepped out into the hallway before turning. "Thanks so much for the invitation. I'll try to do you proud."

"I don't doubt you will." He escorted her to the elevator. As the doors were about to close, he said, "Just one last detail. If you ever call me 'babycakes' again, I'll tell Rhonda Brown you posed for the centerfold in *Playboy*."

"No problem," Charlie grinned, "stud muffin."

The doors slid shut.

Jack didn't start chuckling until he had his apartment door firmly closed behind him. *Stud muffin. The only thing worse than babycakes.*

WHEN SHE PICKED Sallyanne up after school, Charlie suggested going down to the channel to watch the boats go by.

"Mama always made me do homework as soon as I got home, ma'am."

"Well, then why don't we bring your homework with us?"

So they set up chairs and a table down by the wall of the channel. While Sallyanne did her math, Charlie skimmed through the book the fourth grader was reading so she could help with the comprehension questions. But Sallyanne didn't need much help. She answered the questions fully and with imagination.

"You're a really good reader and writer."

"Yes, ma'am." Her face lit up. "I take books out of the library, and the librarian says I read three years above my grade level."

"Have you read the *Chronicles of Narnia*?"

"The first two. I really like them."

"I put the whole set in your room. Tomorrow we'll go to the library."

They both jumped as a fishing boat's horn sounded right beside them. "Hey, Charlie. Who's your friend?" the captain shouted from the helm of the *Rosalie*.

"This is Sallyanne. She's come to live with me for a while," Charlie called back.

"Ahoy there, Sallyanne! Welcome to Corbin's Canal!"

"Thank you, sir," the child called, waving.

"Now we've got *two* beautiful mermaids to greet us when we come home."

Much to Charlie's delight, Sallyanne giggled.

The *Rosalie* was only the beginning of the procession of returning boats. Sallyanne was introduced to every fisherman Charlie recognized. Pretty soon she was reading the names of the boats and asking who the captain was and what they caught. One young man even tossed her a conch shell. It landed unscathed on the grass and Sallyanne touched it as though it were the most delicate porcelain.

"Look at the inside, ma'am. It's like a sunset," she said, showing Charlie the delicate pink-and-yellow interior.

Everything was going smoothly, better than Charlie could have hoped. Then, just before they sat down to dinner, Sallyanne gave Charlie a spelling test she had gotten back from the teacher.

"You got everything right *and* extra credit. That's wonderful!"

"Mama says always do the extra credit, even if you're not sure you're right."

Charlie's respect for Sallyanne's mama was growing by leaps and bounds. She walked over to the refrigerator, pried off her favorite cat magnet and posted the test right in the middle of the metal door. "There. Now everyone will see how smart you are."

Sallyanne's face crumpled.

"Oh, sweetheart," Charlie said, kneeling to put her arms around the girl. "I didn't mean to make you cry. Would you like me to take it down?"

"Mama used to put my tests on the refrigerator, ma'am," a small muffled voice said from her shoulder.

As Charlie felt the little body shaking with silent sobs, she had to blink hard against her own tears. She called back those ancient, awful memories she had pushed into the farthest corner of her mind, and knew what Sallyanne needed most was to be held, to be touched the way a mother would, to be reassured that someone still cared about her. So she held her and told her she was there for her.

"I'm sorry, ma'am," the little girl said when the sobs had subsided.

"You don't ever have to apologize for being sad," Charlie said. "It's called grieving, and you have to grieve for someone you've lost. If you don't, you can't go on with your life."

"Yes, ma'am."

Charlie wiped tears from her own eyes, and said in an especially cheerful voice, "So who wants mac and cheese?"

THEIR DINNER CONSISTED of macaroni and cheese and mashed potatoes, Sallyanne's favorites. When they were halfway done, Charlie broached the subject of the extended McGraw family. Through a conversation with one of the child's neighbors, Rhonda had ascertained that her father was dead, and there had been some estrangement from the mother's family. She had asked Charlie to try to find out more.

"You know, I lived with aunts and uncles when I was growing up," Charlie said, as she spooned out more mashed potatoes. "Do you have an aunt or an uncle? Or maybe a grandmother or grandfather?"

"Granny passed on," Sallyanne said, digging into the butter-laden pile. "I don't remember her very well."

"Did your mama ever mention playing with sisters or brothers when she was little?"

The girl thought for a minute and shook her head again. "No. She said I had cousins, but they were in Alaska."

"Alaska! That's a long way away."

"That's why I never got to play with them," Sallyanne explained.

If she had cousins, she should have an aunt or uncle. "Do you know if McGraw was your mama's last name before she met your papa, or after?"

"No, ma'am."

"Did your mama ever talk about your papa's family at all?"

"No, ma'am. My papa was dead to us."

Charlie almost choked on her pasta. Sallyanne hadn't said her papa was *dead.* She had said he was dead *to her.* Those were two very different things. Maybe the neighbor hadn't paid attention to the wording? "So your mama didn't say your papa had passed on? She said he was dead to you?"

"Yes, ma'am." Sallyanne's fork stopped in midair. "Do you think my papa might *not* be dead?"

The blue eyes were pleading, but Charlie had known too much disappointment in her own younger life to raise Sallyanne's hopes too high.

"When you say a person is 'dead to you,' it *sometimes* means they've done something so awful you never want to see them again."

Sallyanne looked at her plate. "I guess I wouldn't want a papa like that."

"But if you do have a papa, maybe he's changed," Charlie added because she couldn't bear the slump in the little girl's shoulders.

"But he might not want me." Sallyanne went back to her mashed potatoes.

Charlie was feeling out of her depth. She needed to pass this information on to Rhonda immediately. She had a bad feeling about this absentee father. She had come to admire the way Sallyanne's mother had raised her daughter; therefore she trusted the woman's instincts about the father of her child.

"Do you have a picture of your mama?" Charlie asked to redirect the girl's thoughts. "I'd really like to know what she looked like."

"Yes, ma'am," the child said with great emphasis. "It's in one of the boxes Miz Rhonda brought over yesterday. I wasn't sure if I should take it out."

"Sweetheart, that's your room. You can put out anything you want in it."

"Thank you, Charlie."

Not ma'am. Charlie. That was progress.

"You've finished all your homework, right?"

"Yes, ma'am."

"Then can I see the picture?"

They went to the guest room, and Charlie helped Sallyanne open the box with her mother's picture in it. There were several framed photos, mostly of Sallyanne at various ages. "This is my mama," she said with pride as she handed Charlie the largest frame.

The head and shoulders portrait had been taken in a discount store studio. The woman in it was achingly young, probably in her mid-twenties, and had a soft, shy smile.

Her hair was a darker blond than Sallyanne's, and her eyes were brown rather than blue, but the oval of her face, the wide eyes, and the tilt of her nose marked her as the little girl's mother. Charlie idly turned the frame over in her hands. On the cardboard back was a label from the studio that said "McGraw, Leah." Beneath it, in careful script was written: "To Sallyanne, the best daughter in the whole wide world. Hugs and kisses, your loving Mama." X's and O's surrounded Sallyanne's name.

Charlie felt a gentle envy. She had dozens of photographs of her parents, but no written words of love from either of them. Of course, they hadn't expected to die, but then Leah McGraw hadn't expected to either.

"Sweetheart, your mother was very beautiful. And you look just like her."

AFTER TUCKING SALLYANNE in, Charlie went to her office to work. The room seemed empty without Major sprawling on the rug by her chair. She was doing her best to edit the more personal moments out of her memory as well as out of the star-gazing article when the telephone rang.

"Mike!" she said after she heard his hello. "Have you heard about the latest addition to my household?"

"Indeed I have. Isabelle brought me into the loop. It's a fine thing you're doing."

"She's a complete delight." *I only wish her story wasn't so sad.*

"Isabelle also told me about your problem with a dress for the preview party."

"Yeah." Charlie grimaced.

"You need something from a designer. Trust me, I've been to a million of those parties."

"I can't afford a designer dress!"

"You can if it's free. Pick me up tomorrow at 9 A.M. and we'll go see a friend of mine in Manhattan."

"Why would someone give me a dress for free?" Charlie asked suspiciously.

"For the publicity."

"I'm not wearing the label on the outside."

Mike laughed. "Not to worry. Stephen will explain how it works. I'll see you at nine."

THE ENTRANCE ROOM to Stephen Askegaard's atelier was stark, done entirely in pale gray: walls, ceiling, and plush carpet. Three dresses hung from silver hangers under pools of light. A desk occupied by a very thin woman with black hair stood in another pool of light.

"Mr. Phillips. How nice to see you," the woman said, rising to an impressive height. "I'll get Stephen."

"How do they sell clothes here?" Charlie whispered to her neighbor, looking around. "There's almost nothing on display."

"Mike, what have you brought me?" A young man with startlingly green eyes emerged from a concealed door. His blond hair was cut short in back and left long in front so it curved over one eye in a sort of modified pompadour. He was dressed entirely in black: T-shirt, jeans and sneakers.

He and Mike exchanged greetings before he shifted his attention to Charlie. His eyes widened dramatically. Walking around her and looking her up and down, he breathed, "Oh yes!"

"Hello, I'm Charlie Berglund," she said, pointedly putting out her hand.

"I'm sorry, I'm Stephen," he said, shaking her hand with a disarming smile. "I was just carried away by the marvelous possibilities of dressing you."

It was impossible not to smile back.

"Let's get started," he said, leading them through the hidden door and down a hall. "I raced over to the Rose Center after you called so I know the setting. Now we have to choose the fabric."

They entered another gray room; this one had a platform in the middle and metal and plastic chairs scattered around the edges. Mirrors in various configurations covered three walls. Two young women—in black of course—hovered in the background.

Stephen beckoned one forward. "This is Danielle," he said. "She'll take you to the changing room and show you what to put on."

Charlie cast a pleading glance at Mike, but he had settled into one of the chairs and merely raised an eyebrow at her.

The changing room was large and empty except for a small chest of drawers. Danielle slid open a drawer and pulled out a handful of flesh-toned spandex.

"Please take off *everything* and put this on," she instructed as she closed the door behind her.

Charlie shook out the spandex and discovered it had long sleeves, a high zippered neck and ankle-length leggings. She obeyed orders and stripped down to her skin before pulling on the cat suit. Oddly, there was no mirror in the dressing room so she couldn't check to see how revealing her new outfit was.

Danielle led her back to Stephen and Mike. Stephen took her hand and escorted her onto the platform as though she were visiting royalty. She was enjoying the attention until she caught sight of Mike's face. Something in his expression made her turn toward the mirrors.

"Oh my god!" she exclaimed, crossing one arm over

her chest and the other across her crotch. She looked virtually naked in the skin-tight suit.

"Just think of me as your doctor," Stephen said. "I'm only interested in your body in a professional sense. You're nothing more than a frame on which to hang my art."

"Well, if you put it that way," Charlie said with heavy irony.

Stephen gently took her wrists and moved her arms down to her sides. His smile was so warm and understanding Charlie let him do it. Suddenly, he was all business.

"Bring me the dark blue velvet, the silver lamé, the azure silk, the sky blue brocade and the mixed sequins."

Danielle and her clone disappeared through another door while Stephen stalked around Charlie, considering her from all angles. Her hands were beginning to creep upward again when the assistants returned, laden with bolts of gleaming cloth.

For the next hour, Stephen wound, draped, wrapped and pinned more fabrics around her than she could keep track of. It was evident early on that Charlie was not expected to voice any opinions so she spent the time composing article proposals in her head.

Her attention snapped back to the designer when she realized he was writing on her breast with a black magic marker.

"What on *earth?*" she yelped, jumping back a foot.

"I'm writing down your measurements," he said, holding up a tape measure.

"Do you have to write them *on* me?"

He laughed. "It's quicker and easier."

"Oh, fine," she muttered, raising her arm at his request. "Remind me never to go into modeling."

"You're a bit old for that," Stephen said, jotting a number on her elbow.

"Thanks a lot!"

He wrapped the tape measure around her hips.

"Just don't say it out loud," Charlie begged.

He chuckled. "I'm *very* discreet."

She squinted at the number he wrote on her hipbone and frowned. "By the way, I understand you're doing this for publicity. How does that work?"

"Very, very subtly. You only offer the information when asked. The photographers from certain publications will want to know who designed your gown. You tell them 'Stephen Askegaard,' nothing more. If one of the lovely ladies at the party inquires who dresses you, just give them my name because of course they should already *know* who I am." He smiled. "It's very simple."

"I wasn't sure how I was supposed to bring the topic up in casual conversation."

"Believe me, darling, you won't have to. The ladies will be begging you for my name."

The designer took some more measurements and then released Charlie to the dressing room. When she returned in her street clothes, he had a few final instructions.

"Come four hours before the party. Don't bring *anything* but yourself. No makeup, no jewelry, no shoes, nothing. We will create the entire picture here."

"Whatever you say," Charlie agreed. "I just want to go get some lunch."

Stephen took her hands in his. "You will look unforgettable. Trust me."

"He's not going to dress me like Cher, is he?" she asked Mike in the car.

"No. Stephen is extremely talented and very, very subtle. Whatever he does, it will be tasteful and beautiful."

"Some people think Cher's clothes are tasteful and beautiful," Charlie muttered as she paid the parking garage's exorbitant bill.

CHARLIE FORGOT ALL about the dress when she got home. A Federal Express envelope stuffed with neatly filled-out and notarized adoption documents was sitting on her front porch. "That man is incredibly organized," she told Major in awe. "Everything is here. How did he do it so fast?"

Her eyes widened when she looked at his financial statements. He wasn't kidding when he said he'd made some good investments. Jack had certainly kept his end of the bargain. Charlie faxed the relevant documents to Rhonda Brown's office. The social worker was scheduled to meet Jack on Friday while Sallyanne was at school, and so was eager to read the prospective father's autobiography.

If truth be told, Charlie was too.

She started to take it out of the pile of papers, then paused. Oddly, she hadn't hesitated to glance at his financials but reading his autobiography seemed invasive. She pulled it out and laid it on her desk. She obviously needed to know what he had written. But he was so intensely private.

She put it back in the pile.

He could tell her what was in the document himself.

CHAPTER 12

"I GOT YOU a wedding present too," Charlie said, handing Jack a flat gold box.

They were sitting on her back porch where she had just served him lemonade and sandwiches. She wanted him in a good mood for what was going to be a rather personal discussion. They needed to coordinate stories for Rhonda Brown. A pleasure boat puttered through the channel, its motor merely grumbling, and a tangy edge of sea and salt drifted on the air. Major sat by Charlie and gazed hopefully at the food-laden table.

Jack flipped open the lid of the box. She had framed one of the photos of the two of them cutting the wedding cake. The groom had his arms wrapped around her from behind, and was smiling with unholy glee while Charlie appeared to be on the verge of elbowing him in the groin. Jack laughed as he took in the scene. "A true Kodak moment. Thanks." Closing the box, he said, "This isn't the same photo as the one on the table in your living room."

"No. The one in the living room is for public consumption."

In that one, scruffy young Warren Bixby had photographed them as they stood on the steps of the municipal building where the ceremony had been performed. Charlie's cream-colored dress and Jack's silver-gray suit contrasted vividly with the dark oak doors behind them. His arm was around her waist, and she still held her bouquet. Most extraordinary though was that they looked glowingly happy as they gazed at the camera. Warren was a magician as well as a photographer.

Charlie watched Jack drape a cloth napkin over his thigh. She shifted her gaze upward and was mesmerized by the contrast of the tanned skin of his long fingers against the pale granola bread he held. Those fingers had contrasted in much the same way with the skin of her breasts . . .

He turned and focused his eyes on her. "Join me in a sandwich?"

"Um, no thanks, I had a big breakfast. I'll just have some chips," she said, scrabbling in the big wooden bowl of organic sweet potato chips.

"What's got you spooked?" he asked, putting down his sandwich.

"Spooked? Nothing." She took a deep breath. "We have to talk about some personal subjects. And I hate lying to Rhonda."

"It's a little late to develop scruples," he said, tilting a glass of lemonade to his lips.

Charlie tore her eyes away from the ripple in the muscles of his throat as he swallowed. "I've always had scruples. I just use tremendous self-discipline to overcome them," she said with false flippancy.

He chuckled. "Let's get our lies in line then."

With a supreme act of will, Charlie concentrated on the task at hand. They went over the spontaneous wedding story she had made up and got the details right. They discussed Jack's retirement story and nailed down the time frame. When they got to the topic of their philosophy on child-rearing, Jack picked up the pile of papers he had sent ahead.

"I put all that in the autobiographical section."

"I didn't want to read that part without your permission."

"Those scruples again," he said, but there was approval in his voice. He handed her three sheets of paper stapled together. "Go ahead and read it. You'll need to know it all for the interview."

She would rather have read it in private, but Charlie took the papers and settled back in her chair. The beginning was a very sanitized version of a boy's life. His mother and father had divorced when he was ten. He had one younger brother. Charlie was surprised to discover he hadn't finished high school; instead he had a high school equivalency diploma. She was aware of his lack of college education although one would never guess it from knowing him.

His work history was more revealing. He had gone into meteorite hunting at age seventeen. Charlie frowned. She remembered his story of the first meteor shower he had ever seen. But at seventeen how had he even known there *was* such a thing as meteorite hunting? He must have been a very focused young man.

She came to the section on child-rearing. He had written a fairly lengthy essay. She took a deep breath and plunged in. Much of it was similar to what *she* had written since she had given him her essay to read. The penultimate paragraph caught her attention.

Children should be allowed to be children as long as possible. Every effort should be made to shield them from cruel situations and harsh choices that an adult would find difficult to face. It is the parents' responsibility to protect their children even as they teach them the wisdom and judgment that will enable the young people in their charge to make these hard decisions.

There had been nothing like this in her own essay. Every instinct said this was a statement from the heart. Something very bad had happened in Jack's childhood. She finished the essay and put the papers down on her lap.

"Very thorough, if a little bland."

He smirked. "I'm doing my best to fade into the background."

Charlie looked at the length of him stretched out in her chair, at the luminously blue eyes, at the shift of muscle under fabric as he leaned over to set the plate down on the table, and burst out laughing. "You have about as much chance of doing that as the fireball we saw."

"Now how should I take that?" he asked, folding his arms across his chest. "There's the blaze of glory, the brilliance and the heat," he drawled the last word. "On the other hand, the glory is brief and generally ends in total destruction."

"You could take it to mean that you're noticeable."

"Thus grounding my flights of fancy."

"There's another small matter I want to discuss," Charlie said, brushing aside his caprice. She didn't want him charming her just now. "Sallyanne will be expecting us to sleep in the same room since we're married. I'll use the fold-out couch in the living room so you can have my bed. But I won't fold it out until after she's in bed for the night."

"A preemptive strike," he said almost to himself. "A gentleman always takes the couch. You can keep your own bed."

Charlie pushed aside her recollection of the last time he'd played the gentleman. "I have to get up early to get her ready for school, so the couch makes more sense for me."

"I only sleep late when I've been up meteor watching. Don't argue, sugar, unless you want to join me on the couch." He stood up and stretched, exactly as he had on the morning after the first meteor shower.

Charlie locked her gaze resolutely on the tray she was loading with plates and glasses. She picked it up and held it in front of her like a shield. "Would you like to come with me to pick up Sallyanne?" she asked.

"No, let's have the introduction here. I want to be able to talk with her face-to-face, not in a schoolyard or over a car seat."

She nodded her approval and carried the tray into the kitchen. He walked in behind her, and the kitchen walls suddenly shrank around them. Charlie put the tray down with a clatter and looked at her watch. "I'll do the dishes later. I should drop off Major and get going to the school."

He picked up a glass and pulled open the dishwasher door. "See you soon."

Charlie called the dog and fled.

IN A HALF an hour, she was back with Sallyanne in tow. They had discussed the new man in the house, but Charlie held her breath as Sallyanne preceded her through the front door. Jack came out of the kitchen with a smile that made Charlie's internal temperature shoot up ten degrees. The dimple was strongly in evidence, and the ice in his blue eyes had melted completely.

"Hey, Sallyanne," he said, striding over to squat in front of her. "I'm Jack."

Charlie gave herself a mental shake. *All that warmth and sunshine is for Sallyanne, not me.*

"Hello, sir. It's a pleasure to meet you," she said, putting out her hand.

"It's a pleasure to meet you too," he said, engulfing her small hand in his. "I'll be staying here with you as much as I can, but I know Charlie told you I'm real busy with business right now."

"Yes, sir, she did."

"I'm a lucky man to be living with *two* beautiful ladies."

Sallyanne giggled. Charlie snorted. However, she gave him full marks for immediately getting down to Sallyanne's eye-level. Tall men were intimidating as she remembered from her childhood.

"Charlie *is* very beautiful, isn't she?" the child said.

"The most beautiful woman in the world. That's why I married her."

"Let's have some cookies," Charlie said, brushing past Jack with enough force to make him brace his hand on the floor to keep his balance.

He chuckled and swept Sallyanne up in his arms as he stood. She shrieked with delight.

Jack continued to lay on the charm with a trowel all evening.

Charlie supposed she should be grateful things were going so well between her "husband" and her ward but somewhere it hurt that he would smile for a child he considered an inconvenience and not for her.

After Sallyanne was in bed, Charlie took out the sheets for the sofa bed. When she came back to the living room, Jack had already flipped open the mattress. He took the fitted sheet from her and expertly slipped the corner on before smoothing it in her direction.

"I think it went well," he said in a low voice. "She's a nice little girl."

"You're great with children," she agreed, brushing out some wrinkles. "You should have ten."

"Not me, sweetheart." His face was closed. "I'm a wanderer. And wanderers don't make good fathers."

"Speaking from experience?"

"I wish I was."

An odd response. She shook out the top sheet.

"Did you see your father much after your parents' divorce?"

"More . . . questions, Madame Journalist? I thought we'd called a moratorium on those."

He had been about to say something else. In that pause after "more," Charlie had heard a revelation forming. "Sorry. It's one of those occupational hazards."

"When do I get to see the meteor-shower article?" He tucked a pillow under his chin and slid the pillowcase on.

"I decided to honor the spirit of our agreement so I'm not writing *anything* about you." Charlie plumped the comforter she had spread over the sofa bed.

"I see."

"You sound disappointed."

"The auction is coming up soon, so I'm looking for publicity just now. The right kind of publicity."

"Why didn't you say so? I have a rough draft on my computer. I'll print out a copy for you to approve."

"Thanks, sugar. I appreciate it."

Now he was smiling for *her.* The soft light of the table lamp threw shadows over half his face, but she could see the gleam of strong white teeth and the hollow of his dimple. His eyes flickered with something she thought it was better not to put a name to. She arranged the last pillow on his bed. "All done. You can have the bathroom first."

He nodded and disappeared down the dark hallway.

Charlie looked down at the bed they had made together. Instead of perfectly plumped pillows and pristinely flat sheets, she saw the shape of Jack's body under the quilt while his bare shoulders rumpled the sheets. From an indent in the pillow, he smiled at her with those blue flames dancing in his eyes. "An overactive imagination is a dangerous thing," she murmured, turning on her heel and heading for her bedroom.

She closed the door and leaned against it for a moment. Twinkle slunk out from under the bed and sat down to wash his ears. Since she had company, she put on a white, man's T-shirt and a pair of flannel boxer shorts. She decided to burn off the excess energy humming through her by brushing her hair one hundred strokes, something she hadn't done since childhood. So she stood in front of her mirror and started counting.

Fifty-one, fifty-two . . . She was interrupted by a light tap on the door. "Come in."

The knob turned and Jack leaned in the door. "The bathroom is . . ."

He stopped.

Her brush halted in midstroke as she watched the flames she had only imagined before flare to life in those cold eyes. Fire and ice. She had never understood the power of opposites as she did now.

"Damn!" he said. The door slammed, and she was alone again.

Her brush hit the floor with a bang.

JACK TURNED HIS back on the door to Charlie's bedroom and stood for a long moment, remembering the sight of her standing in a pool of light, her long legs bare and her hair streaming down over her shoulders and back, shimmering like a fine chardonnay.

He needed to move. Fast.

Striding over to the French doors, he unbolted, unlocked and unlatched the various security devices with less deftness than usual. Then he was outside, heading for the channel's edge. The breeze from the ocean was bracing. He inhaled it gratefully. Two chairs sat invitingly on a small stone patio but Jack paced along the cement wall that kept the water from undercutting the lawns along the channel.

What had Miguel said about long blond hair? That it could turn into a rope. Her hair was more like a fuse that ignited a nuclear reaction. It fried his brain and made his body want to explode. Inside her.

He needed to take a long, grueling run. But he couldn't leave the doors unlocked, and he was not going to go near her again tonight, even just to get a key. Tomorrow he got to touch her.

Wrong word choice.

Tomorrow he *had* to touch her for the benefit of the social worker. He looked at the water below him, the lights glittering off its wavelets. It looked cool and welcoming. He started to unbutton his shirt, then muttered a curse and started back toward the house.

Rhonda Brown thought Charlie and Jack Lanett both looked heavy-eyed and tired. She attributed it to a long night without sleep, especially when she watched Jack use any excuse to put his hands on his new bride. The man was clearly in love.

One point in favor of the surprise wedding.

By the time she had spent three hours in their company,

Rhonda was convinced the marriage was real and the two of them suited each other well. She had no doubts about Charlie's commitment to parenting. Jack was harder to read. Charlie had warned her he was a very private man, but she got glimpses of the intensity under the control. He was a charmer all right but there was substance there. And one paragraph in his essay had convinced her he was good father material. He had talked about protecting children from adult decisions with total conviction.

"All right, you're approved," she said, closing her file with a snap. "As long as all the other paperwork comes through without a problem."

The smile that lit up Charlie's face chased away all traces of honeymooner's fatigue. Jack picked up his wife's hand and brought it to his lips. "You're going to be a mother," he said softly against her palm.

"And *you're* going to be a *father*," Rhonda said.

"Of course I am. But I understand what this means to Charlie, given her past. This is a tribute to her."

Charlie sat mute, unable to frame a coherent sentence. It was done! Six months from now, she would bring home her new baby daughter. Tears welled up and spilled onto her cheeks; she broke down and sobbed. She felt Jack's arms go around her, and she let him pull her against his chest. It felt good to burrow into his shoulder and have his shirt soak up the salty tears.

But she had to say something to Rhonda so she leaned away and swiped the back of her hand across her eyes. "I'm sorry. I'm just so happy, and so relieved we finally can go forward. Thank you so much."

"Don't thank me, honey. You earned it." Rhonda was putting folders back in her briefcase. "By the way, I'm expecting a response from social services in Tennessee any day now. Then I'll know how to proceed with Sallyanne."

Charlie felt a pang. "So soon?"

"The sooner the better," Rhonda said, giving her a knowing look. "You two are getting attached to each other, and since she's not staying, that's a bad thing."

"I suppose you're right."

"You know she's right," Jack said, tightening the arm he still had around her. "You have a hard enough time giving up the dogs and cats you foster."

How did he know that? Charlie was sure she'd never told him.

But Rhonda was saying good-bye, and Charlie had to focus on being a good hostess. Not that Jack was any slouch in that area; he had been as smooth as silk with the social worker. He had also put on a very convincing show of being an adoring husband. If he touched her one more time, she would start smoking. Charlie decided she was going to take a long run as soon as Rhonda left, preferably on the beach in the frigid surf.

Jack closed Rhonda's car door and lifted a hand in farewell. As he came up the sidewalk toward where Charlie stood on the front porch, he said, "Congratulations on your approval."

"Thank you for doing such a great acting job."

"I'm going to take a—" he began.

Charlie had already started to say, "I'm going to go for a—"

"Run," they finished together.

"Great minds think alike," she said.

Jack frowned. "I want to really push it."

"Don't worry, I won't slow you down," Charlie said, stung. "It's a big beach, and we can go in opposite directions."

He walked past her into the house without another word.

Perversely, she decided she liked the adoring husband act better.

They changed, stretched and jogged to the beach with a minimum of conversation. Charlie pointed him south and watched his stride lengthen. She indulged herself in the view of his backside and muscled legs in fluid motion for a few seconds, then she and Major turned to run north and along the channel.

She got home and showered long before Jack. His gray T-shirt was almost solid black with dampness when he came through the door. "Is that sweat or ocean spray?" she asked.

"Both." He headed straight for the refrigerator and grabbed a bottle of water. After downing half of it, he said, "I needed that."

"Speaking from recent experience, a hot shower is the icing on the cake."

"Do I stink?" he asked with a sudden grin.

"Not at all. You smell like a rose." And he looked utterly marvelous lounging against her kitchen counter as though he belonged there.

He tossed back the rest of the water and wiped his mouth with the white hand towel he had slung around his neck. "I'll go clean up."

He was using Charlie's bedroom to dress when she went to pick up Sallyanne at school. By the time she returned, he had on a crisply pressed pair of chinos and a light blue polo shirt. His hair was still damp and showed a tendency to curl at the longish ends.

He scooped Sallyanne up into a hug and carried her to the back porch where he had put out lemonade and oatmeal cookies. Charlie noticed Sallyanne didn't protest that she had to do her homework, but then Charlie wouldn't have protested either. The three of them spent a delightful afternoon and evening together. After dinner, they played a vicious game of Crazy Eights—with "Nasty Twos" and "Killer Fours." Charlie asked Jack to read Sallyanne her bedtime chapter of *Narnia* and he did so with great drama, changing his voice for each character.

After she said her prayers, Sallyanne asked hesitantly, "Charlie, may I talk to you alone for a minute?"

"Of course, sweetheart."

Jack leaned down and ruffled her hair before he kissed her cheek. "Good night. Sweet dreams."

"What is it?" Charlie asked when the door closed behind him.

"Ma'am, I told a fib before."

"About what, honey?"

"About Major. Well, about dogs." She took a deep breath. "I'm not really allergic. I'm afraid of them, and Mama said it was easier just to say I'm allergic. She said it wasn't really a lie because I'm allergic to them in my brain."

"That's true."

"But it *is* a lie, and I made Major go live somewhere else because I lied. And that's not right." Sallyanne's voice quavered, and tears brimmed in her eyes.

"It's okay. Major is living at Isabelle's house. You've met her so you know how nice she is. He comes here every day while you're in school." Charlie sat on the bed. "Major understands. He doesn't mind at all."

"Really?"

"Really. I'm glad you told me though. Now it's sleepy time. Good night, sweetheart."

CHARLIE FOUND JACK standing on the back porch, looking out at the channel and the lights of the next town up the shoreline. When she came out, he turned. "I'm going to head back to New York tonight."

"Is the couch that uncomfortable?"

"I've got an early appointment."

Charlie studied his face in the light coming through the French doors. "You're making a quick getaway."

He made an impatient gesture. "Face it, sweetheart, you and I are like matches and gasoline—a bad combination."

Charlie suddenly felt like living dangerously. "Why is it bad?" she prodded. "We're adults, we're unattached." She laughed, "Actually, we're *married* to each other. Why is it bad to admit the attraction?"

He paced to the end of the porch and back. "You know as well as I do there's more to sex than just the pleasure of the moment. It creates bonds that have to be dealt with."

"So you feel we've bonded?" Charlie was deliberately pushing him now.

"Not yet."

"What if I don't expect any bonds?"

He laughed. "You've already saddled me with a dog, a daughter, and a trip to China. *Now* talk to me about no expectations."

Charlie waved that away. "Those have nothing to do with sex and you know it."

"Don't they now?" He walked up to her and stood an inch away. His voice took on a husky, caressing quality. "Do you think I'd be standing here right now if you weren't temptation personified?"

"I'm not sure how to interpret that."

"Interpret it like this: you are beautiful, smart and sexy as hell. You are also a trap. You have a cozy house, a child, pets, a Volvo station wagon, and you look good even with all that baggage hanging on you."

"Have you run out of testosterone-saturated clichés yet?"

His mouth tightened but he didn't respond.

"May I point out that you not only built this particular trap, you set it, walked into it and then persuaded me to join you!" Charlie said.

"I'm just trying to escape before the jaws close and I have to gnaw my own leg off."

"*And* anyone who considers children 'baggage' has a warped view of the universe," she continued.

"You won't get an argument from me on that."

"Oh, spare me the tortured soul routine," she said, rolling her eyes. "You're an adult now—in fact, a fairly impressive one—"

"Much obliged."

"—you need to stop letting this deep, dark secret in your past control your life. *Nothing* could be so bad that you can't get through it." Charlie glanced at him and stopped.

He held himself so tightly coiled she thought he might blow up. She braced herself, then relaxed as he turned away to look out toward the black shimmer of the channel. In a voice as cold as the depths of space, he said, "You have no idea what you're talking about."

She had never heard anyone sound so far beyond human sympathy, and she was instantly contrite. "You're right. I don't. I'm sorry I said it."

They stood silent and still for a long minute.

"I'll see you at the party," he finally said, and walked back through the French doors into the house.

Charlie heard the jingle of car keys and two quiet clicks as the front door opened and closed. She stayed on the porch until the snarl of the Land Rover's engine had faded into the night. Only then did she remember to breathe.

CHAPTER 13

"CHARLIE, WAKE UP!"

Charlie reluctantly climbed out of the depths of the sleep she had welcomed after hours of tossing and turning. She pried her eyes open and saw Sallyanne standing by her bed fully dressed. "Morning, sweetheart," she managed. "Did I sleep late?"

"Yes."

Charlie squinted at the clock. *Eight A.M. on a Saturday qualifies as late to a nine-year-old . . .*

"I want to go see Major."

"Sweetheart," Charlie cleared her throat. Her voice had sounded like a croak. "You don't have to worry about Major. He's fine."

"No, I want to go see him. Right now."

"Why?"

"Mama said you have to face your fears. So I promise I won't be afraid of him."

"You know, you're an extraordinarily brave girl. But you've faced enough—"

Sallyanne's chin set hard. "I want to see Major today."

"Do you want to go as soon as I get dressed?"

The little girl nodded.

Charlie wasn't sure this expedition was a good idea, but she didn't know how to dissuade the child, so she pulled on a pair of jeans and a T-shirt and called Isabelle to let her know they were coming. Sallyanne held tightly to Charlie's hand as they walked across the back lawn and knocked on the door.

Isabelle answered and enveloped Sallyanne in a fringe-tangling hug. "Major's in my bedroom, sleeping on his favorite rug so you can wait until you're good and ready to meet him again. Why don't we have some breakfast first?"

"No, thank you, ma'am. I'd like to see Major now."

Isabelle raised her eyebrows at Charlie. "She's a very determined young lady, isn't she?"

At the closed bedroom door, Charlie knelt down in front of Sallyanne. "I want to remind you that Major is a very sweet and gentle dog, but he's also very big, one of the biggest dogs I've ever seen. And he's very loving so he may try to lick you or rub his head against you. If you get at all scared, or even just nervous, tell me right away."

Sallyanne nodded.

Isabelle opened the door, went in and knelt beside the big white dog curled up on the braided rug. When Major saw Charlie, his tail thumped and he started to get up. Isabelle said, "Down!" and held onto his collar. Major looked puzzled but subsided on the rug.

Sallyanne took three steps toward the dog.

He watched her, his ears cocked alertly, and his tail thumping. Five more steps and she was in front of him. She leaned forward to brush the top of his head with her fingertips. Major whined, and Sallyanne jumped backward.

"He's just saying hello," Charlie explained. "He wants to get up and come see both of us, but he's obeying Isabelle because he knows it's the right thing to do."

"He's a good dog," Sallyanne said. "He's a really good dog."

She stepped forward a little farther and this time gave his head a full pat. Major whined again, and although the girl started, she kept her hand on his head. "He's not as soft as I thought he'd be," she whispered, patting him again.

"The outside of his fur is coarse but the underneath layer is like lamb's wool," Isabelle commented. She buried her fingers in the dog's thick fur and showed Sallyanne the soft undercoat. Sallyanne dropped down to the floor to bury her own fingers in the white hair.

"He must get awful hot in the summer."

"It's sort of like insulation," Charlie said, sitting cross-legged and letting Major lick her face as she hugged his neck. "It keeps him warm in the winter and cool in the summer."

"Do you like it when he licks you?" Sallyanne wanted to know.

"Well, it's kind of wet, but it's his way of telling me he's happy to see me so I guess I do."

"Will he lick me?"

"If you get your face close to his tongue, he will."

Sallyanne inched over and sat between Charlie's knees. Major immediately transferred his attention to her small face, lapping a doggy kiss right up her chin, across her lips and up her nose to her eyebrows. The little girl giggled. "Yuck!" Then she put her face closer for another lick.

Charlie felt the tension leave her shoulders as she watched Sallyanne very gingerly put her arms around Major's neck the way she'd seen Charlie do it. The dog licked her ear, her neck and her arm, and Sallyanne giggled even more. Isabelle met her gaze and said, "It looks as though I won't have Major for company anymore. I'll miss him."

Charlie grinned. "You're a peach."

"Can Major have breakfast with us?" Sallyanne asked.

After Major was ceremoniously fed his kibble and the humans ate their corn muffins, they went out on Isabelle's back porch so Sallyanne could throw a ball for him. Soon the girl and the dog were fast friends, and Isabelle and Charlie settled in two wicker chairs to watch them playing on the grass.

"You look tired," Isabelle said. "Is Sallyanne wearing you out?"

"No, I just didn't sleep well last night." She smacked her forehead. "I completely forgot to tell you: Rhonda Brown approved my adoption!"

"Oh, Charlie, that's wonderful." Isabelle leaned across the space between them to kiss her cheek. "Many, many congratulations! Not that I doubted for a moment it would happen. So excitement kept you awake last night?"

"Ye-e-es."

Isabelle looked at her.

"No. Yes and no. I was excited but I was also upset."

"The hunter?"

"How do you always know?"

Isabelle shrugged, making her fringe ripple.

"He brushes off all questions about his life which only makes me *more* determined to find out what he's really like." Charlie sighed. "We had a bit of a fight. I regret some of the things I said, no matter how true they were."

Isabelle laughed. "Sounds as though he's just like a member of your family."

"Well, maybe like a mysterious third cousin you see once every ten years."

"Is he a 'kissing cousin'?"

Charlie tilted her head back to stare at the wrought-iron lantern hanging from the porch ceiling.

"Yes, he is."

"I was afraid of that," Isabelle said, shaking her head. "Oh well, the heart has its reasons . . ."

"The heart is not the body part that's involved here," Charlie snorted.

"So you say. Well, you'd best call and apologize before you lose any more sleep."

"Not a chance."

THAT EVENING, CHARLIE picked up the telephone and dialed Jack's apartment. When she heard the click of the connection, she almost lost her nerve and hung up.

"Hello, this is Jack Lanett."

"Hi, it's Charlie."

"Now how the hell did *you* find out already?"

"What? Find out *what?*" Charlie held the phone an inch away from her ear to mute the roar of Jack's usually mellifluous voice. Then she heard him take a deep breath.

"Why are you calling?" he asked in a quieter tone.

"Never mind. What did you think I found out?"

He muttered a curse. "I suppose you'll hear it sooner or later. Mauritania has laid claim to Sahara-Mars. I've spent the whole damned day in various diplomatic offices listening to more b.s. than you could muck out of a sheep shack."

Charlie stifled a laugh. He was sounding very deep woods Georgia all of a sudden. *Stress must bring out his roots.* . . . "Why does Mauritania think they have any claim to ownership?" She could hear leather creak and guessed he had sat down.

"They don't, really. It's a ploy. I don't know how much of the region's history you're aware of, but both Morocco and Mauritania think they own Western Sahara. At the moment, the world recognizes Morocco as the governing nation. Western Sahara has some groups who are agitating for independence but that's a long way away. However, I made sure to get export permits from both Morocco and Western Sahara, figuring that covered all bases."

"Sounds reasonable to me."

"Well, Mauritania decided to use the publicity surrounding Sahara-Mars to put *their* claim to sovereignty in front of the world. They refuse to recognize the paperwork from the other two countries. Of course, the irony of all this is that no one, including me, knows exactly where the meteorite was found."

"But you can make an educated guess."

"It's only a guess though, and I'm not volunteering it at this point."

"You know, I covered the U.N. for several years, and I still have some sources in the diplomatic world. Maybe I can find out what's going on behind the scenes, and put in a good word for you."

Silence. Charlie tried to figure out how she had offended him.

"That's the nicest offer I've had all day," he finally said in an oddly constrained voice. "You don't have to call anyone; I appreciate just knowing you would."

"Don't be ridiculous! Why wouldn't I call these people?"

"Because you don't owe me anything."

Charlie collapsed onto the couch in exasperation. "I'm not doing it out of a sense of obligation. I'm doing it because I . . ." How was she going to explain what Isabelle had guessed, that he was part of her makeshift family now whether he wanted to be or not. "I'm doing it because I like you." *Well, that was about as lame as an explanation could get.* She braced herself for his ridicule.

"Thanks. I like you too."

She was relieved to hear a smile in his voice although there was just the slightest bit of dry emphasis on the "like."

"All right, I'll take you up on your offer," he said. "Make your phone calls, but don't abuse your connections on my account. I can take care of myself. This isn't the first time I've had government problems."

True, Charlie thought, *but it was the first time they had jeopardized a multi-million dollar sale.* "I'll keep you posted," she promised.

"Now tell me why you called."

"Just to hear your charming voice?"

"I've had my fill of b.s. today."

"Oh, *fine.* I called to, well, to try and put us back on a friendlier footing after last night." Charlie breathed deeply. "The first thing I learned as a reporter was never to write the story without all the pertinent facts. And I certainly did not have all the facts last night, so I had no business criticizing you. I want to apologize for that."

"Nicely said. I accept your apology and extend my own. I was insulting for no reason except I wanted to make love to you in the worst way and knew it was the wrong thing to do."

"Oh," Charlie gasped. His blunt description of his thoughts took her breath away.

"It was pure frustration and inexcusable."

"You're excused. I mean, I accept. Oh, whatever. I have to go. I'll talk to you later." Charlie hung up before Jack had a chance to say another word.

She dropped her head back on the sofa cushion and

tried to get her pulse rate back to normal. An image of Jack bracing her up against one of the columns on her porch and recreating their encounter in the woods flashed across her mind's eye. *That* was *not* the best way to get her nervous system off red-alert.

"I won't sleep any better tonight than last night," she said to Major, "but at least it'll be for a different reason."

JACK LOOKED AT the phone in his hand.

"She hung up on me."

Miguel sauntered into the kitchen. "I'm not surprised. First, you dump your Mauritania problem on her, and then you tell her you're sexually frustrated. I'd hang up too."

"You were eavesdropping?"

Miguel shrugged with patent unconcern.

"She offered to use her connections at the U.N. to help us," Jack said.

"As would any good wife."

When Jack's phone whizzed past his ear, Miguel just laughed.

CHAPTER 14

CHARLIE HIT THE disconnect button and rubbed her temples.

It was two o'clock on Sunday afternoon, and she felt as though the telephone headset were surgically attached to the top of her skull. While she worked her rolodex, Sallyanne was on the back porch with Major and Volume Five of the *Chronicles of Narnia*. Fortunately, Jack had assessed the situation correctly: Mauritania was just grabbing publicity. Every foreign service officer and attaché she had been able to reach assured her Morocco would mobilize its own countercampaign.

Unfortunately, going through diplomatic channels took time.

Time they didn't have; Jack's preview party was in two days.

She was about to autodial Jack's number when the doorbell rang. Ripping off the headset, Charlie stood up and stretched briefly before heading for the door.

Rhonda Brown stood on her front porch.

"I have news," she announced as Charlie let her in.

"Good or bad?"

"It depends. Where's Sallyanne?"

"On the porch reading," Charlie said, starting toward the French doors.

"I'll say hello and come back inside. I don't want her to hear this yet."

Charlie sat down at the kitchen table to wait. When Rhonda returned and sat down across from her, she said, "Okay, spill it."

"We found Sallyanne's father."

"So I was right, he *is* alive! That's great!" Charlie said, even as the pain of the inevitable separation tore at her. Something in Rhonda's expression made her add, "Isn't it?"

"When you've been in this line of work as long as I have, you learn to trust your instincts. I talked with Don McGraw. Something about him doesn't sit right with me."

"Did he say anything wrong?"

"No," Rhonda said, shaking her head. "He said everything he should have, and that's why I don't trust him. I told him to come up here and stay a week to make the transition easier. That way you and I and that husband of yours can look him over before we let him take her back to Tennessee."

"When does he plan to arrive?"

"Late tonight. We'll arrange for them to have lunch together tomorrow. Food always helps smooth over any rough spots in a first meeting."

"So soon?" Charlie needed a minute to digest this. Then she said, " 'That husband of mine' is going to be pretty busy this week; the preview party is Tuesday. But I'll make sure he meets Mr. McGraw."

"You do that, honey. Jack strikes me as a shrewd fellow;

he'd have to be in his line of work. That brings me to the other piece of news."

Charlie felt her stomach tighten.

"One of my colleagues in Georgia called yesterday." Rhonda looked Charlie in the eye. "Jack has a record from his teenage years. It's sealed, so she couldn't read it, but she's got contacts who say it was a serious crime. He did time in a juvenile facility."

Charlie swallowed a gasp and choked.

"You okay?" Rhonda asked.

Charlie nodded mid-cough.

"I didn't tell you any of this, and I'm not going to change my approval of your adoption. I don't believe in holding a kid's mistake against a grown man. That's why records are sealed. But I thought you should know, if you didn't already."

"Thank you," Charlie managed to say. "For not holding it against Jack now."

"You should have let me know, off the record," Rhonda said, interpreting Charlie's comment exactly the way Charlie hoped.

"I had to respect Jack's wishes and the seal of confidentiality."

"You're a reporter; you should know nothing's confidential anymore."

"Even *I* can't get access to sealed records," Charlie said, thinking as she said it, there were other ways to get that kind of information. "Let's talk about Sallyanne's father."

HALF AN HOUR later, they had worked out a suitable plan for the father and daughter's reunion.

Rhonda said her good-byes, patted Major and departed.

Charlie headed back into her office and picked up her telephone headset with a grimace. Neither Jack nor Isabelle answered their phones so she left messages. However, Mike Phillips answered on the first ring.

"Sitting by your telephone?" Charlie asked.

"The wee folk whispered I'd be hearin' from a bonnie lassie soon," he said in a phony Irish brogue. Dropping back into his usual flat Boston tone, he asked, "How's your little guest?"

"That's what I wanted to talk with you about." Charlie gave him a summary of Rhonda's visit, including the bombshell about Jack's juvenile record.

"So you want to know what chance you have of withholding custody if you don't like him?" Mike surmised at the end of her recitation.

"Exactly. If Rhonda is having doubts, I'm not expecting much. I'd trust her instincts ahead of my own."

"It's not my field, but I think your chances are pretty slim. Unless you can prove something substantive against the man that would make him an unfit father. I'll make a few phone calls and get back to you." He paused. "Custody battles are very hard on children."

"A bad father would be worse."

"I suppose so," he said. "Mine was a drunkard, but he'd have a catch with me on a Sunday afternoon."

"You had a mother to take up the slack," Charlie pointed out.

"That I did. She was a saint. Poor kid, would you keep her if you could?"

"I hadn't thought about it until Rhonda told me about her father." Charlie stood up and paced. "I don't want to deprive her of her rightful place in her real family . . ."

"Being genetically related doesn't necessarily make a family."

"Tell me about it." Charlie didn't generally discuss her upbringing, but Mike understood she considered her childhood less than ideal. "I know I've said I wanted a baby rather than an older child. Then I'd be *almost* a birth mother, and I'd know the child's earliest years were good because I would be the one shaping them. Older children can have unknown issues from their past—"

"So you wouldn't adopt Sallyanne?"

"*Of course* I would! But only if her father is truly unfit."

Mike laughed. "That's what I thought you'd say. What about Jack's record? I could contact a few buddies in Georgia and get a pretty good idea of what happ—"

"Thank you but that's his business, not mine," Charlie said with a decisive shake of her head.

"What if he's a child molester? Or a murderer?"

"Do you *really* think he's a child molester or a murderer?" she asked.

There was a long silence. Charlie could visualize Mike pursing his lips as he considered his answer.

"No, I suppose I don't. But I've only met the man for twenty minutes at a fraudulent wedding reception. It might be wise to double check."

"I could find out myself if I chose to," Charlie said, "but I don't choose to."

"You want him to tell you himself," Mike said, with sudden comprehension. "Charlie, Charlie, you're in trouble there."

"Probably." She switched topics quickly. "There's another place I'm in trouble. I called today, and Stephen won't tell me *anything* about this dress he's making. I'm afraid it's going to plunge down to my navel or be completely transparent, or worse!"

Mike let her change the subject but as their conversation ended, he said, "Just remember: wedding rings don't make marriages."

Charlie glanced down at the gleaming band on her finger. "Don't worry. My ring is only valid on Mars."

"WHAT IF I don't like my father?" Sallyanne asked.

"Why do you think you wouldn't?"

"He must have done something awful for Mama to say he was dead."

"That's true," Charlie said slowly. A fishing boat honked but she ignored it. "But you have to give him a chance. For one thing, people make mistakes when they're young. Your father may be very sorry for whatever he did. And sometimes grown-ups do bad things to each other that have nothing to do with their children. Your father may not have been good to your mother, but he may be good to you."

"I'm going to ask him what he did to Mama."

Charlie knelt in front of Sallyanne's chair and rested her hands lightly on the child's shoulders. "He may not answer your question, sweetie. It may be something he doesn't want to share with anyone else in the world, especially his wonderful little girl whom he's just meeting again. You may have to decide about him without knowing the answer."

"But maybe he'll have a really *good* answer."

"I hope so, sweetheart. I truly hope so."

JACK CALLED BACK as Charlie was finishing the dinner dishes.

"Have you had any luck with the diplomats?" she asked immediately.

"Only bad. They must have gone to the same school as Congress; they can talk for hours without saying anything."

She laughed, then summarized the results of her own research.

"That's a hell of a lot more progress than I made," he said when she finished. "So you think I should get hold of Dyson Foley at the U.S. Mission here in New York?"

"I think he's a good bet. He's interested in your case."

"Thanks, sugar. I realize you must have called in some favors. I appreciate your help."

"No problem." Charlie hesitated, then plunged on. "Rhonda found Sallyanne's father."

"Why don't you sound happier about that?"

"Because Rhonda is suspicious."

"Has she met the man?"

"No, but she talked with him by telephone."

"Well, hell, cut the guy some slack. He may hate talking on the phone. People do."

"Actually, she's suspicious because he said too many of the right things, so it's not because he hates talking on the phone." Charlie said shortly.

"Sorry. People have been saying too many of the *wrong* things to me today."

"I know," Charlie said, mollified. "Sallyanne's afraid her father did something awful because her mother excised him from their lives."

Jack's tone was neutral as he asked, "And what did you tell her?"

"That people make mistakes when they're young," Charlie said, putting all the passion of her belief in her voice and hoping he heard it. "That they can't change the past but they can be terribly, terribly sorry. That he could still be a good father to her even if he had done something bad to her mother."

Charlie waited.

"So you think a leopard can change its spots?" Jack said.

"I think one spot does not a leopard make," Charlie said, disappointed by the flippancy of his question. "Anyway, Don McGraw's arriving tonight and coming here tomorrow to take her out for lunch. Rhonda set it up that way."

"You have to give him credit; he got here fast. I've got four meetings scheduled tomorrow, and the party is Tuesday."

Charlie melted when she heard the genuine frustration in his voice. "Rhonda and I will be here, and if we need reinforcements, Mike and Isabelle are on call. So we have it covered. But it's nice of you to think of coming."

"I owe you one."

Charlie remembered the last time he had said that and wished she hadn't.

"All debts are hereby canceled," she said. "I've got to go tuck her in."

"Give her a kiss for me. Thanks again, Charlie."

"You're welcome."

Charlie put down the phone and dropped her head onto her hands in exhaustion. She was struggling to say the right things to a little girl who had lost the mother she adored, she was bracing herself to judge another human being's worth in one short meeting and she had just found out her adoption partner had a secret criminal record.

"I need a big kiss too. And a hug."

The problem is what would come after that.

CHAPTER 15

On Monday, Charlie picked Sallyanne up from school at eleven in the morning. She had decided it would be better for the little girl not to dwell too much on the reunion lunch, but she also wanted to give her time to put on her favorite dress and compose herself a bit. Rhonda had met with Don McGraw in person earlier in the morning and said he seemed "fine."

As they turned into Winter Circle, Charlie spotted a green Land Rover parked in front of Isabelle's house. When she saw the Wyoming license plate, a warmth she preferred not to name flooded through her. *Jack had cleared his schedule!* He opened the front door as soon as she pulled into the driveway. Sallyanne flew out of the car the minute it stopped and hurled herself into his arms.

"Jack, Jack!"

"Hello, sweetheart," he said, spinning her around once before he set her on her feet. Charlie decided he deserved a hug for this, so she walked right up and put her arms around him, saying, "Thank you so much." She meant to step away after a quick squeeze, but when his arms wrapped around her, she allowed herself to rest her head against his shoulder just for a moment.

"Newlyweds." Rhonda, who had just gotten out of her own car, sounded torn between exasperation and indulgence.

Jack slid his hands down Charlie's arms, and snuck in a pat on her rear before he let her go.

Charlie stepped back and adjusted the hair clip holding her bun. *What had Jack said? That they were like gasoline and matches? Right now she felt more like a square mile of dry pitch pine waiting for a lightning strike.* "I know you had a busy schedule today," she said, for Rhonda's benefit. "It was good of you to come."

Charlie looked him up and down as he turned to talk with Sallyanne. His slacks were a fine gray wool, his jacket was the salt-and-pepper tweed she had seen before. He wore a white, button-down shirt and a burgundy paisley tie. The black tasseled loafers were polished to mirror brightness. She needed to remind herself that this was for Don McGraw's benefit, not hers.

"Let's go get you ready," she said, motioning Sallyanne toward the stairs.

Charlie had washed and ironed a blue dress appliquéd with pink and yellow butterflies she had found neatly folded in Sallyanne's suitcase. The child wanted to wear her hair in a French braid, and Charlie had bought blue, pink and yellow ribbons to wind into it. Charlie tied the end of the ribbons into a bow and opened the closet door so Sallyanne could see herself in the full-length mirror.

"You look beautiful, sweetheart."

"Mama said this dress matches my eyes perfectly," she said softly.

"She was right." Charlie gently placed the braid over her shoulder so Sallyanne could see the ribbons.

"That looks so pretty. Thank you, ma'am."

Sallyanne had slipped back into *ma'am*ing. Charlie knelt and hugged her. "We're *all* here with you, sweetheart, and we'll make sure whatever happens you'll be happy." She brushed her knuckles against the wood of the closet door as she said it.

"I wish Mama were here," a very small voice said, muffled now by Charlie's shoulder.

"I do too," Charlie whispered.

Sallyanne was holding tight so Charlie stayed on her knees, gently stroking her small back and dropping little kisses on her hair until Sallyanne let go.

"Will you hold my hand even when he comes?"

"I sure will. Let's have a signal: when you squeeze twice I'll let go, but I won't for any other reason." Charlie stood up, and ceremoniously took Sallyanne's hand in hers. They walked down the stairs side-by-side.

"Will you look at that!" Jack gave a whistle when they stepped into the living room, causing Major to raise his ears. "The two most beautiful women in the world! Sallyanne, that is the most gorgeous dress ever. I've only seen one blue prettier, and that would be your eyes."

Sallyanne gave him a tiny smile.

Jack raised an eyebrow at Charlie, and she nodded. "I'm ready too," she said, as she checked her watch and adjusted her blazer's collar. She had dressed for the occasion in her camel pants suit and blue blouse.

The doorbell rang. Charlie and Jack looked at each other. "He's here." Charlie stated the obvious.

"I'll get the door," Rhonda said. "Then I will retire to the kitchen."

Rhonda and Don McGraw exchanged greetings, and

Sallyanne's father stepped into the living room to face the penetrating stares of two adults, one child and a large Kuvasz.

He hesitated, swallowed and took another step. "Hello, I'm Don McGraw. And you must be Sallyanne." He had a thick accent, southern but with more of a nasal twang than Jack's Georgia drawl. He put down an enormous stuffed pink rabbit he had slung under his arm and knelt in front of the group. "Let me look at you, pretty girl. You have gotten so big and beautiful. The last time I saw you, you were only two years old."

"Hello," Sallyanne said solemnly. "I'm pleased to meet you."

"I was hoping you might have a hug for your papa," Don said as he shook her small hand. "I brought you a present."

He slid the rabbit toward the little girl.

"It's a very big present," Sallyanne observed. "Thank you very much."

"You're very welcome." Seemingly at a loss, Don stood up.

"Hi, I'm Charlie Berglund," Charlie jumped in. "And this is my husband Jack Lanett." She had to work hard to make the second statement sound natural.

Jack and Don shook hands briefly as they appraised each other.

"We're delighted you were able to come so quickly," Charlie continued. "It's good to meet you."

"It's *my* pleasure to meet the pretty lady who's taken such good care of my little girl. I'm much obliged, ma'am."

"Believe me, it was not a chore. Sallyanne is a wonderful girl. She makes the best chocolate chip cookies in the world." Charlie was trying to draw Sallyanne into the conversation, but the child stayed watchful and mum.

"You sure have a nice place here, ma'am," Don said, looking around the room. "I'll bet you made her real comfortable."

"Why don't we sit down?" Charlie suggested, taking the sofa to accommodate herself and the firmly attached child by her side. Major sat at Sallyanne's feet, looking fully alert. Jack remained standing until Charlie gave him a small frown. Then he seated himself on the sofa beside Sallyanne.

While she made small talk, Charlie studied Don.

He was a good-looking man. Sallyanne had gotten her very blond hair and very blue eyes from him. Charlie recognized the smile too. He wore his hair slightly long, brushed straight back with an obvious application of hair gel. His mustache was neatly trimmed. A navy blazer stretched tightly across his shoulders; he looked as though he would be at home in a weight room. He wore a light blue polo shirt and gray flannels. Charlie was almost sure the jacket and slacks were brand new, and she gave him credit for making such an effort. The giant pink bunny was also well-intentioned, if a bit overwhelming.

Don sat with his hands clutching the arms of the overstuffed chair, and shook his head. "I can't believe I'm finally seeing my daughter after all these years."

Charlie thought she saw tears in his eyes, and much of her reserve melted away.

"It must have been very hard for you to be separated from her."

"It was pure misery."

"I have to ask you an important question," Sallyanne spoke unexpectedly.

"Sure, honey bunch. What is it?"

"What did you do to Mama to make her say you were dead to us?"

Don McGraw flushed so red his hair looked almost white by contrast.

"Your father might prefer to answer that question for only you," Charlie said. "Why don't you ask him at lunch?"

The man threw her a grateful glance.

"No, ma'am," Sallyanne said, shaking her head.

Don's high color had subsided, but he swallowed noticeably before he said, "Your mama and I had a big fight. I was really mad so I left for a few days. When I came back to apologize, she had taken you away where I couldn't find you.

"I looked for you and your mama for a year but your mama had made everyone promise they wouldn't tell me where you were. Finally, I quit looking because I figured your mama would come back when she was good and ready."

Charlie sensed Jack stiffen at that flash of still-simmering resentment.

"I haven't been able to be a good father before this, but now I'm going to be the best papa I can, honey bunch."

"What did you and Mama fight about?"

Don's full flush came back. "It was stuff grown-ups fight about: money, a job, your papa spending time with his friends. Nothing important enough to lose you over."

Sallyanne looked doubtful but she was silent.

"Should I take her to lunch now?" Don asked, looking at Charlie and Jack.

"Certainly," Charlie said. "You must be starving, Sallyanne."

"Yes, ma'am," the girl said dutifully.

"We're going to the restaurant at my hotel, sweetie pie.

It's got pink tablecloths and real flowers on every table. Afterward, I thought we'd go to this ice-cream store I found that has fifty flavors. If that's all right with you?" He looked at Charlie again.

She nodded and smiled.

Everyone stood and walked to the door. Sallyanne still had not given the signal to let go, so Charlie knelt down beside her and silently held up their clasped hands with a question in her eyes. Sallyanne nodded and squeezed twice before she released her grip.

Don held out his hand, and after the tiniest hesitation, Sallyanne took it.

As they started out the door, Jack stepped in front of the newly discovered father, forcing Don to stop and look up several inches to meet his eyes.

"I expect you to take great care with Sallyanne. Her well-being is very important to all of us," he said with just a hint of a threat in his voice.

"She's my daughter. I wouldn't let a hair on her head come to harm." Don squared his shoulders and gave Jack just the slightest bump as he brushed past him. Jack stood like a rock, and Don was the one who bounced off from the impact.

"Enjoy your lunch!" Charlie called, glaring at Jack. "And your ice cream!"

"Thank you, ma'am," Don said with a tight smile, as he guided Sallyanne to his rented car.

As soon as the car doors closed, Charlie rounded on Jack. "Major has better manners than you do! Why are you manhandling the guy when he's seeing his daughter for the first time in *seven years?*"

"I don't trust him," Jack said. "I'll bet Leah McGraw had a very good reason for getting as far away from him as she could."

"I don't trust him either," Rhonda's voice came from the doorway.

"Does he have any kind of record?" Jack asked.

"Just standard petty stuff: one car theft, one possession of marijuana, one shoplifting." Rhonda shrugged. "He's cleaner than half my clients."

"He's Sallyanne's *father*," Charlie said pointedly. "He should be given a chance to live down his mistakes, whatever they were. Jack, you, of all people, should sympathize with him."

Jack's brows snapped into an angry line. "What exactly do you mean by that?"

Charlie could have bitten her tongue. She glanced toward Rhonda as a warning to deflect his ire. He grabbed her by the elbow and said, "Excuse me" as he walked her quickly around the corner of the house.

Charlie tried to free her elbow, but Jack's grip didn't slacken.

"Why should *I* sympathize with a man who deserted his wife and child?" he ground out.

"I didn't say that. I *said* you should sympathize with people who have made mistakes in their past and want to—"

"And just what mistakes have I made in my past?" he asked, releasing her arm but continuing to focus his ice-blue gaze on her.

"I don't know because you won't tell me," Charlie said, rubbing the circulation back into her elbow. "But whatever it is, you deserve the chance to make amends, to put it behind you. And so does Don McGraw."

"Some things can't be amended. Not in my life and maybe not in Don McGraw's." He touched her elbow gently this time. "Sorry. But leopards don't change their spots."

He spun on his heel and returned to the front of the house.

"Dig deeper," he said to Rhonda as he strode past her to his car.

Charlie watched him climb in and slam the door without a backward glance.

"Lovers' quarrel?" Rhonda said with a raised eyebrow.

Charlie sighed. "He's on your side about Don."

"And what do you think?" Rhonda probed.

"I think we should see what Sallyanne says about her lunch."

CHAPTER 16

"He ordered me shrimp cocktail, the most *expensive* thing on the whole menu! I didn't like it so he made the waitress bring chicken noodle soup. Then I got to pick *three* different flavors and have hot fudge sauce on two and butterscotch on one. Papa said he thought butterscotch would go better with Denali Moose Tracks ice cream. And he was right because I tried it both ways."

Charlie and Sallyanne were walking on the path by the channel. The little girl could not stop talking about her afternoon with her father; she also couldn't sit still. Don had brought his daughter back right on time. Charlie exchanged pleasantries with him at the door; when she'd explained how Isabelle was set to baby-sit the following day, Don's face had lit up. "I'd be happy to take her after school, if you're busy," he said. "I found a miniature golf course I think she'll like."

"She has to do her homework," Charlie reminded him.

"Yes, ma'am. I'll make sure she does it."

They agreed he would meet Sallyanne and Isabelle at

Charlie's house to supervise his daughter's schoolwork, then take her mini-golfing. They'd return to Charlie's house for dinner. Charlie agreed because she wanted Isabelle's opinion on Don too.

"Did *you* like him?" Salllyanne interrupted Charlie's thoughts.

"Yes." The truth was, she wasn't entirely sure, but had no precise reason for her sense of unease. He was unfailingly courteous, clearly determined to win his daughter's affection, instantly agreeable to whatever arrangements were made on Sallyanne's behalf . . . "And more important, *he* likes *you*. That's what I really care about."

"Jack didn't like him," Sallyanne said.

"Jack's just waiting a little longer to make up his mind," Charlie replied, even as she thought, *she sees everything*.

CHARLIE LET HER head fall back against the black leather seat of the limousine. Rhonda and Jack had infected her with their nebulous doubts about Sallyanne's father. After she had approved the mini-golf outing, she struggled all afternoon to keep their bias from influencing her own judgment. Her eyes drifted closed. *He was very polite when he dropped her off.* She tried to pry them open again. She needed to decide how to behave toward Jack tonight at the party. She should also think of a contingency plan if Stephen Askegaard's design was totally unsuitable. . . .

She went to sleep.

"Miss, we're here."

Charlie startled awake. The limo was parked in front of Atelier Askegaard. She blinked her eyes rapidly. She had been dreaming that the dress was black fishnet and nothing else. . . . *Maybe she could just tell the driver to head straight for Saks?* "It was only a dream," she told herself, and climbed out of the long black car.

Stephen himself met her at the door.

"You look terrified," he said, tilting his head. "I believe I'm offended."

"No, no," Charlie said. "I'm just not a . . . fashion person."

He smiled. "We're about to change that, aren't we?"

"I guess so," she said, following him to the dressing room.

Once again she was instructed to strip down to her bare skin, but this time she was given a short black silk robe to belt on. The fabric was very slippery and she felt precariously covered. However, no one paid the slightest attention to her concerns as she was passed from the hairdresser to the manicurist to the makeup artist in rapid succession. Finally, she was led back to the platform where Stephen held absolute power.

He walked around her, appraising the work of his cohorts.

"It'll do," he said.

"I wouldn't know," Charlie commented. "No one's let me look in a mirror."

"And no one will until the last detail is in place."

"Is my opinion of any importance at all?"

"Would you tell Shakespeare how to write a play?" Stephen asked.

"Oh fine," Charlie grumped, "I'll keep my mouth shut."

"A very good idea. Now off with the robe," he said, smoothly pulling the end of the sash loose.

Charlie grabbed at the black silk as it slid open.

"Hey, this is all I've got on!"

"And we can't put the dress on over it, can we?"

Stephen asked reasonably, as he slid the robe off her shoulders.

Three black-clad women carried in a white cloth bag. A fourth assistant draped a white cloth over her head and face, "to protect your hair and makeup," she said.

"Arms up," Stephen's voice commanded. "Now here. Now down. Now step into these shoes."

Charlie heartily welcomed the slide of fabric over her naked skin. The shoes felt stiff across her toes but were bare from there back.

"Hand out." Something metallic slid onto her wrist. "Let's get that ring off."

"No," Charlie said, closing her fingers into a fist as someone tried to slide off her wedding ring. "It's a meteorite so it goes with the theme of the party."

Stephen laughed. Cool fingers reached under her head cloth and fastened earrings on her earlobes.

"All right, lift the cloth," Stephen's voice came again.

Charlie blinked in the sudden wash of light, and gasped as Stephen slowly turned her around.

The reflection in the triple mirror was a stranger, a woman who walked into a crowded room and started a current of whispers, a woman who announced the winner of "Best Picture" at the Academy Awards, a woman who treated royalty as her equal.

It certainly wasn't Charlie Berglund.

"You're a wizard," she breathed.

Stephen looked pleased but unsurprised. "Exactly. Now walk a bit."

Charlie took two steps and gasped again. Stephen's creation was a long, deep blue column of velvet that flowed over one shoulder and left the other exposed. It fit like a second skin down over her hips, then curved outward toward the hem. A long slit up the side showed a flash of leg when she moved.

Even more extraordinary were the flashes of light. The dress was embroidered with silver and crystal beads in swirling galaxies, blazing suns and shooting stars that glinted to life with the smallest gesture or breath. The bracelet was a vortex of stiff, silvery wires studded with diamonds that seemed to orbit her wrist. More diamonds on long silver wires cascaded from her earlobes. The heels of her Lucite mules gleamed with scattered crystals.

"I look like the Milky Way!"

"You look magnificent," Stephen said. "The upswept hair and the heels add to the drama. What do you think of the earrings?" he asked, turning to his assistant. "Too much?"

"They're a bit over the top but I like them."

Stephen pursed his lips for a minute, then waved his hand. "They stay. And the security is very tight so she doesn't need a bodyguard."

"A *bodyguard?*"

"That's a million dollars in diamonds and platinum you've got on," Stephen explained. "But they're insured."

Charlie looked at her wrist in horror. "Jeez, I hope I don't lose any."

Stephen was conferring with someone else and didn't answer. In a moment, a tiny, jeweled handbag shaped like a space shuttle was put in her hand.

"A touch of whimsy," Stephen said airily.

"I like it," Charlie agreed, examining it at eye-level.

"That's worth another million."

She nearly dropped it. "Take it back. I'll worry about it all night."

"You can give it to Alina here if you get tired of holding it. She'll be at the party to make repairs if necessary."

Charlie smiled at Alina before approaching Stephen to say in a low voice, "I feel a draft. Do you think I could have a pair of matching panties to wear under this?"

"Absolutely not!" he said in horrified tones. "It would ruin the lines of the gown."

"I can't go to a party and meet people with no underwear on," Charlie said through gritted teeth.

"Trust me, you won't notice it after an hour or so."

Stephen looked at his watch. "We've got fifteen minutes. Has she got her lipstick? Absorbent tissue? Perfume atomizer?"

"It's all in the space shuttle."

"What about cab fare?" Charlie muttered.

"It won't fit," Stephen said without missing a beat. Then he gave her his brilliant smile. "You'll be the star of the evening, my dear. Now let us show you how to get in and out of the limo without crushing your gown."

Then Charlie was alone in the limousine, sitting like a statue to avoid ruining the lines of her dress.

As THE LIMO eased around the corner onto 81st Street, the giant globe of the Hayden Planetarium glowed blue-white within the glass cube of the Rose Center for Earth and Space. Huge models of Jupiter and Saturn hung in motionless orbit. Light blazed out onto the surrounding trees, reflecting on the procession of sleek black cars disgorging their passengers in front of the arched entrance.

Even as she admired the dramatic effect, Charlie braced herself for the evening ahead. She reviewed her instructions on exiting the car as it glided to a stop in front of the glass doors. Sliding carefully over the leather seat as the door swung open, she swiveled her legs out before looking up. Instead of the driver she expected, Jack stood with his hand held out to help her maneuver out of the car.

"Oh! Hello, Jack," she said, putting her fingers in his.

He pulled her firmly to her feet, tucking her hand in at his elbow.

"Hello, Charlie. Smile for the cameras."

Jack's smile was pure, easy charm. Stephen had warned Charlie not to talk when the flashbulbs were going off, so she fixed her face in an expression of delight and kept silent no matter what questions the press called out. She even looked up at Jack as though he was God's gift to women just to give the photographers a different pose.

All the while Jack was moving them slowly toward the doors. As they reached them, he held up his hand and said, "This is my wife Charlotte Berglund," in answer to the most popular inquiry.

"Stephen Askegaard designed my dress," Charlie added to address the second most-asked question.

Then they were inside, crossing a polished black floor flecked with silver.

"Nice dress. I see your designer decided this was a theme party," Jack said under his breath.

Charlie had no time to answer as Jack introduced her to the first knot of guests, but she felt as though he had slugged her in the stomach. He thought her beautiful dress looked like a costume.

Once again he introduced her as his wife. People's faces reflected a spectrum of emotions from surprise to speculation. As they moved through the crowd, a ripple of turned heads and whispered comments preceded and followed them. Charlie held her head high and accepted best wishes and congratulations as though she were a happy new bride. Inwardly, she wondered if it would be possible to grind her

Lucite heel into Jack's patent leather-covered arch without anyone else noticing.

He looked magnificent, of course. His salt-and-pepper hair and his smile gleamed under the lights. The shawl-collared tuxedo made his shoulders look even broader and his height more imposing. His black silk tie and cummerbund were shot through with metallic threads that picked up tiny sparks of light as he moved. Charlie spotted crisscrossing Widmannstatten structures on his studs and cufflinks, and seethed: he was wearing a costume as much as she was!

She tried to ignore the frisson of pleasure she felt when he laid his hand on the small of her back in a gesture of possession. He left it there until they encountered Miguel who looked downright menacing in a black tuxedo worn with a black T-shirt underneath.

Charlie was thrilled to see a familiar face and greeted Miguel with effusive delight.

"Ah, 'she walks in beauty, like the night,' " he quoted, raising her fingers to his lips.

Charlie glanced toward Jack. His shit-eating grin had vanished completely.

"I've got to speak with the director," he said. "Take care of her until I get back."

Charlie watched his back as he disappeared into the crowd.

"Jack never did like Byron," Miguel said by way of apology.

"Byron's not the problem. He doesn't like my dress." Charlie sighed.

"Then he's gone blind." Miguel held her hands out from her sides and gave her a thorough scrutiny, ending by shaking his head. "The man's clearly a lunatic. Or maybe he likes the dress *too* much."

"Maybe he's just tense because it's an important night."

"Maybe. All the heavy hitters are here except one."

"Curt Vandermade?" Charlie guessed.

"Yeah. He'll make an entrance right before the unveiling. He likes to create a stir."

As Miguel pointed out interesting guests, Charlie admired the party. The partygoers circulated in the Hall of the Universe, swirling around its color-coded exhibits on galaxies, stars and planets. Some stopped and studied the exhibits, but most were there to see and be seen. The giant globe of the planetarium hovered over all of them, looking like a space ship just touched down on Planet Earth. White-jacketed servers circulated offering drinks and food. *No one in this group was expected to go find their own sustenance,* Charlie thought. The clink of glasses, the hum of conversation and the notes of a classical piece being played by a string quintet mixed and reverberated against the glass and metal walls and stone floor.

Jack materialized at her side from the darkened Hall of Planet Earth behind them. He slid his arm around her waist, resting his hand on her hipbone. She was suddenly very aware that only a thin layer of velvet separated his fingers from her skin.

"I want to introduce you to some old friends of mine," he said, moving her down into the crowd. "Thanks for baby-sitting," he said over his shoulder to Miguel.

"Baby-sitting!" Charlie huffed indignantly.

"Wrong word. How about 'providing protection from circling wolves'?" Jack conceded, as he stopped beside a couple standing near the Willamette Meteorite. "Kate, Randall, I'd like you to meet my new wife, Charlie. Charlie, Kate and Randall Johnson."

Charlie found herself shaking hands with a small, attractive woman with auburn hair and a tall, dark man with killer cheekbones.

"Randall financed a couple of my early expeditions. In fact, I wouldn't have been able to build my business without him."

"It was a risk-free investment with you leading the charge. How could I resist?" Randall said with a noticeable Texas drawl.

Jack shook his head. "He took a major gamble on me," he said to Charlie.

"And it paid off handsomely," Kate chimed in. "It's a pleasure to meet you, Charlie, and best wishes on your marriage. Jack is much too good at keeping secrets from his friends. You and I will have to have lunch together, so I can find out all about your mysterious romance."

Charlie hated lying to people who clearly held Jack in high esteem.

"Sounds great. I'd love to."

"Your dress is spectacular," Kate continued.

"Thanks. Stephen Askegaard designed it as a favor for a friend of mine," she said, looking daggers at Jack.

"I hear you've gotten yourself mixed up in international politics," Randall said to Jack. "If you need any help, I can talk to some folks."

"Thanks, but I very wisely married a well-connected woman. She has a buddy in the American Mission who has been invaluable."

Charlie felt a rush of gratification at the acknowledgment.

A good-looking blond teenager hurried up to the group. "Hey, Jack. This is so cool. Thanks for letting us come."

"You're always welcome at my parties, Clay. You and your brother behave better than most of the adults," Jack said, as the two shook hands.

Kate laughed. "This is my son, Clay. Clay, Ms. Berglund, Jack's new wife."

Clay's eyes widened as he took in Charlie in all her splendor. "Nice to meet you." He shook hands before turning to Jack. "I didn't know you got married."

"Neither did anyone else," Randall said.

"Um, congratulations," the young man said.

"Where's your brother?" Kate asked.

"He's over finding out how much he weighs on the sun," Clay said. "He doesn't think the scales are accurate."

Randall laughed. "I'd better go find him before he takes the scale apart to recalibrate it."

They said their good-byes. As Jack steered her toward another group of people, she heard Clay say, "Wow, Mom, she's gorgeous."

Charlie's lips curved into a pleased smile. At least she could impress fourteen-year-olds.

"You've conquered yet another susceptible heart," Jack murmured.

"My path is littered with them," Charlie said flippantly. Then she sobered. "You know, I've heard of Randall Johnson. He's a *very* powerful man, and much better connected than I am. You might want to take him up on his offer of assistance."

"He's done enough for me already. He doesn't owe me anything more."

"You're very big on this debt thing," Charlie said. "Your friends don't help you because they *owe* you; they help you because they're your friends."

"I just like to keep my budget balanced, sugar."

"Jack Lanett!" A man's voice came from their left.

As they turned, Jack's grip on her became slightly convulsive.

"Dr. Burke, you honor us with your presence," he said, extending his right hand.

Charlie remembered the man as the agitator from Jack's

question-and-answer session. Up close he was even more striking, the jet-black hair contrasting sharply with intensely blue eyes. If she weren't a married woman, she'd consider him compellingly attractive.

The two men stood measuring each other in silence, and for a moment, Charlie had a weird sense of seeing double. Then Jack made the introductions, and Peter Burke politely congratulated them.

"I'd like to set up a meeting with you as soon as possible." The bio-astronomer spoke in the same southern cadences as her husband.

Jack's eyebrows rose. "In reference to?"

"Sahara-Mars."

"I thought the consortium was a dead issue."

"I'd rather discuss it privately," the younger man said, glancing at the tightly packed guests.

"I'm just trying to make sure there's something to discuss," Jack said.

"There is, I assure you," Dr. Burke snapped.

"As long as you're not wasting my time," Jack said, pulling a business card and gold pen out of his pocket. "Tomorrow at five at this address." He scrawled his apartment's street address on the card and handed it to the scientist.

"I know he was obnoxious at your lecture, but you were quite rude to him," Charlie said after they said good-bye and strolled away.

"A little evening of the score."

"He reminds me of you."

"Peter Burke? We're about as different as two people can be."

"Not really. You have the same intensity. And the same accent."

"But he's got a Ph.D. and an attitude."

Charlie laughed at that.

"By the way, what do you have on under this outfit?" Jack asked, splaying his fingers over the join between her hip and thigh and gently kneading the soft fabric.

"Nothing. It would ruin the line of the gown," Charlie quoted airily.

His fingers dug into the velvet.

"Damnation. I've already got enough on my mind."

His grip loosened, but as he slid his arm away from her waist, his fingers brushed low across her buttocks, making her gasp.

"A little treat for both of us," he drawled as he placed her hand sedately in the crook of his elbow.

CHAPTER 17

A RIPPLE OF murmurs began flowing through the crowd. Jack's smile never flickered, but Charlie felt tension in his body as the sound seemed to increase in volume. Jack pivoted to his right, where the whispering was most prominent, and extended his hand. "Curt, a pleasure to see you," he said.

The billionaire who coveted the meteorite. Charlie peered around Jack's shoulder to get a glimpse of him. Her first thought was *he's short*, but standing next to Jack made most people look short. He was fiftyish, balding, had a ruddy complexion, and was surveying her with an avid gleam in his eye. As Jack introduced her, she held out her hand. She almost grimaced when he took it, then laid his left hand over it.

"Trust you to find an exquisitely beautiful wife," he said to Jack. "You've always had the eye of a connoisseur."

Charlie raised an eyebrow but refrained from saying she was not a collectible.

"Charlie's a well-known journalist," Jack said, earning him her undying gratitude. "Hello, Eileen," he continued, greeting Curt Vandermade's agent.

"Jack, I'd like you to meet the world's foremost authority on geological rarities, Dr. Reginald Hollinger," Eileen said.

Charlie caught the skepticism in Jack's eye, and she disliked Dr. Hollinger almost instantly. Tall and very thin with a carefully styled head of snow-white hair, Hollinger responded to Jack's polite greeting by raising his brows, with the air of a scientist observing some low, dull form of life.

"I'd like Reginald to get a look at your space rock," Vandermade said, "just for insurance."

"He'll have the same access to it as all the bidders," Jack said noncommittally.

"You've got a significant problem to solve before the auction," Hollinger said.

"What's that?" Jack drawled.

"Mauritania's claim on Sahara-Mars," Hollinger answered. "A find of this importance might rightfully belong in the country where it fell."

"What he means," Eileen Kushen glared at Hollinger, "is that Mr. Vandermade cannot possibly place a sizeable bid on the meteorite without an *undisputed* transfer of ownership."

Charlie watched Hollinger as he comprehended his faux pas. He tilted his head back and regarded Eileen Kushen down his long narrow nose. At the same time, he hooked his left index finger inside his ear and pulled his ear lobe downward as though he couldn't quite hear what she was saying. *"Precisely,"* he said dismissively.

"Rest assured any such issues will be taken care of before the auction," Jack said. "I don't sell meteorites that don't belong to me."

Eileen turned her glare on him. There was obviously a story *there*.

"Please excuse us, gentlemen . . . and ladies," Jack said, with a glance at Eileen. "My wife and I have to prepare for the presentation of Sahara-Mars."

He slid his hand around her waist once again and steered Charlie through the crowd toward the Hall of Planet Earth. Miguel fell into step with them. Jack nodded to the two guards stationed at the entrance to the darkened exhibit area. The three of them walked up a set of steps, stopping when they arrived at a metal railing.

The railing encircled a small sunken amphitheater. Two flights of black stone stairs leading down into the circle interrupted the sweep of railing on either side. Focused spotlights lit the perimeter, while darkness enveloped the center. Charlie could just make out a dark square column rising from the floor.

Several technicians were consulting with each other on the terraced steps.

"Turn it on," one called out.

Overhead, a huge half-globe set into the ceiling lit up with a display of the night sky. Suddenly, an explosion of meteors streaked across the constellations.

"Great. We've got it," the technician approved.

"Wow!" Charlie said. "That's stunning."

Jack smiled.

"We weren't sure if it was going to work," Miguel said. "Usually, the globe displays satellite images of the earth viewed from outer space. It took some jiggering to get the view turned the other way."

"Mr. Lanett, could you come over here," a technician called from the other side of the amphitheater. "We want to check the lighting on you."

"On my way," Jack responded. "Charlie, why don't you stand with me?"

"I'm flattered, but no thanks. This is *your* show," she said. "I'm going to call and check on Sallyanne. Then I'll hang out with Miguel." She reached for her purse and shook her head in annoyance. "Darn it! I gave my purse to Alina, and it's got my phone in it."

"Here, use mine," Jack said, fishing his cell phone out of his pocket.

"Thanks," Charlie said, accepting the phone. It radiated the warmth of Jack's body heat, just as the car keys had all those weeks ago. This time she closed her fingers around it without hesitation.

Isabelle reported all was going smoothly.

"What do you think of him?" Charlie asked.

"Well, he's a bit of a good ole boy," Isabelle said. "But you can't blame him for where he grew up. He's very nice with Sallyanne." Relief flooded Charlie. *If Isabelle thinks Don McGraw is okay, he probably is.* "However," the older woman continued, "I don't like the way he looks around your house. As though he's calculating something."

So much for relief. "What do you mean?" Charlie squeaked.

"We'll talk about it tomorrow. You enjoy your party!" Isabelle hung up.

Enjoy the party? She was going to stew over that comment for the rest of the night!

Miguel beckoned her over to his post by a huge red boulder in a glass case. From there, she could see the whole open space including the entrance. As the guests began to climb the stairs into the exhibit hall, two tripod-mounted television cameras swiveled, their red "on" lights glowing.

It was truly a photogenic crowd: the men's dark tuxedos

provided the perfect foil for the evening dresses swirling or clinging in a full spectrum of colors. The dramatic lighting brought out the maximum glitter from jewels liberally scattered on ears, throats, wrists, and fingers. Charlie rotated her own wrist, and her bracelet sparked with diamond fire. The chattering voices dropped to murmurs as people filed down the steps of the amphitheater and took their positions standing on the descending stone tiers.

Charlie noticed Curt Vandermade and his group had appropriated space in the front row, as close to the darkened display case as possible. She examined them each in turn. Vandermade stood with his arms folded, scowling at the opaque box in front of him. Eileen Kushen chatted animatedly with the woman standing next to her. *Probably trying to sign up another client.* Dr. Hollinger evidently disapproved of the conversation because he was tugging at his ear lobe again.

The last guests filed down the steps, and Miguel nodded toward someone across the room. The lights at the entrance blinked out. Now, only artificial starlight illuminated the room. As meteorites streaked across the overhead globe, several people "ahh-ed" in admiration. Then a single spotlight speared abruptly down through the darkness and lit Jack standing poised at the top of the staircase opposite Charlie and Miguel.

"Good evening, ladies and gentlemen, and welcome."

He paused.

"Thousands of years ago, men looked up at the night sky, and imagined the gods tossing glowing coals at the world. The coals burned through the fabric of the heavens to create the pinpricks of light we know as stars. On the rarely recorded occasions when these coals fell all the way to earth, they were treasured as gifts from the gods by ancient people in Mexico and revered as holy by Muslims in the Kaaba."

Jack took one step downward, the movement making the polished meteorites of his studs flash.

"We, of course, are interested in fallen stars only for their scientific value," he said with a grin at his eager buyers.

A ripple of laughter went through his audience.

"The meteorite you will see here tonight," he said, sweeping his hand toward the darkened center and creating absolute silence, "is not a fallen star. It is a fallen planet, hurled here by the God of War, the mighty Mars. Perhaps it holds signs of living creatures other than ourselves, granting us hope of company in our lonely universe.

"But whether life is sealed inside this black stone or not, it comes to us from the birth of our solar system, a gift to our ever-questing minds from the gods of space."

The spotlight blinked off Jack as a shaft of brilliant white light blazed down onto Sahara-Mars in its sealed display case.

Even Charlie gasped. Miguel chuckled with satisfaction beside her. "He's quite a showman, our Jack," he said.

A babble of voices broke out as people recovered from the drama, and began to examine the gleaming stone now revolving on the stand in front of them. Several surged forward to get a closer look. Soon the crowd was packed around the pedestal. Jack stood solitary on the steps, watching the spectacle with an impassive expression. Charlie excused herself to Miguel and walked over to her husband. "You were magnificent! Your speech alone should push up the price by several hundred thousand dollars," she said.

"Thanks," he said, continuing to watch the crowd. "As long as they feel they got their money's worth."

There was a flat note in his voice she wasn't accustomed to hearing. Charlie really looked at him, and saw exhaustion in his face and posture. She reached up to lay her palm against his cheek in a gesture of concern. "You look tired."

His eyebrows arched in surprise, but he let her hand rest against him. Then the one-hundred-watt smile was back. "Just a little post-show letdown," he said, taking her hand in his to kiss her palm before he released it. "Don't worry about me, sugar."

One of the television reporters approached brandishing a microphone, and Charlie tried to beat a speedy retreat. Jack captured her wrist in a grip of steel and pulled her close to his side. "Smile for the cameras, Charlie. I want to show off my beautiful wife." Charlie threw an imploring glance at Miguel, but he grinned and held his position.

The interview was mercifully brief and focused almost entirely on Jack and his find. When it was over, Charlie escaped before the next reporter could collar him.

Most of the guests had looked their fill at Sahara-Mars and were drifting back out to the brilliantly lit Hall of the Universe to replenish their drinks. Charlie waited for a lull in the traffic up the steps, then went down to take a closer look at the famous rock. Miguel's sealed case had been set atop a rotating pedestal so a spectator could stand in one place and view the entire meteorite. Up close, the flow structures created by its fiery journey through the atmosphere were more pronounced; the straight lines radiating back from the stone's nose looked as though they had been drawn by an artist's steady hand. Maybe Jack had influenced her, but Sahara-Mars did emit an alien aura. It looked like nothing on the earth.

"Impressive, isn't it?"

Charlie turned to find Curt Vandermade beside her, his

gaze locked on the glittering object revolving in front of them.

"Very," she agreed. "It certainly gives one the sense of being from somewhere far away."

"I have one Martian achondrite in my collection," he said, "but it doesn't compare to this. And of course, ALH 84001 was found by scientists in Antartica so it's out of my reach for now." The man's dark eyes narrowed as he continued, "If you give this to the scientists, they will destroy its beauty, cut it up into slices and stick labels all over it. It belongs where it will be revered for the mystery that it is."

Surprised by the poetry of his passion, Charlie nodded.

"I don't really give a damn about Mauritania's claims," he said, tearing his eyes away from the display. "You tell your husband he's got a buyer."

"I will," Charlie said.

Without another word, Vandermade turned on his heel and climbed the steps to join his entourage. Charlie lingered, and when she heard footsteps on the stairs behind her she started to work up her best social smile.

"What does it say to you?" Jack's breath tickled her neck as he murmured beside her ear. "Does it speak of ancient organisms and visions of the stars or is it just a dead stone?"

"It says, 'I'm from another world, another time, and I've seen more than you'll ever know,'" Charlie said, fascinated equally by his voice and the stone spinning in front of her.

She heard a rustle and then his warm palms cupped her shoulders. He tilted her back against him, then wrapped his arms around her waist to hold her there. She felt the brush of starched cotton, slippery satin and soft wool against her bare shoulder blade. As his chest rose and fell, the hard chill of a stud grazed her skin. She stood, mesmerized by a delicious sense of enclosure, exquisitely aware of the compression of fabrics sliding over her skin and his. Closing her eyes, she could feel his heartbeat against her back and the pulse of his wrists where they pressed against her.

"Hey, *amigos*, I know it's been a long night but it's not over yet." Miguel's deep voice sliced through her trance. "There are still people who want to talk to both of you."

"Tell 'em to go to hell," Jack said without moving.

Charlie chuckled, which had the effect of making Jack's hold on her tighten.

Miguel's laugh rumbled over their heads as he leaned over the railing. "This is a pretty public place to be continuing your honeymoon. The security cameras are filming your every move."

They were so closely locked together she felt Jack's sigh more strongly than if it had been her own. He let his arms drop and stepped back from her.

"When did you become my conscience?" he asked his friend.

Charlie turned and put one hand behind her husband's head, pulling his lips down to hers for a quick kiss of sympathy. "Let's go be good hosts," she said, lacing her fingers in his and leading him up the stairs.

"If you could see the way Jack's looking at your *fondillos*," Miguel said, "you'd know his mind is *not* on the welfare of his guests."

CHAPTER 18

"THERE'S SOMETHING I want to show you that's a long way away. Come with me."

Charlie objected, "But there are at least *fifty* people still here!"

"Miguel will take care of them," Jack said, grabbing her wrist and pulling her firmly away from the Rose Center entrance, where people were saying their good-byes, toward the opposite side of the hall. Miguel was deep in conversation with a group of men, but at Jack's signal, he nodded and headed for the entrance.

Jack smiled at the people who tried to catch his attention, but his stride never shortened. Charlie was struggling to keep up in her elegant but impractical Lucite mules. When they emerged into the hall that connected with the main building of the Museum of Natural History, she braced herself against his forward momentum. "If we're going sightseeing, I've got to get out of these heels." She toed the shoes off and bent down to pick them up.

"Leave 'em here," Jack commanded.

"I don't think so." She held one up and rotated it so he could see the embedded stones as they caught the light. "For all I know, these are real diamonds like that ridiculous evening purse I hope Alina is guarding with her life."

"Here." Jack held out his hand for the offending slippers. Then he was off again, leading them past cases of stuffed mammals, through dark, narrow hallways and around Indian dioramas. "Did you know Admiral Peary financed his expedition to the North Pole by selling a meteorite?" he asked.

"No," Charlie said, wondering what on earth *that* had to do with *this* mad dash.

"It's one of the 'great irons' from Greenland. It took three trips to get it to the United States. For seven years, it sat on a pier at the Brooklyn Naval Shipyard. No one wanted a 34-ton iron meteorite. Finally the president of this museum paid a paltry $40,000 and hauled it through the streets of New York with a team of eighty horses."

They passed by an enormously long canoe peopled with slightly dusty plaster figures in colorful costumes. Charlie recognized their direction now: they were headed for the Hall of Meteorites. It seemed like years ago she had come here to start her research for the article about Jack. "Are you talking about the huge meteorite in the middle of the exhibit here? *Ahnighito*?" she asked.

"That's right. It's one of my personal favorites."

They had entered the dimly lit space devoted to rocks from the sky.

A huge photograph of the moon's surface illuminated the wall in front of them, and hexagonal glass cases lit from within seemed to hover at waist level. At the center of the room, an enormous mass of iron crouched on short concrete piers like a giant prehistoric beast. It hulked above Charlie's head as Jack led her around to the opposite side so they stood between *Ahnighito* and another display of large iron meteorites. The lighting there was even murkier; Charlie could barely make out the labels on the huge stones.

"The natives named it The Tent," Jack said. "And these two, the Woman and the Dog, were part of the same meteor. Peary talked the natives into letting him take them away. The task proved to be so difficult he referred to *Ahnighito* as the 'demonic iron from heaven'." He scanned the cratered giant, and turned to Charlie. "Right where we're standing, there's a blind spot in the security system."

Then he reached out and flicked one of her earrings with his finger. "Too bad falling stars aren't really diamonds."

Charlie caught her breath as he trailed his fingers down her neck.

"It seems your designer studied his constellations," he said, tracing a pattern between the crystals sewn on the shoulder of her dress. "That's Cygnus."

His finger moved slowly downward to the swell of her breast. "That's Ursa Minor." She felt her nipples harden. Jack's smile gleamed in the half-light as he noticed. The crystals threw off sparks in rhythm with Charlie's quickened breathing.

"How intriguing. He's put Orion just below this spiral galaxy." His fingertip followed the spirals swirling over her breast.

As he reached the shower of stars over her nipple, Charlie inhaled sharply. "Are you seducing me in the middle of the Museum of Natural History?" she asked, locking her fingers around his wrist.

"No, sugar, I'm seducing you *in a dark corner* of the Museum of Natural History," he said, his voice falling into a slow southern cadence. He flattened his palm over her breast. "Any objections?"

She hesitated.

He put his other hand on her backside and moved her against him so she could feel his erection between her thighs. "You wear a dress like this, and you've got to expect to get seduced," he whispered against her neck as he feathered kisses down to her shoulder. His teeth and tongue grazed her skin, and she hissed out a moan.

"Any objections?" he repeated.

"I'm sure I have some, but they don't readily come to mind." She let go of his wrist.

He shifted his hand from her breast to the length of thigh bared by the dress's slit, sliding his palm upward along her skin until he cupped her bare buttock beneath the clinging velvet. His fingers brushing against her from behind and his erection pushing against her in front tightened the tension coiling deep inside her. Eyes closed to savor the sensations, she arched hard against him, even as he slid one finger inside her. "Oh God, Jack."

"Look at me."

She opened her eyes. His face was in shadow; she could see only the white of his eyes and teeth, as he said again, "Any objections?"

"None at all," she said.

He groaned in relief and brought his lips down lightly against hers. "You won't regret it," he promised. She felt his finger slide out of her, and she nipped his lower lip in complaint. He drove two fingers back into her. She felt a ripple of orgasm.

"Stop," she gasped. "I want you coming with me."

He slowly withdrew his hand. Her inner muscles tightened again. "Ahhhhhhh," she breathed, unable to forestall the delicious spread of heat.

"Patience, sweetheart," he commanded, taking her head between his hands and planting teasing little kisses everywhere but on her lips. "You don't want to rush a good thing."

"Yes, I do," she said, as she wrapped one arm around his neck and levered herself up close along the length of his body. She rotated her hips hard against him, gasping as the warm steel of male thigh and chest increased her own urgency.

"Mercy!" he moaned. "I give up." His fingers bit into her buttocks as he rocked against the vee of her legs.

Bending her knee, she rubbed it up the outside of his thigh. The velvet caught on the inside of his trouser so she felt nothing but the press of wool and muscle between her legs.

"Jack, I can't wait any longer."

"Then turn around," he rasped.

She obeyed without question. He came up behind her, cupping her breasts as he used his weight to bend her over the shelf supporting the iron meteorites. Hearing the whine of his zipper, she braced her forearms on the cool dark surface. Then his hands were brushing up her thighs, pushing aside the velvet skirt and caressing her bare skin, the clever fingers seeking and sliding into her.

His hands swept down to the crease where thigh met hip and held her. She felt him position himself; then in one smooth stroke, he was inside her. Her orgasm crested instantly. "Oh god," she said on each pulse of her release. *"Oh god, oh god, oh god, oh god."* His rhythm quickened. His motion pushing through the clench of her muscles propelled her beyond the bounds of thought. He drove deep. She felt the pounding of his own climax match hers as he groaned her name, *"Charlie, ahhhh, Charlie!"*

He slid out of her, and Charlie's elbows and knees buckled.

She collapsed face down on the hard melamine shelf.

She felt Jack smooth her dress down over her backside but she was far past any sense of modesty. Then he gathered up her boneless body and carried her over to *Ahnighito*. Bracing his back against the mighty iron, he slid to the floor, cradling Charlie on his lap, his long legs stretched out in front of him. He tucked her head under his chin and held her there. She could feel his heart pounding against her ear, and the rise and fall of his chest gave evidence of his exertions. Tiny aftershocks continued to shiver through her own body, especially when he lifted his hand to idly stroke a wisp of hair back from her face.

"We-e-e-ll," he said, making it last about three syllables.

Somewhere she found the strength to chuckle, albeit weakly. "That's a major understatement," she said.

An answering chuckle rumbled in her ear. "That wasn't meant as an evaluation," he said, flicking her cheek with his finger before letting his hand drop heavily onto her shoulder. "We may have to spend the night here."

"Why? Because they'll lock us in?" Charlie asked, starting to sit upright.

"No. Because I can't move."

She subsided against his chest with a sigh.

He laughed, raising their joined hands to kiss the inside of her wrist.

One little brush of his lips, and every nerve ending in her body paid attention. "I forgot to give you a message from Curt Vandermade," she said to distract herself. "He asked me to tell you, you have a buyer for Sahara-Mars. He doesn't give a damn about Mauritania."

Jack's tone was unpleasant. "That's because he has

more money than Mauritania's entire annual gross product. He can *buy* the country if they won't give up their claim."

"Aren't you glad he's hooked? You'll be able to squeeze maximum cash out of your space rock."

"That's what you think I want?"

"That's what you've told me you want."

"What I *want* is to hand this rock over to Peter Burke free of charge. He may be obnoxious as hell, but he wants Sahara-Mars so he can add to our knowledge of the universe. What I *really* want is to join him in that quest. But I'm not welcome. So I have to give someone like Curt Vandermade the chance to expropriate a valuable scientific discovery so he can fondle it to inflate his own ego."

"I wasn't judging you," Charlie said quietly. "You have a right to realize your dream."

"Dream?" He sounded surprised. "I think of it as a long-term goal."

"Call it what you want," she shrugged. "You're about to achieve it, and I'm impressed."

"Thanks, sugar." He wrapped his arms around her, crushing her against him.

"Mmmmm," she said, as delicious tremors began to take hold of her again. She both felt and heard his voice as he said, "I don't know what the hell is going on here, but I like it."

The tremors evaporated, and her mood took a U-turn.

She knew exactly what was going on here: she was becoming *involved*. She wasn't willing to use a stronger word, *involved* was bad enough. Cradled in his lap in this dusky corner of an enormous empty museum, she felt safe, she felt comfortable, she felt, almost, cherished. Even worse, she wanted to cherish him right back.

She pushed away from his chest.

"Miguel's going to wonder what happened to us," she said.

"Miguel would completely approve of our activities," he replied, running a finger along her bare shoulder. "But I shouldn't leave him to do all the cleaning up."

He boosted her to her feet, and hoisted himself up beside her.

"Where are your glass slippers?" he asked, scanning the floor around them. He spotted them under the display shelf and scooped them up. Holding out his other hand to her, he said, "Back to the ball, Cinderella."

As JACK CHECKED in with Miguel, Charlie gladly handed over her earrings and bracelet to Alina who was waiting in the nearly deserted hall with purse in hand. Tomorrow she would have the dress and shoes delivered back to Stephen Askegaard.

Jack escorted her to the waiting limousine, helping her into the back seat and ducking in to sit across from her.

"Bellefont first," he said over his shoulder to the driver. "Then back to Manhattan."

Charlie bent her head to hide her pleased smile.

"You were incredible tonight," he said, pushing a button to raise the privacy screen.

"Wow. My lovers usually only call me *great* or *fantastic*," she teased.

"No, I meant at the party. You handled it like a pro."

"Even in my costume?"

He grimaced.

"I was being an idiot. When you got out of the car looking like a movie goddess, I felt like I'd been kneed in the gut." He gave her a look. "You know damn well you're stunningly beautiful."

"You're too kind."

"There's one thing I didn't get to do tonight." He shifted onto the seat beside her.

"Just one?" She arched an eyebrow.

He chuckled and twisted sideways, then grasped her hips and slid her back toward him. He sank his fingers into her hair and suddenly the hairdresser's work of art began to uncoil. He took his time, pulling out the pins one by one and tossing them on the carpeted floor.

Charlie sat with her eyes closed and her head thrown back, lost in the exquisite pleasure of his slow release of the tight chignon. The memory of their first night under the stars surged through her, merging past with present sensation until she couldn't remember exactly where she was. When he had removed every hairpin, he draped her hair across her shoulders and back, combing his fingers gently through the twisted strands to untangle and smooth them.

For a long moment, he withdrew his hands. She was about to beg him not to stop when she felt him gather up her mane and twist it into a rope.

"Just like Rapunzel," he said in an odd voice.

"Are you going to braid it again?"

"Not this time. I want to see what it looks like spread across black leather."

"MA'AM, SIR, WE'RE here." The driver's voice came through the car's intercom as the car glided to a stop. Charlie fumbled her feet back into the Lucite slippers and scooped up a handful of hairpins. Jack watched her as he adjusted his cuffs.

"Maybe I'll put you up in the sky as a constellation," he mused. "Like Zeus did for his favorites. Then I could stare at you all night long."

"I hope you're a better artist; only about three of those constellations look anything like their names."

"Oh. I wouldn't miss a single curve," he said, leaning forward to run his hand down her hip to her thigh. With his thumb, he gently stroked high on the inside of her leg through the velvet. "I'd put a supernova right here because you are very, very hot."

"Wicked man," she said, brushing his hand away. "You and horny old Zeus would get along well."

He laughed as he opened the car door for her. On her front porch, he tilted her chin up to give her a quick kiss. "Sweet dreams, sugar." And he was gone.

She walked into the living room to find Isabelle reading by the fireplace with Twinkle in her lap. The older woman looked up and after a quick survey of Charlie, shut her book with a wise smile. "I'll find out all about it in the morning."

"No, don't go! I want to hear what you think of Don McGraw," Charlie protested. "And what you meant by the way he was looking at—"

"Tomorrow," Isabelle said, stowing her book in her tote bag and wrapping a wool shawl around her shoulders. She headed for the door.

"Thanks so much for taking care of Sallyanne," Charlie said.

Isabelle waved over her shoulder.

Charlie went up to check on the little girl. The beads on her dress clicked together softly as she bent over the sleeping child to smooth her hair back and drop a kiss on her forehead. She gently pulled the blanket up to cover the small shoulders, and lingered a moment to savor the sweet curve of the little girl's cheek.

She walked slowly back down the stairs with Major padding along beside her. As she passed the full-length mirror in her bedroom she gasped. Her hair cascaded over her shoulders in wild waves and her dress looked like someone had balled it up in his fist, which wasn't far short of the truth. "No wonder Isabelle beat a hasty retreat. And what am I going to tell Stephen Askegaard?"

JACK SPRAWLED IN the shadows in the back of the limousine trying to forget what he and Charlie had been doing just minutes before. Leaving her at her front door had taken all the willpower he could summon. *If Isabelle hadn't been waiting in the house . . .*

He had it bad.

Even worse, the party had made him see her as a *partner.*

He had begun to construct a scenario in which she played a role in his life, and that scared the hell out of him. It scared him because her generosity and willingness to forgive reminded him too much of his mother. But his mother hadn't had the strength to support her love. Charlie had it in spades. She was strong and determined and stubborn and gorgeous and smart as a whip and . . .

And she wanted to have children and a house and pets and a loving husband.

He didn't need this right now. He needed to focus on untangling Sahara-Mars from the diplomatic snares of Mauritania and selling it for as much cash as possible. In fact, his first meeting tomorrow morning was with Dyson Foley, Charlie's contact.

Charlie's contact. He shook his head.

There was entirely too much of Charlie in his life.

CHAPTER 19

THE NEXT MORNING, Sallyanne woke up talking.

"Papa, Miss Isabelle and I saw you and Jack on television. You looked so beautiful, and Jack looked really, really handsome. Papa said you were the most beautiful woman he had ever seen. We went mini-golfing. I got a hole-in-one on the hole with the windmill where you have to wait until your ball can go between the blades. Papa's ball hit the blade, and he got mad because he had to start over again."

By the time they were dressed and eating breakfast, Charlie had heard every detail of Sallyanne's evening with her father, some several times over. Don McGraw was clearly well on the road to overcoming the girl's doubts about his treatment of her mother. She had picked up the *New York Times* from the front porch and was idly paging through it to see if there were any familiar bylines when Sallyanne squealed.

"Look, it's you and Jack!" she said, pointing with her spoon.

Sure enough, on the front page of the Metro Section was a photo of the two of them standing in front of the Willamette meteorite, chatting with Kate and Randall Johnson. "Clever photographer," Charlie muttered.

"Why?"

"Well, because he got a lot into one photo. There are the two people giving the party, two of the more interesting guests, *and* a large meteorite."

"Do you think Jack would let me see Sahara-Mars?"

"He'd love to show it to you," Charlie said. "I'm not sure when your father plans on returning to Tennessee, but maybe he would wait until after the weekend and we could all go to New York City on Saturday?"

Sallyanne looked down at her cereal.

"What's the matter, sweetheart?"

"Couldn't he live here?" the little girl asked. "I don't want to move to Tennessee," she said, beginning to cry.

Charlie's chair crashed backward as she scrambled to gather the sobbing child in her arms. She had never felt so helpless in her life. It seemed highly unlikely Don McGraw would move to New Jersey. She knew from hard experience there was no solution to Sallyanne's dilemma other than just toughing it out. She hated that a nine-year-old girl had to tough *anything* out.

"Oh, sweetheart, I promise to come visit you." It was the only promise she knew she could keep. "I've never been to Tennessee, and I hear it's really beautiful." She was babbling.

"Th-th-thank you, ma'am. W-w-will you bring Major too?"

"Of course." It would be a long drive. She hoped Major liked riding in cars. Sallyanne's sobs finally subsided. She washed her face, finished her cereal, and went off to school with only slightly reddened eyes to mark the trauma of the morning. Charlie, however, came home and flung herself sprawling onto the couch. Major dug his nose under her wrist, looking for attention, and she could barely lift her hand to stroke him. "Parenting is hell!" she said, making the dog swivel his ears in sympathy.

The telephone rang, and Charlie groaned.

She let the answering machine pick up, but hauled herself off the couch when she heard Isabelle's voice. "I'm coming over with some zucchini bread," Isabelle said. "We'll talk about Mr. McGraw."

Charlie put a kettle of hot water on to boil just as Isabelle appeared at the back door, with two loaves of freshly baked bread wrapped in organic cotton dishtowels.

"Yum, it's still warm," Charlie said as she cut into a loaf.

"I had some extra zucchini from the co-op and couldn't bear to see it go to waste," the older woman explained as she sat down at the kitchen table and dunked her herbal tea bag in a mug of hot water.

"*Everyone* has extra zucchini," Charlie said. "Just don't leave any in its natural state on *my* porch."

Isabelle's silvery laugh rang out, but then she grew serious. "Now let's talk about Sallyanne and her father."

"Yes, let's. I want to know what you really think of him."

"He's a very polite young man; he held my chair, cleared the dishes and *ma'am*-ed me until I thought I'd scream."

"I hear a 'but' in your voice."

"Now wait, I've got more good things to say about him. Young people are so impatient." Isabelle deliberately sipped her tea. "He was very attentive to Sallyanne, encouraged her to talk about all sorts of things, wanted to see her room and so forth. He was always very careful to ask my permission before taking her anywhere, even in the house."

"So where's the 'but'?"

"He has an odd way of looking around your house. As though he's assessing it."

"Maybe he's just interested in the place his daughter's living," Charlie said. "You know, making sure it's safe and comfortable."

"Not *that* kind of assessing. Rather the 'how much did this cost' kind of assessing," Isabelle clarified. "But more importantly, Major doesn't like him."

Charlie blew out an exasperated snort. "I love dogs, but I'm not going to base my opinion of a person on what a Kuvasz thinks. Major growls at Jack too."

"Does he? Now I wonder why that could be?" Isabelle raised her eyebrows at Charlie.

"Never mind. You must have a better reason than that."

"Animals have very sound instincts about certain people. There's something the tiniest bit frightening about Don McGraw, something just below the surface he's being very careful to control. Don't you feel it too?"

Charlie broke the fragrant slab of bread into several pieces and then left it on the plate. "Honestly, I haven't spent enough time with him to say yes or no. I'm afraid I just don't *want* to like him, because he'll take Sallyanne away."

"Well, dear, you need to make up your mind quickly because the man is doing his very best to win over his daughter, and I'd say he's succeeding admirably. She moved the big pink bunny from the closet to the bed last night."

"I noticed," Charlie admitted. "I'll spend the afternoon with them. Is it so wrong to want to give him the benefit of the doubt?"

"No, it isn't." Isabelle patted her hand. "You've got a

good head on your shoulders. Just don't let your own lack of a father cloud your judgment."

"I'll try." Charlie's shoulders rose and fell in a sigh. "Even if we *all* decide we don't trust Don, Mike says it would be extremely difficult to keep him from taking her unless we could prove he's an unfit father."

Isabelle poured some hot water into Charlie's mug and dropped one of her own tea bags in it. "You look as though you could use a pick-me-up. This is my special blend; it has a secret ingredient to counteract lack of rest."

"It wasn't *that* late when I got home," Charlie protested.

"I wasn't born yesterday. I know very well what you and Jack were up to last night."

Charlie felt her cheeks burning.

"It doesn't shock me, but it worries me," the older woman continued.

Charlie took a gulp of the tea, and almost gagged. "What's in this?"

"Herbs and spices," Isabelle said airily.

"It tastes more like mud," Charlie eyed the mug skeptically, "and stagnant pond water."

"You're trying to change the subject, and it won't work."

"All right. *Why* does it worry you that I, um, was up to something with the man to whom I am, after all, married?"

"Because you're getting as attached to him as you are to Sallyanne."

Charlie started laughing. "The way I feel about Sallyanne and the way I feel about Jack are a bit different."

"Obviously. But the strength of those feelings is what concerns me, on both counts." Isabelle reached across the table to lay her hand on Charlie's. "Jack is a lovely, lovely man, but you know as well as I do that he's hiding something. And you know as well as I do your marriage is nothing more than a useful facade."

"Better than you think," Charlie muttered. She wanted to jump up and escape Isabelle's well-meant warning, but she couldn't bring herself to pull her hand away from the older woman's warm clasp.

"Protect yourself, my dear," Isabelle said.

It was too late for that. As she lay staring at the ceiling last night, Charlie realized she wanted Jack in bed with her when she awoke. She also wanted him swinging Sallyanne up in his arms, and feeding Major bits of cheese, and pointing out constellations in the sky. She wanted him to trust her enough to tell her about his terrible past, and it didn't worry her at all that he had one.

She angled the ring on her left hand so it glinted in the morning sunlight. "Jack told me I could keep the ring when this is all over. Do you think it would be all right if I did?"

"So it's that bad," Isabelle said.

"I think so." Charlie took a sip of the horrible tea and grimaced.

"Well, we'll just have to see what we can do to keep that ring on your finger for the right reason."

"It's a nice thought, but completely impossible," Charlie said.

"Remember, I'm a lobbyist. My specialty is persuading people it's in their own best interests to do exactly what they don't want to do."

"Oh great, now you have to brainwash a man into being my husband. I appreciate the offer, but—"

"There's no brainwashing involved; he just needs to be shown the benefits of making the right decision," Isabelle said serenely, patting Charlie's hand before she picked up her fork.

"No lobbying Jack," Charlie said, giving Isabelle a level stare.

Isabelle just said, "Hmmm," and sipped her tea.

JACK WATCHED PETER Burke on the security camera's monitor.

It irritated him that the man walked through the building's lobby as though he owned the place. But Peter always walked that way; probably as far as he was concerned, there was no reason he shouldn't. Jack envied him for that feeling and for a lot of other things. Peter had the life Jack should have had.

The camera's view changed as the elevator doors slid open. Jack swung the door open, and met the scientist in the hallway.

"Dr. Burke," he said, holding out his hand.

"Mr. Lanett," Peter Burke said, gripping Jack's hand hard. "We meet again."

"I hope under more constructive circumstances. Come in."

Jack led the way to the living room. This was his last and least welcome appointment of the day. "What can I pour for you? Coffee, water, soda?"

"Nothing, thanks. It's late and I'm sure you want to know what my offer is."

Peter sat in one of the armchairs, stretching his legs out in front of him and crossing them at the ankles. Jack picked up a bottle of water and sat down opposite. He had to stop himself from matching the other man's pose.

"Go ahead."

"I represent a consortium of three universities, a museum and a private investor."

Jack's eyebrows rose at the last. "What does the private investor expect to get out of this? A tax deduction?"

"He expects to add to the knowledge of our solar system."

Jack snorted.

"You find it impossible to believe a man can be motivated by something other than cash?"

"Not at all. There are other temptations: power, fame, sex."

"You're a cynic, Mr. Lanett."

"I'm a realist, Dr. Burke. I'd say you fall into the 'fame' category."

The younger man suddenly sat forward. "Even if my consortium succeeds in buying Sahara-Mars, I may never get to touch it, and that's fine. As long as another scientist using proper scientific procedure makes the first cut into that rock, I will have done what I needed to do."

"Your altruism is an inspiration. Now what's your offer?" Jack tilted the water to his lips without taking his eyes off the man across from him.

"My offer has two parts. You should listen to both of them. First, the money." He named a very respectable figure. "However, we are also willing to offer you assistance in clearing the meteorite's ownership."

"What if I don't need your help?" Jack said, smiling.

The scientist looked taken aback. "Mauritania has made a very serious claim to ownership—"

"No, it's made a completely baseless claim. I'm not worried about it."

"I see."

"You're a lousy negotiator, Dr. Burke," Jack said, rising easily and walking to the bar. He poured a mug of coffee and carried it over to his guest. "You look like you could use some caffeine."

The other man took the mug, put it on the table and stood up. "Are you rejecting this offer because *I'm* making it?"

"Why would I do that?"

"Because we're—" The younger man stopped.

"On opposite sides of the fence?" Jack finished for him.

Peter shook his head and looked away.

"Sit down," Jack said as he went back to his own chair. "I'll accept your offer—the cash, that is. But I want to know the name of your private investor."

"I can't tell you that," the younger man said, still standing.

"Then the deal's off."

"Then it's off," the scientist said through gritted teeth. He pivoted toward the door.

Jack laughed. "Now *that's* something I admire more than altruism," he said.

Peter hesitated. "What?" he finally snapped.

"Protecting your sources. Sit down, you pain in the ass. You're giving me a stiff neck."

"You're jerking me around," Peter said, but he sat.

"Maybe. Have some coffee." Jack took a swallow of water. "Here's the deal: I'm having an attack of altruism myself. I want to sell to your consortium, but you've got to sweeten the offer, and I need one guarantee."

"What's the guarantee?" Peter sipped the coffee.

"That your private investor is not Curt Vandermade."

"I can guarantee that."

"Good."

"And I'm prepared to go *slightly* higher in price."

"As they say in Georgia, now you're fryin' hog guts in moonshine," Jack said, with a grin and a drawl thicker than molasses.

The bio-astronomer looked pained. "I grew up in Georgia too, and I've never heard that particular expression before."

"You must have kept better company than I did."

HE PUNCHED A speed dial number into his cell phone. "Hey, *amigo*, I just sold Sahara-Mars to the good guys."

"I never doubted you would," Miguel said. "That's why I told you to put the 'gift to science' clause in the contract with Sotheby's."

"If you're so smart, why did we sign the contract with Sotheby's in the first place?"

"To drive up the price, of course. If those scientists knew what a soft touch you are, we'd have gotten nothing for our treasure. By the way, what *are* we getting?"

Jack named the sum, and Miguel whistled.

"You got your pound of flesh, *amigo*."

CHARLIE WATCHED DON McGraw and Sallyanne checking math problems at the table on the back porch, their matching blond heads nearly touching as they bent to their work. *How could anyone decide they didn't belong together?*

Don had arrived after school with a small bouquet of daisies for her and a chocolate lollipop in the shape of a butterfly for Sallyanne. He immediately sat down with his daughter to supervise her homework, accepting only a glass of milk and a cookie. Now their voices wafted in through the open French doors, and Charlie noticed Sallyanne's accent deepened when she was with her father.

Even their voices went together.

They closed the books and stowed them in Sallyanne's backpack. "Charlie," Sallyanne said, coming to the door.

"I'm finished with my homework. Papa wants to know if we can all three take a walk on the beach?"

"Sure," Charlie said, slipping into the beach sandals she kept by the door. Major raised his head hopefully, but she didn't want any distractions from her observation of Don, so she gave him the stay signal. He dropped his head back to the rug with a disgusted *erf.*

Don carried in the dishes and carefully loaded them into the dishwasher. When Charlie smiled her thanks, he looked gratified.

It was a glorious day to walk on the beach. As they strolled toward the sea, gulls easily rode a surprisingly gentle breeze, hovering almost at eye-level over the water of the channel. When Sallyanne took Charlie's hand and swung it jauntily between them, her day was complete.

She almost didn't notice Sallyanne was holding Don's hand as well.

CHAPTER 20

SALLYANNE LET GO of their hands to run ahead, scanning the sand for seashells.

"I saw you on television last night," Don said. "You looked real pretty."

"Thank you," Charlie said, turning her face upward to enjoy the sunshine.

"I read about the party in the newspaper today. It's amazing what people will pay for a chunk of black rock."

"I suppose so, but it *is* from Mars."

"No offense meant, ma'am," he said, picking up a broken clam shell and hurling it into an oncoming wave.

"None taken."

It was too beautiful a day to be offended. The sun sent sparkles dancing off the waves, the air blew clean and salty, even the gulls' cries seemed raucous rather than mournful. Sallyanne raced the surf up and down the shore, shrieking when the cold water splashed up her bare calves.

"Don," Charlie plunged in, "what are your plans for her?"

"Plans?" He picked up another fragment of shell and tossed it in the water. "I'm going to take her home to Tennessee and be her papa."

"Do you have a house there?" She hated to be so blunt, but she needed to build a picture of what the girl's life would be like.

"I stay with Sallyanne's grandmother when I'm home. It's not as nice as your house, but the cookin's good."

"When you're not home, where do you live?" Charlie asked neutrally.

"Wherever there's work." He shrugged. "A man has to go where the opportunities are."

"Would Sallyanne live with her grandmother then?"

"Until I got set up with a permanent position. Then I'd send for her. She's a pretty little thing, isn't she?"

Charlie watched the little girl, her hair flying in the wind. "She's the most beautiful child I've ever seen," she said. "She's also sweet and brave and loving. Your wife did well with her."

"You're saying I didn't?"

Charlie shook her head. "I don't hold the past against anyone. People make mistakes. That doesn't mean you can't try to fix them."

"Sallyanne told me you grew up an orphan."

"That's true, so I think having a father is very important."

"I missed my little girl something fierce when Leah took her away." He kicked a piece of driftwood out of his path. "I guess you understand, because I think you like her a lot."

"Would I be able to talk to her grandmother?" Charlie asked. "I assume that's your mother?"

"Sure, you can talk to her, if you come down to Tennessee. She doesn't have a phone, and she wouldn't talk on it if she did."

"Oh, I see." *Does the lack of a phone indicate a lack of other creature comforts? But then who am I to decide a telephone is a requirement for a good life?*

"She's a stubborn old woman," Don continued, not without affection. "She doesn't own a television either, although I've offered to get her one."

"So she's old-fashioned?" Charlie asked.

"Except for the washer and dryer. She was happy enough to get rid of her washtub and roller when the electricity came in."

Charlie swallowed.

"But we've got a movie theater," Don continued, "and a McDonald's, and Walmart is only a half an hour drive. Sallyanne'll have everything she needs."

"What about school? Is there a local one?"

"Naw, they regionalized us years ago. But there's a school bus that stops right in town."

"What do you think of the school?"

"School's school," he said, shrugging. "Readin', writin', arithmetic. Sallyanne's real smart; she'll do just fine."

"Look what I found," Sallyanne said, running up at that moment with her hand held open. "An almost-perfect scallop shell."

The white shell with pinkish-brown stripes fanned across her small palm.

"There's just a tiny little hole right here," she said, pointing.

"You've got good eyes, honey bunch," Don said. "I can barely see that itty bitty hole."

"Do you want to take it home?" Charlie asked. "I'll put it in my pocket."

"Yes, please," Sallyanne said, handing over her treasure.

Then she took Don's hand and chattered happily about her day at school.

Charlie watched and listened. Don's description of his life in Tennessee had been unappealing; surely he knew that. *Why does he want me to think Sallyanne's life with him will be less than satisfactory?*

"Charlie, what flavor ice cream cone do you want?" Sallyanne's voice penetrated her mental debate. "Papa's going up to the sweet shop on the boardwalk."

"What? Oh, mint chocolate chip would be great," Charlie said.

Don jogged across the sand while Charlie and Sallyanne followed more slowly.

"My papa's really nice, isn't he?" Sallyanne said happily.

"I think so," Charlie answered. *I hope so.*

THE TELEPHONE RANG, and Charlie handed Sallyanne the napkins and silverware to finish setting the dinner table for three.

"Jack! How did all your meetings go?" she said, delighted he had called.

"Fine. I've sold Sahara-Mars."

"Before the auction? I didn't know you could do that."

"I had an escape clause in my auction contract, if I sold it to a research institution."

"That's where you really wanted it to be! So Peter Burke finally found the money?"

"Yes."

Charlie could hear a smile in his voice. "You made him

miserable before you sold it to him, didn't you?" she guessed.

"Payback's a bitch."

"If I hadn't seen his behavior at your lecture, I'd feel sorry for the man."

"Save your sympathy. I just got off the phone with Curt Vandermade."

Charlie whistled. "I'll bet he hates to lose."

"It was ugly." Jack hesitated. "Do you want to break the story on this?"

Now it was Charlie's turn to hesitate. *What an offer!* Jack's attitude about her profession seemed to have taken a turn for the better. On the other hand, the direction of Sallyanne's life hung in the balance. "I'd love to but I couldn't do it justice right now." She lowered her voice, "Don's here for dinner. I could recommend the second-best person for the job."

"I guess I'll have to settle then."

Charlie gave him a name and telephone number before she added, "Thank you so much for asking me. I'm sorry I can't do it for you."

"Sallyanne comes first. A child should always come first. Good night."

Charlie put down the telephone. He hadn't said a word about last night. She tried to console herself with the fact he had offered her a story. He had even approved of her refusal to take it.

Maybe that was better than sex?

The evening passed pleasantly enough. Before he left, Don asked if he could come by in the morning after his daughter went to school to "discuss her future." Charlie agreed, and they set a meeting for nine o'clock. She suggested including Rhonda but Don demurred, saying, "You know her the best of anyone here. I want to talk to you."

The next morning, he arrived promptly at nine with a box of Dunkin' Donuts.

"I've always been partial to the cinnamon," he commented as Charlie arranged them on a plate. "Sallyanne likes Boston Crème so I bought a bunch of those too."

"I love the marble frosted ones," Charlie said, leading the way into the living room. Major was right on her heels.

"Can I give the dog a bit?" Don asked as he sat down and reached for his favorite.

Charlie wanted to be friendly so she nodded.

Don broke off a piece of cinnamon doughnut and held it out. Normally, Major would have swallowed it whole in three seconds flat. Instead, he lowered his head and stared at Don.

"Go on, Major," Charlie said, giving him a nudge with her knee.

The dog looked up at her before stalking over to take the proffered treat. He immediately returned to Charlie's side.

"Sorry, he's still learning his manners," Charlie said, thinking back to what Isabelle had said. *Major really does not like Don.* "Would you like some coffee?"

Don took the mug and cleared his throat. "Ma'am, you've taken real good care of my little girl, and she's crazy about you. I feel terrible taking her away."

"I appreciate that, but I knew her stay was only temporary." Charlie gripped her mug tightly. "As much as I've come to love her, I want her to be with her family."

"Family's important; but I can't give her all this. I don't live where she can go to the beach. I don't have a house with a room she can have all to herself. She'd be living with her grandma most of the time because I've got to work."

"It may not be ideal, but I'm sure she'll love her grandmother too," Charlie said, even as she wondered where this conversation was leading.

"What I'm saying is," and now Don leaned forward, resting his elbows on his knees, "I love my little girl more than life itself. I love her so much I'm willing to give her up to you so she can have a better life."

"Oh." Charlie felt both relieved and terribly sad. Don had confirmed everyone's mistrust of him as a genuinely interested parent, but that left Sallyanne without a father. "Having Sallyanne live with me is only temporary," she repeated. "Rhonda brought her here because it was an emergency." She didn't add that she wasn't even a real foster parent.

For a moment, Don looked nonplused. Then he smiled.

"I can see how much Sallyanne means to you. I know you'd like to adopt her."

Would you keep her if you could? Mike had asked. *Of course*, she had said. And suddenly, she had no doubts. Even if it meant she could never adopt a baby from China, she wanted to hold onto Sallyanne with a fierceness that shook her to her core.

"I will need to cover my expenses for coming up here." Don's voice interrupted her thoughts. "And there will be some legal costs. And it must be worth something for a father to give up his daughter."

"Yes?" *Could he really be suggesting she pay him to keep his child?*

"I figure $50,000 would be fair."

"I see." She tried to keep her shock from showing. As appalling as his offer was, she wondered if she should clean out her savings account and pay him. It might be the easiest way to get him out of Sallyanne's life. Instead, she stalled. "I'll have to think about it. It's a lot of money."

"Not compared to that Mars rock your husband's got,"

Don snorted. "You can't put a price on a child; what I'm asking is just help me get started someplace new where I won't be reminded of my loss."

What you're asking is to be bought off. Maybe we could use this to our advantage in a custody battle? She needed to consult with Rhonda and Mike.

"I understand, but I've got to talk with my husband," she said.

Don's face flushed crimson as he muttered something unflattering about Jack. He stood up. "Don't talk too long, or I may change my mind."

"No, I won't. Thanks for the doughnuts." Charlie wanted him out of her house before she said something to antagonize him. The man was beneath contempt.

He stopped on the porch and turned to level a finger at her. "I'll be back after school to spend some more time with *my* daughter. Maybe I'll take her back to the motel with me. She might like to spend the night with her papa."

That was a threat, and Charlie didn't respond well to threats. "I'm going to keep this polite for Sallyanne's sake," she said in a deceptively calm voice. "She stays here until her social worker says otherwise."

"I'm her father. I have rights, and if you make trouble for me, my expenses will go up." He put his face too close to hers. "I know you don't want my little girl to think her papa doesn't love her so you're not going to say a word about any of this to her. Are you, pretty lady?" Then be grabbed her chin and pushed her head from side to side in a travesty of agreement before she could jerk out of his grip. He laughed and turned away to walk down the steps, squaring his shoulders as though he had won a fight.

Charlie watched him get into his rented car.

Don McGraw wouldn't know what hit him by the time she was through.

CHAPTER 21

CHARLIE'S FIRST IMPULSE was to call Jack but she quashed it as selfish; he had enough on his mind, and this wasn't his battle anyway. He did a good job of playing father, but dealing with the girl's real father was her own responsibility.

The fury Don McGraw had evoked was so intense her hands shook.

She dialed Isabelle, then Rhonda, then Mike and called a council of war.

An hour later, everyone was seated in her living room, listening intently to her description of Don's offer. "The worst part is, I actually considered accepting it," Charlie finished. "I've gotten as sleazy as he is."

"Honey, you're not even close," Rhonda said. "But I don't think I can do much with the family court judge. Right now, it's your word against his."

"You don't want to take this to court," Mike said. "The girl would get dragged into it, and we don't want her to be made any more miserable. Rhonda, I think you and I can get creative and handle this ourselves."

Mike explained his plan. "McGraw's a petty criminal, and he thinks he's smart. But I don't think he's a match for an overpaid New York lawyer and a tough-talking New Jersey social worker." Mike raised his brows and looked at Rhonda; she gave a single nod of agreement. He continued, "I'll borrow the conference room at Haywood and Mayer in Spring Lake. Rhonda, you're going to wear your most intimidating ensemble and bring a bulging briefcase. I'll drag out one of my power suits."

"What about me?" Charlie asked.

"You won't be within ten miles of the place." When Charlie opened her mouth to protest, he held up his hand to stop her. "If Don calls you before I call him, tell him to talk to your lawyer and give him my number." Mike turned back to Rhonda. "I don't know a damned thing about family law, so you'll give me a crash course in the jargon. And we'll need every form necessary for Don McGraw to sign over his rights to Sallyanne, so no court in the United States would hand her back to him."

"Forms I've got," Rhonda said.

"We'll set up the meeting for tomorrow. I don't want this character hanging around any longer than is absolutely necessary."

"For a lawyer, you're okay, Mike," Rhonda said, rising majestically and handing him her business card. "Let me know what time, and I'll be there."

After ushering her to the door, Charlie came back and said, "Why can't I be there?"

"Because we may have to use tactics that aren't strictly legal, and you have to be able to deny all knowledge of them," Mike said with a grin and a crack of his knuckles. "And you might be shocked by some of my language."

"What about this afternoon?" Isabelle cut in. "Sallyanne will expect her father to be here. Surely you don't want him in the house after—"

"We'll go bowling," Charlie said, decisively. "It's public, and we won't really have to talk to him. We can even eat at that new bowling alley. Will you come too, Isabelle?"

"I haven't been bowling in years—"

"Please?"

"I was going to say, 'so I could use some brushing up,'" Isabelle continued.

SALLYANNE LOVED BOWLING, and never noticed Charlie and Isabelle kept their distance from her father. Don easily beat all of them, which put him in an affable mood so he carried the conversation at dinner. As they walked down the hall to leave, Charlie exchanged a congratulatory smile with Isabelle.

Just then, she felt a grip like a vise on her wrist, and she was jerked to a stop.

"You two go on," Don said to Isabelle and Sallyanne. "I need to talk with Charlie for a minute."

Charlie nodded to Isabelle. There were plenty of people within yelling distance.

Don kept his hold on her as he waited for his daughter to go out the door. Then he shoved Charlie against the wall. "What does your lawyer want with me?" he demanded, squeezing her wrist harder.

"Please let go of me," Charlie said calmly.

"You tell me what that bloodsucker wants, and I'll let you go."

"Mr. McGraw, there are a lot of people around. If you don't let go of me, I will scream."

He stayed where he was for a long moment, increasing the pressure on her wrist until she could feel the bones grind together. Then he let go and took one step back.

Charlie pointedly massaged her wrist before saying, "My lawyer has advised me not to discuss the matter with you."

Don flushed scarlet and stepped into her again. "I don't like lawyers," he hissed. "And I may just change my mind if you don't watch it."

"I'll take that chance," Charlie said, sliding away from him. "Don't come in my home when we get back. Tell Sallyanne you're expecting a phone call, then leave."

"Watch yourself," he said, and stalked out the exit.

Much to her relief, Don followed her instructions, but her heart almost broke at the disappointment on Sallyanne's face as her father drove away. The telephone rang shortly after they got into the house.

"Charlie, it's Jack."

"It is *so* good to hear your voice."

"Sugar, you sound like you had a *really* bad day. What's going on?"

Charlie whacked herself on the forehead at her slip. "Nothing at all. I just missed you." *Weak, very weak, even if it was true.*

Luckily, he bought it. "Any particular parts of me you missed especially?" he drawled.

So now he wanted to flirt. "No, just a general sense I hadn't had my daily dose of smug, self-satisfied male."

"Oh, I'm feeling very self-satisfied," he said with a low chuckle. "For all kinds of reasons. Really, sugar, how many men have made love on a 34-ton iron? It's a meteorite hunter's greatest fantasy."

"Actually, we did it on a display shelf between two much smaller meteorites." She wasn't going to give in to his telephone seduction. "Tell me another reason you're feeling self-satisfied," she said, trying to ignore the heat his words were stoking deep in her gut.

"All right," he said. "I signed the contract selling Sahara-Mars to the scientists."

"Can you retire now?"

"If I cut back on caviar."

"That's wonderful!" she said, smiling. "Any progress on the Mauritania issue?"

"Your buddy has gotten the right people together. Believe it or not, Burke has put some pressure on too; he's working the angle that Mauritania doesn't have the scientific expertise to analyze the meteorite properly."

"I'm glad he's on your side now. He's a tough opponent, a lot like you."

"Miguel just arrived," Jack said. "I'll talk to you tomorrow. Give Sallyanne a big kiss for me. And sugar, this is what I want to give you."

Before he hung up, he whispered two sentences that made Charlie's cheeks burn scarlet.

THE FOLLOWING MORNING, on her way home from school drop-off duty, Charlie's cell phone rang. She punched the "hands-free talk" button and said hello.

"They've stolen Sahara-Mars."

"Jack?"

"The bastards stole Sahara-Mars. Right out of the goddamn Museum of Natural History."

"*Who* stole it?" Charlie swung the car into an empty parking place and killed the engine.

"According to the letter, an extremist faction from Mauritania."

"Oh no! Have you talked to the police?"

"The police. The F.B.I. The C.I.A. And the State Department. I'm about to go over and watch the museum's videotapes. Museum security says the thieves bypassed the alarm system and knocked out the guards with some kind of gas."

"That sounds too professional for a political faction from Mauritania. They aren't usually that organized."

"They knew enough to take it in the case. So hopefully, the meteorite will still be intact."

"What can I do to help?" she asked. "I could try and call—"

"There's nothing you can do, sugar." He took a deep breath and exhaled slowly. "Nothing at all. I'll call you later."

Charlie was surprised when she pulled into her driveway fifteen minutes later; she had no recollection of driving there. She rested her forehead against the steering wheel and continued to rack her brain for a way to help Jack. She knew a few people in the New York City Police Department, but they were mostly street cops . . . *a case this high profile will get plenty of attention from the police anyway.* Jack had said the F.B.I. and C.I.A. were involved already. *I could do some research on Mauritanian politics* . . . but Dyson Foley would know more than she would.

She banged her head once on the steering wheel. "Ow! I hate this. I can't do anything for Jack. I can't meet with Don McGraw. What *can* I do?"

Opening the car door, she sniffed the fresh spring air.

"Go for a run with Major. That's what I can do."

Soon she and the Kuvasz were speeding across the

sand, scattering seagulls like confetti. As Charlie settled into her rhythm, she forgot the dog, the seagulls and the ocean.

If the meeting with Don went according to plan, she would be a mother much sooner than she had anticipated. Rhonda would never take Sallyanne away from her now, hazardous profession or no. Of course, she probably wouldn't be able to adopt from China. Usually if an adoptive parent already had a child that disqualified them. She searched her heart for any lingering regrets about not having a baby to cradle in her arms and found none. Sallyanne was a real person with a real need. The baby was only a dream.

Now she had to get serious about finding another source of income. *The Average Adventurer* had two articles completed, one in draft form, and three sets of notes she'd written on expeditions taken in the last three months. Maybe Jack would consider that book now that he knew her better. . . .

Jack. Somewhere in the back of her mind had lived a little hope that with time and some really great sex, she might persuade him their marriage could become real. He was wonderful with Sallyanne, but a child represented everything he claimed not to want, home, hearth, family.

He'd run the other direction now.

She stumbled as a physical pain lanced through her chest.

How stupid am I? First Nick, now Jack. " 'Love is a universal migraine . . . blotting out reason,' " she gasped as she hit her stride again. "I can't remember where I read that but it's accurate."

Major barreled into her as he raced the surf up the beach.

"Watch it, boy!" she said, staggering. She stopped and

gave his damp head a rub. "I guess I'm adopting you and Twinkle too. Since Jack won't be staying, I need to keep the rest of the family unit together."

That decision made, she started to run again, imagining her new life with Sallyanne. *It will be fun to decorate her room with her . . . and take her to the library to pick out books.* Summer was coming so they could build sand castles on the beach, play with Major, eat ice cream on the boardwalk. . . .

She jumped three feet as her cell phone vibrated on the waistband of her shorts.

"Hello?" she panted.

"Charlie, it's Mike. Don signed the papers. It took a little persuading, but he's leaving for Tennessee tomorrow."

"That's great," Charlie said, bending over to relieve the sudden cramp in her side. "How did it go?"

"He didn't like being railroaded. He was quite angry— wait a minute."

Charlie heard Rhonda's voice in the background.

"Rhonda says she's going straight to the school to meet with the principal and explain some of the situation. She'll make sure they know only two people are authorized to see or pick up Sallyanne: you and herself."

"Does she think Don would try to take her?"

"Most kidnappings are by family members," Mike answered. "We've got to be careful. And Charlie, it's not going to be easy, but you have to decide what to tell her about her father."

"I know," she said, the tightness in her chest now having nothing to do with her exertions. "Does Rhonda have any suggestions?"

"She'll come by to talk with you about it after she stops by the school. Good luck. And congratulations on becoming a mother!"

"Thanks." She hit the "disconnect" button. "I'm a mother!" she said to Major. "I'm a *mother!* Not exactly the way I planned, but I have a child."

An elderly couple strolling hand-in-hand on the beach smiled quizzically at the tall young woman dancing a jig at the edge of the surf as a huge white dog capered around her, barking excitedly.

CHAPTER 22

CHARLIE STARED OUT at the channel through the kitchen window as she framed and reframed her discussion with Sallyanne. She heaved an enormously relieved sigh when Rhonda finally arrived.

"You've got yourself a daughter now," Rhonda said without preamble as she stepped inside the door. "Are you sure you and Jack are ready for this?"

"What do *you* think?"

"I think if you aren't, it's too bad because that little girl needs you." Then she enveloped Charlie in a bear hug that smelled of tropical flowers. "This story has a happy ending. I can feel it in my bones."

"If I can get past this afternoon, I'll agree with you," Charlie said against the woman's shoulder as she hugged her back.

Rhonda stepped out of their embrace. "Is Jack going to be here when Sallyanne gets home?"

"I'm afraid not," Charlie said. "He's got a major problem on his hands right now. Sahara-Mars has been stolen. He found out this morning."

"When trouble comes, it always comes in threes," Rhonda commented. "Let's talk. There isn't much time till school lets out, and you'll be handling a tough conversation alone."

She gestured to the couch, and Charlie nodded. They both sat, and Rhonda continued, "The best policy is to tell the truth. Up to a point. Don't mention the money, but *do* tell her that her Papa just wasn't prepared to be a father. When Jack comes home, have him tell her that he *is*. Don't try to sugarcoat it too much. Sallyanne's too smart."

"I know. I'm so afraid of what she'll ask me."

"She'll only ask what she's ready to handle. She's smart enough for that too." Rhonda took an appreciative look around the room. "You know, I'm going to miss your place when this case is closed."

"You'll be coming back, won't you?"

"As little as possible, and only officially. I don't want to disrupt the relationship you're building with the child."

"I'm really touched by your trust, but I *want* you to come and see her . . . and me!"

"I can't be spending extra time on a child whose future is secure. There are too many others who still need my help," Rhonda said sternly. "But I'll do my best to work you in occasionally."

Charlie felt tears gathering.

"We have two other issues to deal with, young lady," Rhonda said, pretending not to notice Charlie's wet eyes. "And don't think you can get me to ignore either one. The first is your Chinese adoption. Do you and Jack still want to go through with that?"

"Will we be able to? Isn't it difficult if you already have a child?"

"I can't guarantee anything but I believe a strong argument can be made for extenuating circumstances."

"Oh, that would be wonderful. Thank you!" Charlie breathed, then hesitated, "but we'd want to talk to Sallyanne about it first."

Rhonda nodded. "Good idea. Now what about your traveling? Can you cut back on that sooner rather than later?"

"I talked with my agent. She's going to shop a few ideas I came up with. And I'm looking for a good topic for a book. Until that comes through, I've got several more *Average Adventurer* articles ready to go. I figure I can start up the column again when Sallyanne's old enough to go rock-climbing with me."

Rhonda started to sputter but caught the teasing glint in Charlie's eye. The telephone rang and Charlie checked the caller ID. "It's Sallyanne's school," she said, snatching the handset out of the cradle. She listened for a few minutes, asked a couple of questions, and hung up.

"That was the principal, Mrs. Falcone. Don came to the school to say good-bye just a few minutes ago," she told Rhonda. "Mrs. Falcone explained she couldn't allow it, and he went ballistic. It took two gym teachers, a custodian and the assistant principal to get him off school grounds."

Rhonda pulled her cell phone out of her briefcase and scrolled through her speed dial numbers. "I'm going to make sure the police put a patrol car outside your house until that man is back in Tennessee."

Charlie bit her lip. "Shouldn't he be allowed to say good-bye?"

"Honey, I deal with this kind of thing all the time. It's nasty, and you can't get sentimental about it." Rhonda stopped as someone answered her call. After she made the arrangements, she put the phone away. "You watch your-

self. Don's angry and that makes him dangerous and un-
predictable."

"I know, but it's going to hurt her if he leaves without—"

"She has you and Jack now. You'll make things right."

After Rhonda left, Charlie made a quick survey of the
cul-de-sac before she went out to her car. She wished she
were as confident as Rhonda that she would say the right
things.

"WHEN IS PAPA coming by?" Sallyanne asked as she fastened her seatbelt. "I got a hundred on my math test, and I
want to show it to him."

"Mmmm, we have to talk about that when we get
home," Charlie said as she made sure all the car doors
were locked. "That's great about your math test!"

There was silence from the back seat.

"Did you get any other tests back today?" Charlie prodded.

"He's not coming, is he?" a small voice asked.

Charlie sighed and swung the car into a parking space
by the boardwalk.

"Let's take a walk, sweetheart," she said.

Sallyanne's face was a mask of indifference over a
world of hurt. When Charlie put her arm around the girl's
shoulders, she could feel her rigidity. She walked her over
to a bench that looked out toward the ocean, and sat her
down. Charlie perched sideways, but the little girl stared
straight out to sea.

"Your Papa loves you," Charlie started. "He just realized he can't make a home for you. He travels a lot for his
job, and he doesn't have a wife to help take care of you."

A tear flowed down the child's cheek. "People shouldn't *say* they love you when they *don't*."

"He *does* love you. He came all the way from Tennessee just to see you and to make sure you were safe and happy. He believes you'll be happier here than with him. Real love sometimes means giving up what you love."

"He shouldn't have come."

"He needed to come. He needed to see you."

Charlie decided to turn the conversation in a different direction. "Would you like to stay with me and be my daughter? I think we get along well, and I've always wanted to adopt a little girl. You don't have to decide right this minute. Take your time and think about it."

Sallyanne swallowed hard and nodded. "Yes, ma'am, I'd like that a lot."

"Oh, thank goodness!" Charlie said, sweeping the girl up in her arms and onto her lap, tears of sheer relief spilling down her own cheeks.

"What should I call you?"

"Sweetheart, you can call me whatever you want." Charlie hugged Sallyanne, then held her away so she could see her face. "I can't take the place of your mama; her name will always be special. You can keep calling me Charlie."

The girl shook her head.

Charlie tried to think of something else. "Why don't you call me Ma'am?"

"But you always tell me not to."

"Truthfully, I've gotten to like it when *you* say it. You have such a pretty accent."

"Really?" Sallyanne said, looking at Charlie dubiously.

Charlie nodded. When Sallyanne kept on studying her, she added, "Ma'am has the same letters as 'mama,' just in a different order."

Sallyanne's face lit up. "And you're my mama in a different order."

Charlie's heart leapt, then sank fast as Sallyanne's face crumpled. "I'm not going to call Jack Papa because I don't like that name anymore," she whispered. "I'll call him Daddy."

Charlie winced. What a tangled web she had woven.

Just then, Sallyanne put her head down on Charlie's shoulder and sobbed out her sorrow at losing two parents. Charlie forgot about Jack and wept with her. She'd give anything to take away such suffering. All she could do was resolve to bring enough joy to the little girl's future to throw a softening haze over her memories of loss.

When Sallyanne finally lay limp and silent against her shoulder, Charlie picked her up and carried her to the car, carefully fastening the seatbelt across her lap.

"Let's go home," she said, brushing back the hair clinging to the girl's wet cheeks. "To *our* home."

SALLYANNE INSISTED ON doing her homework, even though Charlie said she'd write a note to the teacher if she didn't want to. She asked to go to bed early, and went upstairs to put on her pajamas and brush her teeth. Charlie followed her upstairs a few minutes later, and discovered a large object wrapped in a garbage bag sitting at the top of the stairs. She touched it and realized it was the stuffed pink bunny.

Sallyanne came out of the bathroom and saw Charlie looking at it. "I don't want it."

"Don't worry, I'll take care of it," Charlie said, taking her hand and leading her into her room.

The child knelt beside her bed and asked God to bless her new ma'am and daddy, Major, Twinkle, Isabelle,

Rhonda, Mrs. Gencarelli from the apartment building, her cousins and grandmother in Tennessee, and her mama in heaven. Blessings for Papa were conspicuously absent. Well, Charlie didn't blame her for the omission. And they could talk about forgiveness when Don's desertion was farther in the past. She tucked her new daughter into bed, and kissed her good night, hoping the child was so exhausted she wouldn't lie awake wondering why her own father didn't want her.

She went downstairs and poured herself a glass of white wine to take out to the porch. She needed some quiet time to figure out how to deal with the suddenly complicated issue of Sallyanne and Jack.

The moment she closed the refrigerator door, the telephone rang.

"Charlie, it's Jack. I want to bring the security videotapes from the museum down there for you to look at. There's something nagging at me about them, and I can't put my finger on it. I'm hoping you can catch it."

"Anything I can do to help," Charlie said with a flutter of pride; he considered her powers of observation better than his.

"Good. I'm on the turnpike already."

"Um, Jack. I've . . . well, actually, *we've* adopted Sallyanne," Charlie said, deciding it was better to tell him part of the truth immediately. "Don's going back to Tennessee tomorrow."

"The hell he is! What kind of father inserts himself back into his daughter's life and then abandons her five days later?"

"A bad one. This is best for Sallyanne in the long run. I'm sorry to involve you in this, but you're going to have to sign a few papers for the adoption. Don't worry, it won't affect our divorce proceedings later."

There was a long silence. "Isn't it going to be hard when her second father walks out on her?" he finally said.

"Yes, but by then she'll be settled with me and secure that I won't leave her," Charlie said, knocking on the wooden kitchen table for luck.

"I'll see you in an hour," he said and disconnected.

Guilt at forcing Jack to walk in and out of Sallyanne's life swamped her. She remembered all too vividly coming back to whatever bedroom had been hers temporarily only to find her suitcases neatly packed. Her foster mother of the moment—the women always got the job—would more or less gently break the news that she was being sent somewhere else. *Somewhere nicer, of course.* The desolation and the sense of failure—if only she'd been better they would have kept her—were so piercing that she often couldn't even cry. Charlie pushed away the terrible memories.

Jack's absence couldn't be helped, but Sallyanne would never have any reason to doubt that Charlie loved her. Never.

She prepped the coffee maker before she escaped out to the porch. She sat in the rocker, soothed by the gentle brush of the night breeze against her cheeks and bare arms. She was still rocking when she saw headlights sweep around the cul-de-sac. She got up and walked around to the front of the house as the engine's growl died into silence, and a car door opened and slammed.

The glow of the car's interior light glinted on Jack's hair as he reached into the backseat of the Land Rover to pull out a white bag and a briefcase. When he closed the back door, he looked up and saw Charlie.

"Sugar, you are a sight for sore eyes," he said, a slow smile pulling the corners of his mouth upward.

In three strides, he was there with his arms wrapped

around her. She slid her arms around his waist and leaned close against him. She could hear the uneven rasp of the breath in his chest and feel the strong pulse of his heart against her cheek just beneath the soft, skin-warmed cotton of his shirt. With each breath she drew in the faint scent of an exotic soap, the detergent used to wash his shirt and the warm, distinct smell of the man whom she wanted with all her heart and soul. Just as she was about to say something she'd surely regret, he sighed and loosened his grip.

"Was I suffocating you?" he asked ruefully.

"I was breathing by osmosis," she joked, not wanting him to let go.

He did anyway, shifting his hands upward to cradle her face as he kissed her forehead. "Sorry. You just looked . . . welcoming . . . standing there in the moonlight." He stepped back, bending to pick up the neglected briefcase and bag.

"I was sitting on the back porch," Charlie said, leading him back around the house. "Would you like coffee, wine or something stronger?"

"Coffee," he said. "Thanks."

"Sit down, and I'll bring it out."

"Sounds good to me."

When she returned, he was leaning back in the rocker with his legs stretched out in front of him, his eyes closed and his arms relaxed on the wooden armrests. He shifted upright as soon as she set the coffee tray down on the table.

"Any progress?" she asked, putting a mug in his hand.

"None whatsoever. I'm hoping you can shake something loose from these tapes."

Again she felt that flush of gratification. Jack Lanett did not accept help easily. Yet here he was asking her for it. "Let's look at them."

He shook his head. "First, tell me what happened with Don McGraw."

"That's kind of long and involved. What it boils down to is he gave up all rights to custody."

"Does the police car parked in the cul-de-sac have anything to do with this long and involved story?"

Charlie sighed. "You noticed."

"Yeah, sugar, I noticed. Care to elaborate?"

She elaborated, telling him about everything except the confrontation at the bowling alley.

"You didn't think I might want to know McGraw was trying to blackmail you?"

"It wasn't your problem," Charlie said. "I didn't want to bother you with it. You have enough on your plate right now."

"And is Sahara-Mars *your* problem?"

Charlie swallowed the rest of her wine in one gulp. "That's different," she muttered.

He exploded out of his chair. His blue eyes burned cold. "Different how? Different because I trust you and you *don't* trust me?"

He stood very still for a long moment before he said, "You're right not to trust me. You know why? Because I'm the son of a drunk and a wife-beater. My father beat my mother every time he had a few. And I'm likely to do the same to you. That's what children of abusers do."

"That's ridiculous," she protested. "I've never seen you drunk! And I'm certainly not afraid you'll hit me. In fact, I've never seen you drink alcohol at all except for some champagne at the party for Sahara-Mars."

"That was tonic water," he said. "And you have no idea what I'm capable of."

"As a matter of fact, I know a great many things you're capable of, but I have no intention of pandering to your ego by telling you what they are." She was trying to ease some of the tension that vibrated almost tangibly around him. She stood up. "Nor do I believe the children of alcoholics or wife-abusers are doomed to follow in their parents' footsteps. You're way beyond that."

"That's truer than you know." And suddenly the cold, bleak depths of space were back in his voice. He stepped off the edge of the porch and turned his face to the sky as though looking for something.

Charlie followed him and his gaze but saw only the usual moon and stars. She looked back at him, longing to reach out, to prove his unexpected revelation changed nothing for her. Her hand was halfway across the space between them when she dropped it to her side. Something about his stance repelled contact; he wouldn't be receptive to her touch. "I don't care what crimes your father committed," she said quietly. "I care about you."

"What about the crimes *I've* committed? You might care about those." He lowered his head to look at her.

She shook her head. "Whatever they were, they're in your past. I trust the man you are now."

"Evidently not enough." He walked back onto the porch and retrieved his briefcase. "Where's your VCR?"

JACK SLAMMED THE first videotape into the player with the resentment of a man acting against his will. Charlie tried to focus on the shifting scenes of the interior of the Museum of Natural History even as she racked her brain for the words that could make it across the suddenly vast gulf between them.

Mostly the tapes showed empty corridors and exhibit halls with the occasional guard strolling through them. A couple of cryptic phrases regarding codes and arming scrolled across the bottom of one screen.

"That's when the thieves disarmed the system. They knew the code." Jack spoke suddenly, making her jump.

As the second tape neared its end, a group of six men dressed in black from head to toe came around a corner into full view of the camera. They walked briskly but without haste; clearly they knew where they were going and weren't concerned about anyone stopping them.

"The guard monitoring these screens was knocked out by nerve gas. They didn't care about the camera, the bastards," Jack commented.

The tape ended, and Jack stalked to the television set to feed in the third. It picked up the men as they entered the Rose Center and made their way toward the Hall of Planet Earth where the Mars rock hung suspended in its protective case. "Now they disarm the extra security system we put in place around Sahara-Mars. I hope whoever sold them that information made them pay through the nose." Jack's fury sizzled in his voice.

Charlie watched the figure at the head of the group lift a hidden panel in the wall, then tap a long sequence on the keypad. She was so focused on his actions she almost forgot to watch his companions.

But an odd movement caught her eye.

Four of the group stood scanning the huge exhibit space under the sphere of the planetarium. A fifth man positioned himself behind the typist, either coaching or checking up on him. Absorbed in his observations, he absently raised his left hand toward his ear. When his curved index finger encountered the fabric of his mask, he turned his head toward his raised hand as though surprised to see it. He made a self-conscious adjustment to his headgear, then shoved his hand into his trouser pocket.

"Wait. Rewind that," Charlie said urgently.

Jack looked at her questioningly and pointed the remote at the VCR. "Is this far enough?"

Charlie nodded and watched the men walk into the Rose Center and disarm the special security system again. "Once more."

As the man reached for his ear the third time around, Charlie said, "That tall man behind the guy disarming the system. I think that's Dr. Hollinger, Vandermade's expert."

"Why?" Jack said, sitting forward.

"Back it up again. You see how he raises his hand toward his ear almost as though he intends to scratch it? Hollinger has this odd mannerism where he hooks his index finger in his ear and pulls down on it. He did it twice at the party. And that's what the tall guy seems about to do."

"I *knew* I'd seen that gesture before. I couldn't come up with when or where." Jack replayed the scene twice. "You're right! Vandermade's definitely involved. This won't stand up in court, but it doesn't have to," he added.

"What does that mean?" Charlie asked, made uneasy by his tone of voice.

"Nothing you need to worry about."

Clicking off the television, he rose and hit the VCR's eject button. For a few moments, he stood idly turning the black plastic cartridge in his hands. Then he slapped it against his palm sharply as if to punctuate a decision.

"Jack . . ." Charlie began, pushing herself up off the couch and hoping she would say the right thing. "I—"

"I have to get this back to New York." He cut her off. "Thanks for your help."

"Don't walk out," she said, stretching a hand out to him.

He stood like stone beyond her reach. "I've got things to do. This is *my* problem."

Better not to remind him she had just given him the tool to solve it. "Jack," she tried again. "I just—"

He was loading the tapes back into his briefcase. "Another time," he said without looking at her. "By the way, that white bag out on the porch is for Sallyanne. I was going to give it to her in the morning, but you can do it for me."

"Stay," she said, as the wonderful, excruciating realization hit that he had *planned* to.

He looked at her for a long minute. "Give her a big hug for me."

He pulled open the French doors and was gone.

Charlie slowly sank back down onto the sofa cushions, listening as the roar of the Land Rover's engine receded into the night. He had finally told her something about himself because she had hurt him. He *wasn't* grateful not to have another problem dumped in his lap, especially a problem with "baggage."

He was *hurt.* How could that be?

She went out on the porch to retrieve the abandoned bag. The white plastic was emblazoned with the multi-colored Toys "R" Us logo. It rustled loudly as she pulled out a large, light box. "Gone with the Wind Barbie" flowed across the clear plastic front in elegant script. Behind it stood a doll dressed in an exquisitely detailed antebellum ball gown, with tiny pearl jewelry at her ears, neck and wrists. Static electricity glued the receipt to the box. Charlie peeled it away and read the location and time of purchase. His own dream was in jeopardy, but Jack had stopped on the turnpike tonight on his way from New York City to buy the perfect doll for a little girl.

She hugged the box to her chest and sobbed.

CHAPTER 23

1:23 A.M. CHARLIE kicked the covers off and hurled herself out of bed. She obviously wasn't going to get any sleep so she might as well get some work done. She visited the kitchen and poured a glass of white wine before she stalked into her office and flipped on the computer. As she waited for it to boot up, she noticed the wine glowed weirdly blue in the light of the computer screen, reminding her uncannily of Jack's eyes.

Shoving the keyboard aside, she put her elbows on the desk and stared at the icons marching up and down the monitor. What could she say to Jack to undo the damage she had done? *Nothing.* Nothing she could say would convince a man who didn't want to be convinced.

She had to *do* something to prove she trusted him completely.

"I can't throw myself off a cliff and hope he'll catch me, Major," she said as the big dog pushed his head onto her lap. "I'm a writer, I need to come up with a metaphor. What shows trust?"

She sipped the wine thoughtfully.

"Vulnerability. What shows vulnerability to a man who thinks he's capable of physical abuse?"

She took a swig of Chardonnay.

"Helplessness. I have to make myself deliberately vulnerable and helpless. Ugh."

Putting down the wineglass, she stroked Major's white fur absently as she considered the best way to demonstrate *vulnerable* and *helpless*. When something Jack said long ago triggered a wild idea, she groaned and shook her head. "I can't do that. It's about as vulnerable and helpless as a woman can be, but I can't do it." She cradled Major's head in her hands and looked into his eyes. He licked her hand.

"I really love this man. So I have to do it."

She rested her face against the dog's warm head.

"This is going to be really humiliating if it doesn't work."

SALLYANNE ATE HER breakfast kashi as usual. She wasn't silent but she was subdued. True to her word, Charlie had removed the stuffed rabbit although she had not thrown it away. It was well-wrapped and stashed as far under the eaves as she could shove it; someday Sallyanne might want the only evidence she had of her biological father.

"Anytime you want to talk about your father, I'm here to listen."

"Yes, ma'am."

"Want to help me wrap the birthday present for Christina?" Charlie asked.

"No, thank you, ma'am. I'd like to take Major outside for awhile."

Sallyanne had been invited to a classmate's sleepover party later that day. Rhonda had recommended that she go, saying that pizza and friends would distract the child from her troubles. Charlie watched through the kitchen window as Sallyanne played tag with Major. Taking a deep breath, she dialed Miguel's number.

"Charlie, *mi amor*, you are a genius. We all knew there was something we were missing on that videotape."

"The man annoyed me so I guess I was watching him," Charlie said. "I have a favor to ask you."

"I am entirely at your service."

"Jack is a little upset with me. I didn't keep him informed about a situation here . . . with the best of intentions, but it was the wrong thing to do. I need to get into his apartment to talk with him privately tonight. Could you help me arrange that?"

"I wondered why the mention of your name made him go ice-eyed."

"So you've noticed he does that too?"

"I've known him a very long time. But Charlie, he is not a man who listens well when his mind is already made up. I'm not sure that *talking* to him will solve this 'upset.'"

"Well, I may do a bit more than just talk," Charlie admitted. "So I need privacy."

Miguel chuckled. "You are an intelligent woman. But we're going to see Dr. Hollinger this afternoon. Jack may not be in the best of moods when he gets home. Maybe you could delay your 'talk' a few days."

"I can't. I only have tonight free." *And I might lose my nerve if I don't do this now.*

"All right, tonight it is. I will make sure Jack comes back to his apartment alone."

Charlie wrote down all the codes and instructions for entering the mini-fortress that was Jack's apartment.

After she read them back, Miguel said, "You are a good thing for Jack. *Buena suerte.*"

"Thank you for saying that. I need all the encouragement I can get."

"THE MAN IS seriously paranoid," Charlie muttered as she entered yet another string of numbers on yet another keypad. The door to Jack's apartment swung open without any sirens blaring, and she heaved a sigh of relief.

She couldn't resist walking over to the pallasite Jack had shown her at their second meeting and kicking on the display light. The embedded crystals threw their otherworldly glow over her fingertips as she traced their irregular shapes. Jack's long fingers had followed the same path. Her breathing quickened as she remembered him threading his hand through her hair and teasing her with his private collection of meteorites.

Stop avoiding the task at hand, Charlie told herself, even as she was grateful for the memories that made her plan seem slightly less insane. She turned off the light and squared her shoulders. Hefting the bag of silk neckties she had bought on her way to Jack's apartment, she ordered herself, "To the bedroom."

She walked down the long corridor, peering into the rooms opening off it, as she searched for Jack's sleeping quarters. Two bedrooms clearly had not been used recently. A third had a stack of towels neatly folded on the bed, ready for a guest. They were all furnished in the style of the living room, with chrome and steel chairs, black-lacquered chests and bedside tables. And low platform beds. *Damn.*

"Why couldn't the landlord be an antiques dealer with a specialty in Colonial furnishings?" she muttered, as she headed for the last door. "A four-poster bed would make me very happy right now."

"Whoa, this is even better!" she amended, as she walked into the master suite.

While the rest of the room sported the usual chrome and glass, the bed was straight out of the Arabian nights. The heavily carved headboard and footboard were inlaid with mother-of-pearl and semi-precious stones and draped with thickly tasseled silk cords. Jewel-toned silk pillows embroidered in intricate gold patterns glowed against the dark wood. A silk bedspread with the brilliance of stained-glass spilled across the wide mattress.

Charlie flipped up the hem of the bedspread to discover that the elaborate bed had been installed right over the built-in platform.

"So, Jack, this is *your* personal fantasy," she said, surveying the opulence with her hands on her hips. She laughed. "Now I'm going to take it just a little bit further."

She dropped the bag of ties on the bed and randomly pulled out a navy blue paisley. Threading it through a cutout in the footboard, she debated whether she needed to attach a second tie for length and decided that one would do. She tied the wider end to the wood and laid the narrower portion out diagonally toward the center of the mattress. After repeating the process three times, she took a deep breath and stood looking down at the empty center of the bed. Picking up the end of the bright blue tie extending from the right side of the headboard, she made several loops and laid it back down. The rest she left alone.

She checked her watch, squinting at the dial as she calculated how long it might take Jack and Miguel to confront the dishonest Dr. Hollinger.

"*Now.* I've got to do this *now*," she said loudly.

Dropping onto the edge of the bed, she yanked off her sandals, jerked her T-shirt over her head, unhooked her bra and dropped it on the growing pile of clothes on the floor.

"This is a metaphor. Nothing but a metaphor," she chanted as she unbuttoned and unzipped her shorts and pushed them and her panties down around her ankles in one swift motion. Stepping out of the last of her clothing, she bent down and scooped up the bundle, stuffing it in the canvas bag with the unused neckties.

Finally, she pulled the tortoise shell clip out of her ponytail and shook her hair down around her shoulders, partially covering her nudity. *Lady Godiva had the right idea,* she thought wryly.

Scooting into the center of the bed, Charlie put the sole of one bare foot beside the navy paisley necktie, and took another deep breath.

"Just tie the knot the way they showed you at Wilderness Survival," she encouraged herself. "Loop it around, down and through. Now loop it back up and through. Then pull here."

The silk tie tightened around her ankle.

She moved her right foot to the red paisley tie attached to the other side of the footboard and swiftly completed the same motions.

She sat a moment with her knees bent inward and her ankles splayed apart.

Ever so slowly she slid backward across the smooth silk of the bedspread, gasping slightly as she hit a rougher patch of heavy embroidery, but continuing so that gradually her knees were drawn down and apart and her legs were spread.

Charlie lay back and placed her left hand on the yellow and blue striped tie extending from the left side of the headboard. She easily finished the knot and pulled it tight.

Did she really want to do this?

She put her right hand in the still-loose loops of blue

silk. Once she pulled the end of the tie, she was here until Jack decided to turn her loose. Or not.

All the possible variations of how Jack might react pinwheeled in her brain. She wanted to provoke a strong response, and as she glanced briefly down at her bare thighs stretched across Jack's gorgeously colored bed, she was surer than ever that this would do it.

The real question was: *Did she love Jack enough to risk total humiliation?*

She closed her eyes and yanked on the tie.

TWENTY MINUTES PASSED. Charlie tried to relax into the soft slither of silk on her bare backside, but her breasts and stomach and the hollow between her legs felt all the more exposed by contrast. She attempted to move her knees closer together, but the ties were too short to allow more than a fraction of an inch of increased modesty. She tested the loops on her right wrist, and succeeded only in pulling them even tighter against the bones and tendons.

The folks at Wilderness Survival would be proud, she thought, then choked on a giggle. And a couple of the instructors would definitely enjoy seeing her in this position.

She tried to distract herself by examining the collection of exotic swords and daggers arrayed on the wall beside her. The grips were highly decorated and the scabbards gleamed with silver, gold and gemstones. She was admiring the jeweled snake coiling around one particularly ornate hilt when the alarm system emitted a soft beep, signaling that the correct code had been entered. Footsteps sounded loudly, then were muffled as someone walked across bare wood and soft carpet. *No voices.* Charlie silently blessed Miguel for that.

She squirmed against her bonds as she heard the footsteps echoing down the hall, suddenly wishing she hadn't been in such a hurry to pull that last knot tight. There was a moment of silence, and then the footsteps moved away.

Damn. She couldn't stand much more of this torture. Should she call out to him?

She heard the refrigerator *whoosh* closed, and the footsteps came swiftly down the hall again.

The door she had so carefully left ajar at just the same angle she had found it flew open, and Jack strode in. He was dressed in a black blazer, black shirt and black slacks. Putting a bottle of water down on the dresser, he shrugged out of his jacket and began to unstrap the shoulder holster concealed underneath. The sight of the gun made Charlie gasp.

Jack whipped around, his right hand reaching for the pistol as he bent his knees into a dangerous crouch.

For a long moment, he froze. Then his hand dropped, and he straightened.

"Well, well, well. What have we here?"

He sauntered over to the foot of the bed and let his eyes roam up and down Charlie's spread-eagled body.

"Hello, Jack."

He laughed.

"Hello, sugar."

As he came closer, Charlie could see the blaze of restrained exultation in his eyes, like a general who's just won one battle but faces another, more difficult one the next day.

"That's an interesting knot," he said, his long fingers toying with the loose end of the tie around her left ankle. "It seems securely tied."

Charlie cleared her throat. "Very. The average adventurer knows her knots."

He dropped the tie and trailed his fingertips up the inside of her calf to her knee as he took a step forward.

Charlie swallowed hard as he continued to move his touch upward along the exposed skin of her inner thigh. She shifted her gaze upward to his face and lost her ability to breathe. The blaze in his eyes had multiplied tenfold, and he was staring down at her body with a hunger that made her long to free her hands to cover herself.

She closed her eyes to block out the vision of naked desire, then wished she hadn't. All she was aware of now was the slow, inexorable progress of his hand toward the warm, dark throbbing between her legs.

As his fingers danced across the join between thigh and hip, she moaned softly.

Then his fingers were sliding down along the folds of her center, against the most exquisitely sensitive place on her body, and deep inside her.

She arched up from the bed like a bow, driving his fingers deeper. "Oh God, Jack!"

He slowly withdrew his fingers, only to slide them in once again. And again.

Her hips rocked upward and she groaned, "Yes, yes. Again."

As he left the inside of her body, he flicked the outer nub and laughed triumphantly when an orgasm ripped through her. The silk ties bit into her wrists and ankles as her inner muscles clenched like a fist, then spilled a pool of warm release which spread in ripples from her center outward.

She lay limply with her eyes closed, a few quivers of leftover sensation rippling through her. *How had that happened?*

"I see you've been thinking about me," Jack's voice drawled from above her.

Charlie forced her eyes open. He was standing right beside the bed, and as she looked upward, she noticed that the black wool of his slacks was pulled taut over his arousal.

"All day," she managed to rasp out. "And all last night too."

He laughed again, and sat down on the edge of the bed. His weight rolled her toward him slightly, and he splayed his left hand across her belly and left it there.

Suddenly, all the laughter left his voice. "Care to tell me what this is about?"

"It's a metaphor," Charlie said.

He slid his hand up to cup her breast. "You know, I have a hard time seeing a naked woman tied to my bed as a literary device."

She wished he would stop circling her nipple with his fingers. It made it very difficult to explain her message. "It's a metaphor for trust. I want to show you I trust you. That I have no fear that you're like your father."

"Trust." His fingers stilled. "Here I was thinking it was a metaphor for 'Take me, I'm yours.'"

"It is," Charlie whispered. "I trust you to do anything you want with me. I *am* yours."

His expression darkened at her last sentence. Then he looked down at his hand resting on her breast. "So you wouldn't have a problem with it, if I just lay down on top of you, unzipped my fly and drove myself inside you right now?"

"No problem. Do it," she said, her eyes locked on his. "Whatever you want."

He shifted his hand to her other breast, stroking it softly so that she had to swallow a whimper of pleasure. He was no longer looking at her. Instead, he stared toward the curtained window for a long moment.

When his gaze shifted back to her, she smiled at him, knowing her heart was in her eyes.

He got up abruptly and walked over to the wall of knives. Drawing a curved dagger from its silver-and-leather case, he turned and sliced through the necktie holding her left ankle with such swiftness that she jumped.

"*Now* you're afraid?" he asked, walking to the right side of the bed. He scythed through the second necktie.

"No." Charlie drew her knees together.

He quickly freed her two hands, then unhooked a dark blue silk bathrobe from his closet door and tossed it to her. She pulled the bathrobe on, and stripped the remains of the neckties from her wrists and ankles.

"What are you trying to prove?" he asked, crossing his arms with the dagger still dangling from one hand.

What was she trying to prove? Charlie took a deep breath.

"I'm trying to prove that when I didn't tell you about Don's threats, I did it because I thought you had enough to worry about. I knew if I told you, you'd drop your own concerns and come racing to help because that's the sort of person you are. You'd already done enough; I didn't want to be a further burden to you."

Jack uncrossed his arms and put the dagger down on the bedside table.

Charlie swallowed and went on. "But that doesn't work. If you love someone, you can't choose when to let him in and when not to. You have to trust him enough to let him decide. I wanted to prove I trust you enough to do that."

She had never seen anyone go so still. If Jack was breathing, there was no outward sign of it. Suddenly, he dragged in a long draught of oxygen, and spoke. "Did you just say you love me?"

"Yes," she said quietly. "Yes, I love you."

He laughed.

Charlie flinched inwardly. But Jack had turned away to pace across the room to his closet, and didn't see the hurt in her expression.

"You can't love me," he said, spinning around. "You don't know me." He laughed that ugly laugh again.

Charlie pushed herself off the bed. He stalked to within three feet of her and said, "Sit down. I'm going to tell you what I really am. Then see how much you trust me."

She stood for a moment, her eyes locked with his, before she sank back down. *What made Jack believe he was so far beyond the reach of the most powerful of human emotions?*

"I told you my father was an abusive husband when he drank," he began, shifting his gaze back to the window. He seemed to be conjuring up a past so awful he couldn't stand to look at it straight on. "My mother did her damnedest to keep me out of their battles but as I got older, my father got drunk more often. Once I knew what was happening, I tried to defend her. My father was a big man so he'd just slam me against the wall, and go back to beating Mama."

Charlie felt tears sting her eyes.

"When he finally gave me a concussion, my mother went to a lawyer and filed for divorce. She even had a restraining order put on him. But we all know restraining orders aren't worth the paper they're printed on if no one's there to enforce them."

Jack stopped. Charlie watched him gather his breath and strength for the rest of the story.

"I came home from school one day, and found my mother unconscious on the kitchen floor. Her face was covered with blood, her clothes were in shreds, and I could see a bone in her arm sticking out through her skin. I called an ambulance and as soon as she was in it, I went back inside the house. I got a shotgun from my father's gun case, and I went from one bar to another until I found him."

"Oh God . . ." Charlie gasped.

"I told him I was going to kill him for what he'd done to my mother. He laughed. He was so drunk he *laughed*. I shot him right in the chest."

"Did he die?"

"Yes. A shotgun blast at three feet does a lot of damage. So at age fourteen, I murdered my own father."

"That's not murder, that's self-defense!"

"It was premeditated murder." He leaned down and gripped her shoulders hard. "Do you *understand*? I took that gun and went looking for my own father with the sole purpose of killing him. I didn't want to scare him. I didn't want to hurt him. *I wanted him dead*."

He let go of her and straightened to pace over to the dresser. Bracing his hip against it, he shoved his hands in his pockets and continued. "I got a lot of sympathy. The lawyer bargained it down to manslaughter. I was a juvenile so I went to a juvenile prison. But it was *prison*."

"Is that where you saw the meteor shower?"

"Yeah. My first night there, I was lying in bed staring at the bars in a tiny window seven feet above me, when the sky exploded. It made an impression."

"Those meteors saved you. They gave you something to focus on while you were shut up in jail. No wonder you're so passionate about your work."

"I'm so passionate, I want to retire from it," he pointed out.

"What happened to your mother? Is she still alive? Do you ever see her?" Charlie said, brushing aside his interjection.

"Mama recovered. She even had a baby nine months

later because along with beating her, my father had raped her."

"Oh no!"

"Oh yes, I have a baby brother. Not that I ever knew him. When I got out of prison, I went to say good-bye to Mama. Then I never went back home again."

"So you haven't seen your mother or your little brother since you were a teenager?" Charlie could not conceive of having a mother *and* a sibling and choosing to cut them out of your life.

Jack's shoulders moved in a sort of half-shrug. "As often as I can persuade her, I fly my mother to some nice hotel and meet her there. But I can't stand the sight of Molena, Georgia. And I don't include my brother because I don't think he needs to know the convicted murderer in the family."

"But your mother understood why you had done what you did?"

"She understood and she blamed herself."

"That's a lot of blame to shoulder." Charlie pulled the robe tightly around her, trying to imagine a household where fear of physical injury was the prevailing emotion. It made being an orphan seem almost easy. "It seems to me your father is the only one who was guilty. You and your mother were his victims."

"The law frowns upon individual citizens deciding who's guilty and then carrying out a death sentence," Jack said.

"But the law didn't protect you or your mother, so what other choice did you have?"

"At the time, I didn't think I had any."

She could see in his eyes he had gone away to his own private hell. But she refused to leave him there. She got up and slowly walked over to him. With equal deliberation, she wrapped her arms around his unyielding body, and laid her head against his chest.

His heart beat loudly against her ear. They stood motionless for a long minute. Finally, he slipped his hands out of his pockets and circled his arms around her back, pulling her tightly against him. She thought she felt him feather a kiss over her hair. Then he slid his hands to her shoulders and moved her away from him. He walked to the door before he turned. "Thanks for the sympathy . . . and for the . . . 'show of trust.' I enjoyed it."

Charlie blushed.

"But none of it is necessary," he continued, smiling without warmth. "You were quite correct about Hollinger being involved in stealing Sahara-Mars. When we confronted him, he admitted his guilt pretty quickly. Unfortunately, he no longer had the meteorite in his possession, so now we're going to pay a visit to Vandermade."

Charlie couldn't have cared less about Sahara-Mars just then.

"You forgot to mention one other thing I offered you," she said quietly.

He thrust his hands back into his pockets but looked straight at her. "Sugar, I'm very flattered by your sentiments, but I don't return them. You're looking for something I haven't got."

BY THE TIME Charlie walked into the living room, her head was high and her shoulders were back. Jack was standing in front of the empty marble fireplace.

"Good luck with Vandermade," she said. "Let me know how it goes."

"I will."

She looked at him full on for just a moment. "If I were

you, Jack, I'd get in touch with your brother. He might actually be proud to have you as a member of the family."

"I don't think so," he said with implacable conviction. He accompanied her to the door. "Drive carefully."

AFTER CHARLIE WALKED out of the apartment Jack's eyes never left the security monitor as her image progressed from hall to elevator to lobby. He watched the empty lobby long after she was gone, then dropped into the nearest chair, his elbows on his knees and his palms pressed hard against his eyes.

CHAPTER 24

TWO GUARDS SWUNG open enormous wrought-iron gates, and Jack gunned the Land Rover through them. "Why doesn't Vandermade invest in electronic gates?" he asked Miguel, in the passenger seat.

"Because having human beings manning the portals reinforces the Master-of-All-I-Survey image he has of himself." Peter Burke spoke from the backseat.

Jack had reluctantly agreed to let the scientist come because he had gotten them in to see Hollinger. Now he had to admit Burke would add to the intimidation factor; the professor wore a charcoal-gray suit with a brilliantly white shirt and red tie, and he wore it with the arrogance of the CEO of a multinational corporation.

The Land Rover ate up the long winding road to the Vandermade mansion, and the three men were ushered into the billionaire's library. Books climbed the walls for two stories, interrupted only by one immense leaded glass window. A mahogany desk the size of a ping-pong table dwarfed the man who rose from behind it.

"Jack!" Curt Vandermade said, walking around the desk, hand outstretched. "I was devastated to hear about the theft."

"You know Miguel," Jack said, gripping Vandermade's hand for a split second. "And this is Dr. Peter Burke."

"The eminent bio-astronomer," Vandermade acknowledged. "And your nemesis, Jack. How strange for you to come calling together."

"We've joined forces in the interest of science," Peter said.

"Oh?" Vandermade cocked an eyebrow. "Gentlemen, have a seat."

No one sat. Vandermade couldn't conceal the flush of color on his face at their blatant disregard of his command.

"We paid a visit to Dr. Hollinger yesterday," Jack said. "He made a surprise appearance on some videotapes from the Museum of Natural History, and we thought he might shed some light on the disappearance of Sahara-Mars."

Vandermade's color intensified but he didn't move.

"It turned out he was quite well-informed on the subject, and we have a very fine recording of our discussion, thanks to Miguel's camera work," Jack continued.

Miguel nodded in mock appreciation of the tribute, and pulled a slim plastic case from the inside pocket of his jacket. Leaning forward, he placed it on Vandermade's desk. "I made a copy on DVD for you, in case you'd like to see it."

Now Jack sat down in a large leather chair.

He rested his elbows on the overstuffed arms and crossed his legs, the very picture of a man in control of the situation. Miguel and Peter remained standing, flanking him. "We believe you would prefer not to have that recording find its way into the hands of the police and the press, and we're prepared to offer an exchange."

"I can discredit Hollinger in an instant," Vandermade said, snapping his fingers. A vein was pulsing in his temple. "Nothing he says will stand up in court."

"You blackmailed him into stealing the security codes," Jack said. "As a scientist, he had access to the staff at the Museum, and he used *your* money to bribe them."

"I can make your life *very* unpleasant," Vandermade jabbed a finger in Peter Burke's direction. "Princeton's always looking for large donors. I'll insist on some personnel changes in exchange for my donation."

"Don't waste your time," Peter said coolly. "I've got tenure."

"And we all know it's impossible to get rid of a professor with tenure," Jack said.

"I'll make sure you never get a graduate degree at any university in this country," Vandermade hissed.

"There's always the University of Djibouti," Jack shrugged.

"What about me?" Miguel asked. "I feel neglected."

"You're just a damned Spic," Vandermade spat. "I'll have you deported."

"I was born in Union City, so that's as far as you can deport me." Miguel laughed. "Although I think that's the worst threat you've made so far."

Jack and Peter chuckled.

"What about that beautiful blond wife of yours?" Vandermade sneered.

Jack was out of his chair and across the five feet between them in an instant, his face mere inches from the other man's. "If you hurt Charlie in any way, all the security guards you can hire will not stop me from killing you," he said through clenched teeth.

"*Hurt* her?" Vandermade laughed nervously. "I'll *buy* her.

Every woman has her price, and it's generally surprisingly low."

For a moment, Jack leaned in even closer, and Vandermade involuntarily shifted back. Miguel took one step toward the two men, then relaxed as his friend straightened.

"I'd like to see you try," Jack said as he strolled back to the chair and sat down. "This conversation has become a waste of my time. Let's make the exchange. Get the meteorite."

"Where's the original video?" Vandermade said, folding his arms across his chest.

"In a safe-deposit box. Where else would it be?" Jack asked, raising his eyebrows.

"You expect me to give you the meteorite before I get the original? And how many other copies are there?" Vandermade asked. "I'm not a fool, gentlemen."

"Perhaps I didn't make the terms of the exchange clear." Jack stared at Vandermade for a long moment. "You give us the meteorite you stole, and in exchange, we will promise not to release the video to the police or the media. However, the original recording will remain in my possession."

The billionaire stood abruptly, his fists clenched, his face almost purple. "You've made a very powerful enemy today," he said, his voice shaking with rage. He twisted and stabbed his finger on a button set into the mahogany surface behind him. "Bring the meteorite to my office," he barked.

As they waited, the only movement in the room came from the pulsing vein in Vandermade's forehead. Finally, the paneled double doors swept inward, and two men in dark suits side-stepped into the room, carrying the glass and steel cube between them. They took it to a round, leather-topped table and lifted it carefully onto the smooth surface. Vandermade flicked his fingers at the men, and they went swiftly out of the room, pulling the doors shut behind them.

Peter strode over to the table. "At least your goons had the sense to steal the meteorite in its case. You didn't open it, did you?" he asked sharply as he searched for the light switch.

"They'd have to use an acetylene torch," Miguel said. "I built that case, and they'd never figure out how to open it." He walked to the table and ran his fingers along one edge of the cube. The interior light came on, and Sahara-Mars gleamed darkly in its frozen flight.

Jack watched the scientist devour it with his eyes, and a sympathetic smile played around his mouth. "Well, gentlemen, we have what we came for. Miguel?"

Miguel swept the case off the table and walked to the doors Peter held wide.

"Curt," Jack said, turning back toward the desk, "I hope I never again have the misfortune of being in the same room with you."

Then he strolled through the doors, leaving them gaping open behind him.

THE LAND ROVER rolled up to the glass doors at the entrance to the Rose Center.

A phalanx of security guards met it, but Miguel refused to hand over his precious burden, so the three men entered the sleek, modern foyer surrounded by a cordon of uniforms. Museum-goers turned to watch the silent procession as it passed under the giant silver sphere of the planetarium and up the steps to the Hall of Planet Earth.

Another group of guards stood at the top of the steps to keep visitors out of the hall, parting to let the meteorite and its escort through. Miguel walked to the pedestal and set the case on top. Pulling a small set of tools from his pocket, he made several adjustments, punched a series of numbers into a keypad and stepped back.

Sahara-Mars once more spun glittering in the brilliant light of a simulated sun.

"Let 'em in," Jack said to the guards holding back the considerable crowd.

As the curious onlookers formed a line between the velvet ropes, Jack and Peter stood and watched. One young boy read the plaque aloud to his older brother, " 'Inside this meteorite could lie the answer to the question: is there life on Mars?' How cool is *that*?"

"It's an alien egg," his brother said, flapping his hands like jaws. "It's going to hatch and eat us all. Watch out!"

"You dork," the younger boy said, scornfully. "It's not that kind of life. It's like amoebas or something."

Jack watched the boys examine his meteorite. "I have a brother," he said, after taking a deep breath.

"I do too," Peter said. "He likes to pretend I don't exist, so I go out of my way to annoy him whenever possible."

Jack turned to stare at the man beside him.

"Yeah, I know you're my brother," Peter acknowledged. "I figured it out years ago."

"Why the hell didn't you say so?"

"Why the hell didn't *you?*"

Jack's gaze shifted back to Sahara-Mars. "Because who would want a brother who'd murdered his father?"

"That's ancient history, and the bastard got what he deserved," Peter said. Suddenly he grinned. "Besides, *you dork*, I want a brother who catches stars."

"What?" Jack glanced sideways.

"That's what Mama told me my big brother did. She'd take me outside for every meteor shower we could see and tell me that my brother was out there catching all those stars falling to earth. For years, I visualized you as some sort of cosmic baseball player."

"I don't believe this! Why didn't Mama tell me you knew?"

"Because I wasn't going to force myself on you."

"We're *both* dorks," Jack said, a matching grin lighting his face as he grabbed his not-so-little brother and wrapped him in a bear hug.

Miguel strolled up, his eyebrows arched in inquiry. "Are we celebrating the return of Sahara-Mars or something more private?" he asked.

The two men turned toward him. "It's a family reunion," Jack said.

"It's about time," Miguel said, shaking Peter's hand. "Jack would never admit this, but he's been following your career with brotherly pride. Even when you were complaining loudly about his commercialization of scientific materials."

Peter shrugged. "I didn't get to break his toys when we were young, so I had to find ways to make up for it when I got older. By the way, where did you get the name 'Lanett'? It makes you sound like some shady cardsharp."

"The bus I took out of prison passed through it. Population 7,897. It seemed pretty snappy to a juvenile delinquent."

"Let's go have lunch and celebrate," Miguel said, chuckling.

"Great idea! Especially if Jack's buying."

"We have a lot of lost time to make up for, little brother," Jack said, his tone serious as he gripped Peter's hand. "And we'll do it, but there's something else I have to make up for first."

Miguel locked eyes with his old friend. "Would that something have happened last night?"

Jack nodded. "I owe her an apology . . . and a thank-you," he added, glancing at Peter.

"I'm glad you've come to your senses, *amigo*," Miguel said, smiling. "Go mend your fences. I'll take care of your *hermanito* here."

"Remind me to tell you to stay out of my business the next time I see you," Jack said. "In the meantime, I owe you a thank-you too."

As Jack cut through the shifting crowd of meteorite gazers, Miguel said to Peter, "I think your brother has finally decided to rejoin the human race."

CHAPTER 25

CHARLIE HAD BEEN very grateful that Sallyanne was out when she got home. She'd gone straight to her bed where she'd tossed, turned and cried all night.

This morning she just felt spent.

After picking up Sallyanne and getting the scoop on the slumber party, she retreated to her room with Major padding along behind her. When she stopped in front of her dresser to stare at her reflection in the mirror, he flopped down on the bedroom rug with a long-suffering sigh.

Puffy eyes. Hair carelessly twisted into a lop-sided bun. Still wearing her pajama shirt tucked into a pair of ratty blue jeans. She noticed the gleam of her so-called wedding ring, and her breath caught on a sob. She slid it off her finger and held it up at eye-level, tilting it back and forth to watch the criss-crossing lines flicker in the morning sunlight. Then she tossed it onto the dresser where it settled with a small vibrating clatter.

"Face it, Charlotte Elizabeth Berglund," she said to the

mirror, "you just don't inspire long-term commitment in the male of the species."

She thought she'd learned that lesson. Certainly Nick and her husband Greg had done their best to instill it in her. Of course, she'd hoped Jack would be different, that he would have the strength and good taste to appreciate her unique qualities. She snorted at her reflection. "Where'd I get that idea?"

Charlie couldn't bear the pain in her own eyes so she turned away, her hands pressed to her gut as she tried to physically soothe the agonizing ache of Jack's rejection. A sob wrenched itself from her throat, and she doubled over. An image of Sallyanne floated through the haze of misery, and she found the strength to stand straight again. She glared at the mirror. "You've got a daughter to worry about. Moping is not an option," she said, heading for the shower with a determined stride.

She would get dressed and take Sallyanne shopping at the local bookstore.

That would cheer both of them up.

As she lathered her hair, she allowed herself to consider the fact that Jack hadn't called, even to let her know what had happened with his visit to Curt Vandermade. "Cold-hearted creep!" she said aloud as she ran her fingers through her hair to rinse it.

"Are you sad about something, Ma'am?" Sallyanne asked when Charlie joined her for a glass of milk in the kitchen.

Charlie's heart gave a little lilt every time Sallyanne called her "Ma'am." "No, sweetheart, I think I'm just coming down with a cold," she said.

"Take some vitamin C," the little girl said wisely. "It works real well."

Major sat up abruptly. A low growl rumbled in his throat as he looked toward the door into the living room.

"What is it, Major?" Charlie asked, heading into the other room. Everything seemed fine. "He must have had a nightmare," she said to Sallyanne, as she patted the big dog's head. He sat down, but his eyes were open and his ears were cocked forward.

Sallyanne carried her glass to the sink, then went to retrieve her book bag from beside the front door. Charlie was wiping down the table when she heard the little girl cry out, "Papa!"

Charlie raced into the living room, but she was too late. Sallyanne had already unlatched the French door. Don McGraw was stepping inside as she skidded to a halt. "Don, you're not supposed to be here," she warned, wishing the police guard hadn't left when they assumed Don was on the plane to Tennessee.

"My little girl thought I didn't want to say good-bye to her," he said, sweeping Sallyanne up into his arms and hugging her. "I couldn't let that stand."

"I sympathize, but we have a legal agreement," Charlie pointed out. Major punctuated her statement with a growl. She laid her palm on top of his shoulder to calm him.

"Well now, don't they say possession is nine-tenths of the law?" Don said with a smile as he held his daughter against his chest. "I believe I am now in possession."

"What does that mean, Papa?"

"It means you and I are going to be together, honey pie."

"You're squeezing too hard," Sallyanne said as she started to squirm. "Please put me down."

Don let her slide to her feet, but kept his arm firmly wrapped across her chest.

"I'm going to call the police," Charlie said, starting for the telephone.

"I wouldn't do that, missy."

She turned to see him pull a hunting knife from behind his back.

Sallyanne screamed. Major hurled himself forward and Charlie shrieked, "Down, Major!" as she saw the knife flash toward the dog's head. Don's hold on Sallyanne loosened, and Charlie yelled, "Run, Sallyanne! Run to Isabelle's!"

She just had time to see the child stumble off the porch when she felt Don's arm snake around her waist. He yanked her back against him and held the knife to her throat as he dragged her away from the door.

"You shouldn't have done that, pretty lady. Now we're going to have to go see Isabelle, aren't we?" He spoke right into her ear.

Charlie stood very still. Out of the corner of her eye, she could see Major's body stretched out on the floor. She couldn't tell if he was breathing, but she couldn't see any blood. Don pressed the knife closer against her neck and let his free hand roam up to close around her breast.

"Maybe I'll take you with us. You'd make a real fine whore until Sallyanne gets old enough to make some money for her papa."

When Charlie didn't respond, he slid his hand downward between her legs. She tried to twist away but he laughed and forced his hand between her thighs. "Or maybe you'll decide to pay me the money I asked you for," he whispered in her ear as he pushed his fingers hard against the denim of her jeans. "Except the price has gone *way* up."

"I'll pay you," Charlie whispered. The knife was so

tight against her throat she was afraid to speak any more loudly.

"We'll discuss my terms later. Now let's go see Isabelle."

Don let go of her crotch and started to move her toward the back door. A flicker of shadow on the throw rug caught her eye. *Please let it not be Sallyanne,* she thought. Then the French doors crashed open, the glass shattering.

Jack Lanett stood braced in the doorway.

Charlie almost flinched at the expression of lethal intent etched on his face.

"Let her go," he said in a deadly flat voice.

Charlie felt Don shift behind her. She closed her eyes for a moment. Then her brain kicked into gear, and she began to run through every extreme survival course she'd ever participated in. Of course, any self-defense course she'd taken advised a woman not to try to defend herself when a man was holding a knife to her throat . . .

She opened her eyes and smiled weakly at Jack. He might be a coldhearted creep, but she was glad to see him right now.

Jack's gaze never wavered from Don McGraw's face. "I called the police before I came in, McGraw. They'll be here soon, and I'm not moving until you let her go."

Don pressed the knife even harder against her throat. Charlie gagged.

Jack twitched at the sound.

She felt something warm tickling her throat and realized with a shock she was bleeding. *That did it.* She wasn't going to let him slit her throat without a fight. She did a quick mental calculation, blinked at Jack twice, then cut her eyes down and to the left in hopes that he would understand her signal. *Please understand, Jack!*

Taking a deep breath, she slammed her head back into

Don's face and thrust her hands up between his right arm
and her neck. As she pushed outward with all her strength,
she jammed the heel of her sandal down on the arch of his
foot and threw herself to the left and downward. The handle of the knife struck hard against her head as she fell. She
rolled behind her favorite armchair and lay there with pain
radiating through her forehead.

"You goddamn bitch!" she heard Don McGraw scream.

The sounds of a scuffle drifted through her consciousness. Then Jack was looming over her with the knife
gripped in his right hand.

"Charlie? Are you all right?" Jack's voice seemed to
come from a distance. "Charlie! Answer me!"

"I'm fine," she managed, her palm pressed to her temple.

"Are you sure you're fine?" He sounded worried.

She did her best to smile up at him, but when she moved
her vision went black around the edges. His expression
went from concern to fury, and he disappeared from her
line of sight.

"Don't kill me! I wasn't going to hurt her. I just—"
There was a frightening thud and then silence.

"Charlie!" Jack was kneeling beside her, his hands
gently probing her head and neck. "Where are you hurt?
Christ, you're bleeding."

"It's just a cut. It's my head that hurts."

"Let me get some ice."

Finally, Charlie heard sirens, their wail slicing through
her aching skull.

"You've got to get up," Jack said, as he used his left
hand to hold a dish towel filled with ice against her head.
"Come on. I'll help you."

He wrapped his right arm around her rib cage and
hauled her up to a sitting position. "Ow!" she complained.

"Come on. Up!"

Now he supported her against his body and straightened, bringing her with him to a standing position. Her head was pounding, but her vision had cleared. "Major!" she said, seeing the dog still sprawled on the rug.

"He's breathing," Jack said as he walked Charlie closer. "Did Don stab him?"

"There's no blood," Charlie said. "He must have hit him with the handle of the knife." She looked curiously at Don McGraw where he slumped unconscious against the wall. "What did you do to him?" she asked with an utter lack of sympathy.

"I had to knock him out so I could take care of you."

Suddenly, reaction to the violence crashed into her, and she collapsed against Jack, sobbing. "Oh God, Jack. I thought he was going to hurt Sallyanne. I thought he'd killed Major. I was afraid he was going to stab me. I was so glad to see you, but I was so terrified."

"Shhhh." He dropped the ice and held her against him with infinite tenderness. "Shhhhh, sugar. It's all right now. It's over."

Charlie let go of her head and grabbed fistfuls of his shirt, trying to wrap herself in the warmth and safety of his body. His arms tightened around her, and he kissed her hair and murmured soft words of comfort. Then he said, "The police are here, sugar. There are a lot of guns pointed at us so move slowly. They don't know who I am."

Charlie opened her eyes and lifted her head slowly.

Jack stepped back and raised his hands, his gaze never leaving her. She turned to face five men in dark uniforms with guns aimed straight at Jack.

"Don't shoot. He's the good guy," she said. "The one you want is over there." She moved her arm in slow motion to point toward Don's slumped body.

"You sure, ma'am?" one officer asked, his rifle still
locked on Jack.

"I'm sure," she stated firmly, and sighed in relief as four
muzzles were slowly lowered, and the fifth swung toward
Don.

Controlled chaos erupted. Two ambulances arrived in a
blaze of light and sound. The police tried to rouse Don
without success. "Someone really wanted him out," one
officer muttered as he bent over the inert man. One of the
ambulances carried Don's unconscious body away under
armed guard.

Jack beckoned the other medical crew over to Charlie.
They shone flashlights in her eyes, asked her who was
president, and tried to persuade her to come with them for
X rays. She refused to go despite Jack's threats to strap her
to the stretcher. She wasn't leaving without seeing
Sallyanne.

The technicians handed her an ice pack and gave Jack a
long list of warnings and instructions before they reluctantly left empty-handed.

Charlie was more concerned about Major than herself.
The big dog's eyes were open, but he showed no desire to
stand up. When Mike appeared and volunteered to take
Major to the vet, she gratefully agreed. He and one of the
policemen carried the big dog carefully out through the
open French doors. She heard him tell a couple of reporters
she could see hovering outside the house to get lost.

Through it all, Jack's arm stayed wrapped firmly
around her waist, his body warm and solid against her side.

As the police continued to mill around the house, Jack
led her over to the couch and sat her down beside him. He
reached up and tilted her head onto his shoulder and said,
"Just rest for a minute."

But the doorbell rang, and the front door banged open.

Sallyanne raced into the living room and threw herself at Charlie while Isabelle, Ernst and two policemen followed at a slower pace.

"Ma'am, Ma'am, are you all right?"

Charlie wrapped her arms around the sobbing little girl and kissed her. "I'm fine, sweetheart. Are you all right?"

"Yes, Ma'am. How's Major?" Sallyanne pulled away to look around. "Where is he?"

"Mike took him to the vet. He'll be okay," Charlie said, mentally crossing her fingers.

"Daddy!" Sallyanne said, shifting to hug Jack.

If he was surprised by his new name, he didn't show it. "Sweetheart, I'm glad to see you safe! I heard you were very brave and ran as fast as you could to Isabelle's house."

"I was so scared. I cried when I got there," Sallyanne confessed.

"Perfectly understandable," Jack said, shifting her weight onto his lap.

"Before she started crying she told me everything I needed to know. That's why the police came so quickly," Isabelle said, leaning down to examine the lump on Charlie's forehead. "I have a wonderful poultice for swelling. After I fix some coffee for everyone, I'll get it for you."

Ernst stood before them. "So Jack, you saved our Charlie. Good man." He reached out and shook Jack's hand.

"She's *my* Charlie," Jack said, looking up at the older man.

"So I see," Ernst said. "While Isabelle serves coffee, I will sweep up all this glass."

"I can do it," Charlie said, struggling to get up.

Jack's arm became a band of steel around her.

"You're not going anywhere, sugar. You've probably

got a concussion, and you're going to accept Ernst's very kind offer."

"Thanks, Ernst," Charlie said, subsiding. In truth, she just wanted to close her eyes. Sallyanne was holding onto her hand, and she stroked the little girl's knuckles with her fingertip. "I love you, sweetheart," she whispered to her new daughter, and then followed her impulse to shut her eyes. The pounding in her head lessened as she let her mind drift, soothed by the soft swish of Ernst's broom, the clink of broken glass and Jack's heart beating against her ear.

"WAKE UP, CHARLIE."

She struggled back to consciousness, wincing as pain shot through her temple.

"Are you awake?" Jack's voice was low but insistent.

"I'm awake."

"I wanted to make sure you weren't unconscious. And I want to put Sallyanne to bed."

Charlie opened her eyes to see Sallyanne curled against Jack's chest sound asleep. The sky outside the damaged French doors was midnight blue, and two lamps glowed softly in her quiet living room.

"What time is it?" she asked, carefully lifting her head.

"I'm not sure. My watch is behind your back," Jack said.

"Your poor arm!" Charlie said, leaning forward so that he could pull it out from behind her.

"It's eight thirty," he announced as he flexed his fingers. "I'm going to take her upstairs."

"Let's put her in my room," Charlie said, pushing herself off the couch. "If she wakes up or has a nightmare, I want to hear her."

When she turned, he cursed under his breath. "You have

a lump the size of a robin's egg on your head. Let me get some ice. And Isabelle's poultice."

"No, you take care of Sallyanne."

Charlie found the miracle concoction, got some fresh ice and joined him in her bedroom. Together they settled the girl under the covers of the four poster bed. She lingered a moment, tucking the quilt in and stroking the child's hair. Thank goodness Don hadn't injured her in any way, and thank goodness Sallyanne hadn't heard his comment about turning her into a whore.

She looked up to see Jack looking at the ring she had thrown on the dresser that morning. It seemed a lifetime ago. As she watched, he flipped it in the air, caught it and dropped it in his shirt pocket. A pain worse than anything Don had inflicted tore through her. *He's taking back his ring.*

He turned and gestured for her to precede him out of the bedroom.

Charlie walked into the living room and went over to inspect the plastic Ernst had taped over the broken door panes.

"Let's go out on the porch," Jack said in a low voice. "It's warm. We can leave the doors open."

As she stepped through the door, she could barely breathe. *Jack took back his ring, the one he had told her she could keep.* Her vision blurred, and she tilted her head back in feigned appreciation of the night sky.

He leaned against one of the columns, his hands thrust in his trouser pockets, and stared out toward the channel. "We got Sahara-Mars back," he said.

Charlie propped herself against the opposite column and cleared her throat twice before she said hoarsely. "Congratulations. Was it hard to convince Vandermade?"

"No. We had a tape of Hollinger's confession. He knew we meant business."

"Was the meteorite damaged at all?" Her reporter's instincts rescued her from silence.

"No. Nothing short of a nuclear bomb would get it out of Miguel's case." Jack's gaze shifted to Charlie. "You should sit down."

"It feels good to stretch my legs."

"I took your advice," he said after a moment's silence.

"What advice?" Charlie couldn't remember giving Jack any advice.

"I talked to my brother. As a brother," he added.

"That's great. How did it go?"

"Fine. He already knew."

"But he hadn't contacted you?"

"He thought I should be the one to make the first approach."

She was happy for him, but couldn't pursue the topic. She finally said, "I'm very, very grateful you came this afternoon, but I don't understand why you were here."

Now *he* looked skyward. "I came to see you."

She choked on a laugh.

Pushing off the column, he walked over to her and gently clasped her shoulders. He looked down at her and frowned at the swelling on her temple. "I should have killed the bastard."

"He's not worth going back to jail over," Charlie said.

Suddenly, he crushed her against his chest. "When I came up to these doors and saw him with his hands on you, I didn't give a damn about the consequences. The only reason I didn't attack him was because I was afraid he'd cut you with the knife."

Charlie looked up at him, but his face was in shadow

and she could see nothing of his expression. "I appreciate your restraint."

She felt him draw a deep breath.

"I came to see you to apologize. For being a fool. For being a *dork*," he said with a ghost of a laugh.

"A *dork*?"

"Only a dork would turn down a woman tied to his bed," he said. "Only a fool would refuse to admit he's in love with the woman tied to his bed. And only *I* could be both at the same time."

"But you took your ring back," Charlie said, utterly bewildered.

"I took my ring back because this time I'm going to put it on your finger and mean it."

He released her to reach into his breast pocket. The ring glinted between his fingers as he took her left hand in his. "Yesterday you said you loved me. Has that feeling managed to survive everything that's happened in between?" His grip on her hand tightened noticeably as he asked his question.

"Why would you think it hasn't?" she asked quietly, even as a warmth she could only describe as joy radiated from her chest outward through her bones and muscles and blood.

"Because for the first time since our wedding, you weren't wearing my ring. *Something* made you take it off."

"I took it off because nothing you said yesterday made me love you any less. I didn't need to be reminded of that."

"I'm so sorry," he said. He brought her hand up between them. "Once I put this ring back on, it stays there. Forever. You understand that?"

Grinning like an idiot, Charlie nodded.

Jack did not answer her smile. With utter solemnity, he

said, *"With this ring, I thee wed,"* and slid the silvery band onto her finger.

He locked her into his arms and let all the pent-up loneliness and fear and self-doubt flood out of him in a kiss so deep she thought she would drown.

She threaded her fingers through his hair and held his head away from hers long enough to whisper, "I love you."

Then his mouth came down on hers, and there was no more conversation.

Overhead a single meteor streaked silently across the sky.

EPILOGUE

Four Years Later

THE STUDENTS AT Princeton always joke that the university's Latin motto translates as, "God went to Princeton." On the morning of graduation day, Charlie almost believed it. After a solid week of rain, the sun had come out in the thoroughly rinsed blue sky and shone on a campus carpeted in grass so green it looked like astro-turf. The kaleidoscopic mix of stone, brick and marble buildings around Cannon Green glowed brightly in the clear June light, creating a perfect backdrop for the steady stream of students in flapping black gowns hurrying toward the commencement procession.

As she joined the crowd, Charlie could not help thinking that a similar scene had been repeated for three centuries. These young men and women were part of a long and grand tradition. And today Jack was joining them. In a few hours, he could rightfully put a whole string of initials after his name.

"We've got to hurry and find Daddy before we sit down," Charlie said, swinging Mari up onto her hip.

"Gosh, you've gotten heavy. We're going to have to stop feeding you so much."

She tickled her younger daughter's rounded stomach and enjoyed Mari's giggles. The little girl had a smile that could light up an entire room, and everyone who knew her did their best to bring it out. Not that making Mari smile was difficult; she was an effervescently happy child.

"Want me to carry her?" Sallyanne offered, holding out her arms. The slim thirteen-year-old came almost to Charlie's shoulder and was the spitting image of her mother Leah.

"Thanks but you don't want to wrinkle your dress. You look absolutely beautiful," Charlie said, admiring the pale blue silk sheath Sallyanne had picked out during their last trip to China. She couldn't resist reaching out to run her hand affectionately down her older daughter's smooth cheek.

"Hello, lovely ladies," a deep voice drawled from behind them. "You'd better get moving or you'll miss the big event."

"Uncle Peter!" both girls called.

"Why are you wearing that dopey hat?" Sallyanne asked, eyeing the odd, floppy decoration on her usually cool uncle's head.

Peter grinned, and Charlie wondered yet again how she had repeatedly dismissed the strong resemblance between Jack and his brother. *Of course, when I first met Jack, he didn't grin much.*

"I'm wearing this dopey hat to match this dopey robe," Peter said, flapping the sleeves of his orange and black marshal's gown. "Only the most intelligent people get to look this stupid."

Charlie laughed. "Wait until you see Daddy. He looks just as ridiculous."

She had teased Jack when he shrugged into the long, flowing black robe with the velvet stripes marking his doctorate on the sleeves, but secretly she thought he looked like a Renaissance prince. Even the absurd mortarboard perched on his salt-and-pepper hair looked dashing. She had wicked plans for talking him into wearing the robe with nothing underneath it.

Charlie had sent him off to join his colleagues while she got herself and the girls dressed. Now she wanted to give him a kiss because she was so proud and happy . . . and because she always wanted to kiss him.

"There you are!" As if conjured up from her thoughts, she saw him striding toward them, black satin rippling around his trouser legs. Her heart skipped a beat at the sight of this stunningly handsome man who by some amazing good fortune was her husband.

He swept her, Mari and Sallyanne into his arms all together. "I thought my beautiful women had forgotten me."

"Daddy!" Mari said, holding out her arms to him. "Ma'am says you look ridicklus."

"Hmmmm," he said as he swung the girl easily from Charlie's hip to his, and kissed her soundly.

"*You* look good enough to eat," he said to Sallyanne, as he brushed a kiss on the top of her head to spare her teenaged dignity.

"*Ridiculous,* eh?" he said, arching an eyebrow at Charlie. "Have you no respect for my newly-elevated position in the world?" Then he pulled her close against his side and whispered in her ear, "You know, Ph.D.s make very inventive lovers."

His breath against her neck made her shiver.

He felt her reaction and chuckled smugly. "*That's* more like it. Now you'd better go," Jack said, handing Mari back to Charlie. "Miguel's got seats in about the tenth row on the left."

They found Miguel without any difficulty since his head towered above the spectators around him.

"Are you sure that chair can hold you both?" Charlie whispered as Miguel reached out to take Mari onto his lap, making his flimsy folding chair creak ominously.

"You'd think with the billions of dollars in their endowment, Princeton could afford decent chairs," Miguel said. "But if it collapses, it will relieve some of the solemnity of the occasion."

The music began, a joyous but dignified processional. The graduates entered, led by another orange-robed marshal. Jack strode down the aisle as though he'd been doing it all his life.

"*All* got dopey hats," Mari said, causing the people around them to muffle laughs.

"Yeah, but Dad makes the hat look good," Sallyanne whispered loyally.

By the time all the speeches were made, including one entirely in Latin, Mari was squirming in Miguel's lap. Charlie shifted the little girl onto her own.

The day before, in a more intimate ceremony, the Ph.D.s had individually received their orange and black "hoods," which were worn around the neck and down the back, over their academic robes. As the graduate school dean had called, "Jackson Burke Lanett," Charlie had marveled at how far her husband had come from the boy who created a new identity for himself from the name of a bus stop. Now Jack wore "Lanett" as proudly as he did his hood.

"Would the candidates for the degree of Doctor of Philosophy please stand?" an official announced from the podium.

"Watch, sweetheart," Charlie said to Mari.

She reached over and took Sallyanne's hand, pressing it as she exchanged a smile with her older daughter.

As the group of scholars rose, the orange in their hoods flashed brilliantly in the sunshine. Jack stood tall and straight, making the other Ph.D.s around him seem pale and puny. President Stillman intoned a Latin phrase that declared that they were now officially Doctors of Philosophy.

Tears spilled down Charlie's cheeks. Jack had done it! He had found the legitimacy he had craved for so many years. Her husband had earned the respect of his fellow academics. Although Charlie didn't need any of those things to love him, she rejoiced in his accomplishments because they made *him* happy.

As the rest of the new doctors sat, he remained standing, searching the crowd behind him until his eyes met Charlie's. Smiling, he put his hand to his lips and blew her a kiss.

"Dad looks stoked," Sallyanne whispered.

After the ceremony, they made their way to a previously appointed rendezvous by one of the tiger statues at the edge of Cannon Green. Mari climbed around the tiger's paws as they waited for the graduate to join them. Then they were going to meet Isabelle, Rhonda, Mike and Ernst at Mediterra for a celebratory lunch.

Charlie waved as she caught sight of Jack and Peter cutting through the crowd of students and proud parents.

As Jack walked up, she grinned and said, "Congratulations, *Doctor* Lanett! I'm so proud of you!"

As she reached up to kiss him, he swung her off her feet and spun her around, laughing. As he lowered his mouth to hers, he murmured against her lips, "Are you going to call me 'Dr. Lanett' later tonight?"

"Jack! Behave!"

"Hello, President Stillman," Charlie heard Sallyanne say. She elbowed Jack under cover of his robe and turned to face the university's president.

"Jack, I had to come say congratulations before the reception begins. You *are* seriously considering our offer of a position here, aren't you?" the tall, dark-haired woman asked as she shook hands.

"Don't kid yourself, Jack, she doesn't really care about you," Peter said. "She just wants to keep her most popular visiting lecturer of journalism."

The president laughed. "I need to persuade Charlie to teach more classes. We're getting too many complaints from all the students who can't get into her course."

"That's just because they think it's going to be a gut," Jack teased his wife.

"Aren't you concerned about having these two in the same department?" Charlie said, gesturing to the brothers.

"The prospect *is* a bit daunting," President Stillman said, as she eyed the two tall men standing shoulder to shoulder. "However, a little sibling rivalry is healthy in a faculty. It spurs them on to greater efforts."

"President Stillman! The receiving line is forming already!" another gowned man called as he jogged up to their group.

As the president was escorted away, Miguel shook Jack's hand. "Well, *amigo,* now you're way too smart for your own good. Congratulations!"

Jack gripped his friend's hand fiercely. "I wouldn't be here without you. You know that."

"Just remember that when I need a meteorite authenticated," the big man said, giving Jack a staggering clap on the shoulder. "Since Sahara-Mars didn't give us the definitive proof we crave, I'm still searching for that sign of life in a space rock."

"Won't you miss it, Jack?" Peter asked. "Traveling all over the world, tracking down leads, wondering if the next meteorite you find will be the big one, the scientific break-through?"

"Not at all, little brother," Jack said, wrapping an arm around Charlie's waist as he watched Sallyanne helping Mari duck under the bronze tiger's chin. "I've got all the stars I need right here."

The sizzling debut from
Nancy Herkness

A Bridge to Love

Kate Chilton thought she had it all. But shortly
after her husband's death, she discovers a letter
from another woman: his mistress.

Furious at his betrayal, Kate decides to get even
and accepts a far-from-innocent invitation from
a playboy millionare. And as one wild night
quickly turns into another, what began as a fling
becomes something else entirely.

"SIZZLING SEX, DAZZLING DIALOGUE,
UNFORGETTABLE CHARACTERS—
A BRIDGE TO LOVE IS A BOOK TO CHERISH."
—DEIRDRE MARTIN,
USA TODAY BESTSELLING AUTHOR OF *FAIR PLAY*

0-425-19126-5

Available wherever books are sold or
to order call 1-800-788-6262

B437

BERKLEY SENSATION
COMING IN AUGUST 2004

Sweetheart, Indiana
by Suzanne Simmons

Socialite Gillian Charles has inherited a town. The only catch is she has to live there. What can a small town offer a Big City girl? For starters, a handsome, single man named Sam Law.

0-425-19779-4

Undead and Unemployed
by MaryJanice Davidson

Betsy Taylor may be the Queen of the Vampires, but she still has bills to pay. But landing her dream job selling designer shoes won't help this undead royalty stay out of trouble.

0-425-19748-4

The Heiress of Hyde Park
by Jacqueline Navin

A governess's daughter and a young lord have fallen in love, but he must marry an heiress. If only they had a fairy godmother to secure their fate...

0-425-19778-6

Goddess of Spring
by P.C. Cast

To save her failing bakery, Lina trades souls with Persephone, the Goddess of Spring—and starts to fall for hunky Hades.

0-425-19749-2